THE RED
SERGEANT

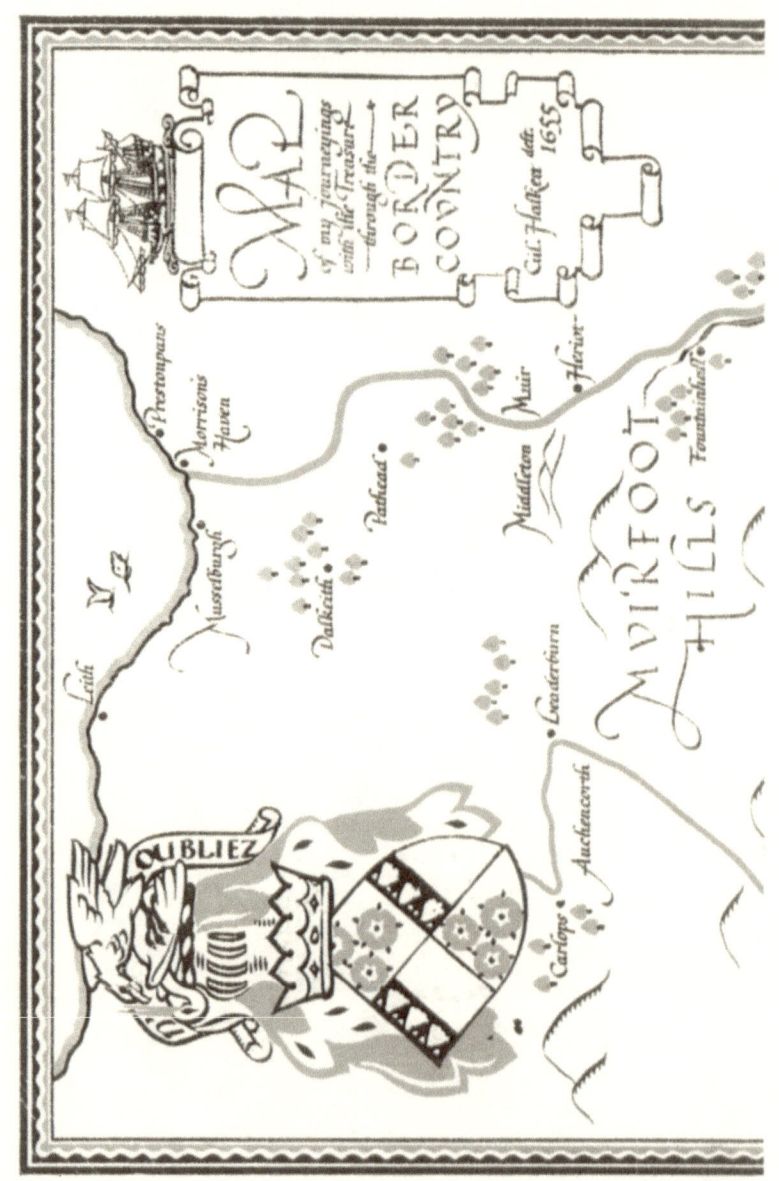

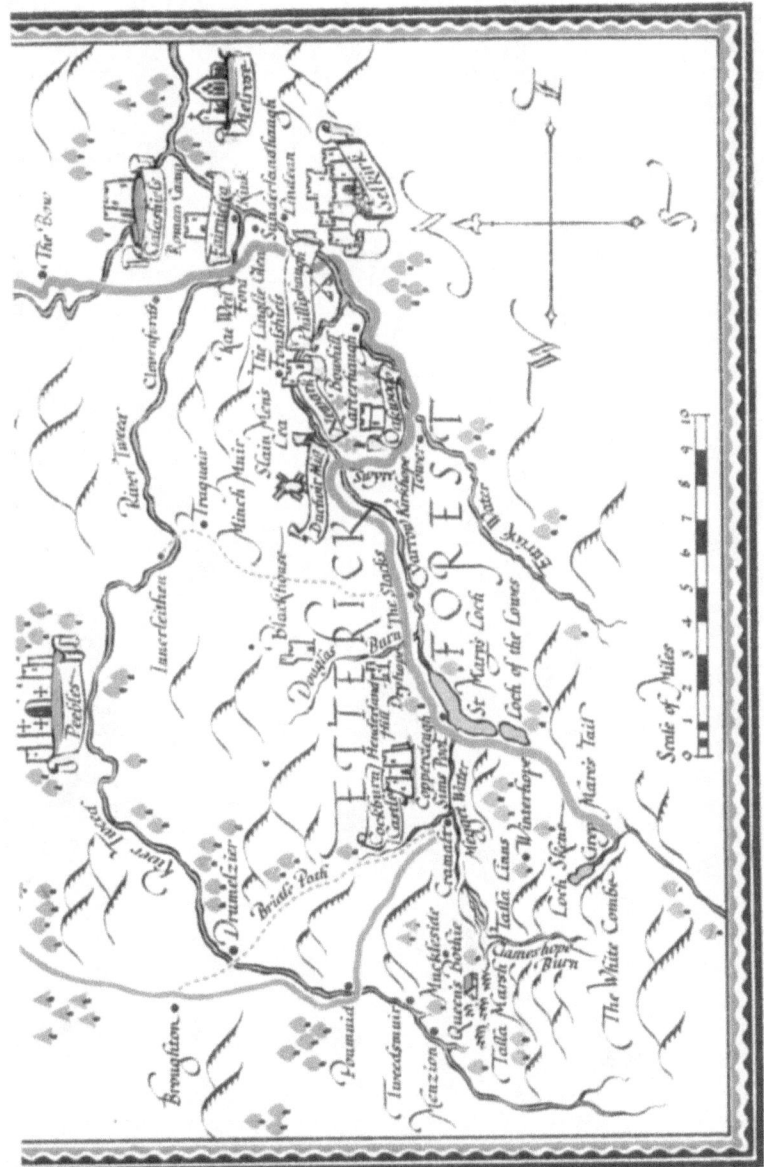

THE
RED SERGEANT

A Novel by JAMES LORIMER

THOMAS NELSON & SONS, Ltd.

LONDON, EDINBURGH, NEW YORK
TORONTO, AND PARIS

First published September 1931

TO

A.I., A.S.M., and J.B.L.

You, dear Trio, who know the ground traversed
in this narrative, will be among the few on whom
Gilbert Halkett's love of the geography of his
story may not pall. For, scattered over the
world's face as you now are, each place will call
up memories of days we spent together.

You will be grateful to the writer, whose manu-
script I have tried to transcribe with fidelity, for
telling how your old acquaintance, John Gwyn,
figured in Montrose's first expedition, as (all
men know from his memoirs) he did in the
second.

Of special interest to you also is the fact that
the Cavalier met that other character, not known
to historians, though told of credibly in those
Highland traditions which we loved to listen to
in our nursery days, the Red Sergeant.

Perhaps some day one of you will put colour
into Gilbert Halkett's sketch of him by telling
what your memory has salved from the old tales.

J. L.

CONTENTS

Contents

THE RED SERGEANT

CHAPTER I

SIM CLEGHORN PLAYS HERMES

AS I stood handling the books that September morning in the town of Linlithgow, you could not have found in broad Scotland a lad less likely to be launched on a life of adventure.

Yet, if I had not been so entirely absorbed in the little academic eddy, I might have reflected that the great happenings in the land would not leave the student untouched.

It was the darkest of days for the Covenant.

Little more than a year before, the Marquis of Montrose, disguised as a horse-boy, had entered Scotland to raise the standard for the King. The story of that horse-boy is like that of the well-eye on the mountainside. He became an irresistible torrent. He swept our armies before him at Tippermuir, Inverlochy, Auldearn, and Alford. Then, but a month before the day on which I begin my story, he put our last hopes to wreck by his victory at Kilsyth, by which he laid the whole of the south country, even as he had laid the north, helpless at his feet.

Men spoke of it as a visitation of the Almighty that, the while these indignities were being endured, the Scottish army should be in England, and we have to depend for our defence on the poor stuff out of which soldiers fit to face Montrose's Highlandmen could not be made.

They might with more reason have seen the visitation of God in the plague. It beset the whole of the south country that year and took all heart out of our policy, civic and military.

The very books, which were my concern at the moment, spoke of it. They had come by carrier's cart the night before. The carrier was stopped at the burgh boundary, and not till he had showed a writing from the Town Clerk of Edinburgh, warranting a package as having come unopened from the ship at Leith, was he allowed within the bounds. Such was the dread of being smitten by what men still call the Great Sickness of the year 1645, that I doubt whether even that box of bloodless books would have been passed on to me, had they not been sent from that eminent man, Alexander Henderson.

Maister Henderson, the Rector of the Town's College of Edinburgh, was at his work in Westminster, but his heart lay aye close to the College and its affairs.

Now, early in May of that year, we students had been dismissed in the midst of our session because of the number of folk who were dying from the plague in the city, and were commanded to meet for the new session in Linlithgow, which, unlike even its neighbouring burgh, Stirling, had not been touched by the plague.

You may be sure this was a matter of concern to the Rector, responsible for the whole conducting of the College, yet tied to London, partly because of the feebleness of his health, but more because of the heavy weight of affairs that could be carried only there by him, Scotland's greatest man.

He had written to the regents fully anent all major matters, including those " circles " of honour which he had himself instituted. These, in spite of the confusion of the transference of a great multitude of students to that little town, it was his dearest wish should be carried on.

A letter from him I had in my pouch was of a different kind. My father, Andrew Halkett, and the Rector had been intimates through the days when Maister Henderson was minister of Leuchars. Though our home, the Mains of Dairsie, was on the estate of the Spottiswoodes, the fellest enemies of the Covenant, that made no difference to the friendship. The Rector had ever shown a tenderness toward me, and, since the death of my father, had been as good as my guardian. To name the latest mark of his kindness, it was at his instance that I, though only a magistrand, was given charge of transporting from the library in Edinburgh what books we needed. So it came that I was at Linlithgow, before the coming of my fellows, to have them certified and housed in St. Michael's Kirk, where the regents were to prelect.

In his letter, beside another matter, on which I am
yet to touch, he told how he had gathered those books
to add to the library donated in bygane years by
Maister Clement Little, that these were for the use of
the magistrands, of whom he hoped there would be some
in the first circle and I myself even among the *exortes*
there.

It touched me to reflect on the great man, his thoughts
set on our poor company, wandering through the streets
of London and bearing back such volumes as I then
was handling—the great folios of Aristotle, the Typo-
graphia Regia copy of Juvenal's Satires just printed at
Paris, the mighty Plato of Marsilius Ficinus, and such
like.

As I stood there in my lodging, with these mentors of
the student's untroubled life set up on the table and
curving round me like a barricado, the Fates were ready
to clip that life short with their shears. The Fates at
times choose curious ministers. As I looked up to place
a volume in the space between the Sphere of Johannes
de Sacrobosco and the Dialectus of Ramus, I found the
space already filled by the head of Sim Cleghorn. I
had heard no footfall, yet there was the man, like a
satyr in the groves of the Academy, immovable and
voiceless, but bending on me the quizzical look which
Dairsie used to say was born with the man. Now Sim
was the Spottiswoodes' steward, and it was just about
as safe for him to be in my lodging as it would have been
had he been seen walking up the High Street of Edinburgh. Linlithgow was strong for the Covenant. Till

a day or two before, it had held in its prison these two leaders among the Malignants, Lord Napier and Sterling of Keir, and, of all the Malignants, the Spottiswoodes were deepest in the affairs of the King and Montrose.

" Sim," I cried, in amazement at the sight of his grizzled visage, " whaur in the warld did ye spring frae, an' whattan madness brings ye here ? "

" Oh, I just slippit past the wifie when she gaed wi' her gird tae the wall," he replied. " Ye were that thrang wi' thae auld-farrant buiks that it was fine tae look at ye."

" Yes, yes," I broke in; " but what brings ye here? It's ill tae risk yer craig for some daft cantrip."

" Nae foolishness, Maister Gibbie, I'se warran' ye, brings me," he went on with a creishiness of manner which I sorely disliked. " I've a message frae Sir Robert for the young laird, an' ye'll free ma craig frae peril the moment ye tak' it frae me for him."

" Me tak' a message tae the camp o' yer great man at Bothwell ! " I cried. " I like yer impidence, Sim. Gang yer ways and rin yer ain errands. It wad better become ye tae pass a word to the young laird on Clydeside than tae waste yer time botherin' a body wha has nae concern wi' sic affairs."

" Ay," he rejoined sourly, " but ye see Maister John is *no* wi' the lave on Clydeside. He's in Embro'. That's the fac', and that's what maks me come, like a coo wi' the branks on, e'en tae you—Maister Halkett."

It was the first time Sim Cleghorn had ever called me by my surname, and that too with the title of respect tacked on to it. He dropped his usual half-sneering, half-surly manner as he used it, and I could not doubt that his affection and concern for the Spottiswoode family, the one sign of softness in him, was somehow touched by what he told me.

" John Spottiswoode no wi' the lave ! " I cried out. " Dae ye tell me this when wi' my ain e'en I saw him in this verra toun, twa-three days gane, by the side o' the Maister of Napier when he enlarged Lord Napier from the prison ? Did I no think it like the lad tae mak' sic a public protestation o' his malignancy ? Man, Sim, a'body kens ower weel o' hoo he followed oot that protestation an' was ane o' the pairty that received the submission o' the Toon Cooncil o' Edinburgh ootside the city walls. A'body kens hoo the imprisoned lords were set free, and hoo the hale company arrived at Bothwell the day afore Sir Robert cam' wi' the Marquis's patent as Captain-General of Scotland. I've little doot Dairsie was figuring in the grand display on Bothwell Haugh the day aifter. Ye'd better seek him on Clydeside."

He heard me out and then said, " Haud a wee. Ye've gotten it richt up tae a pint. Maister John had a private affair tae cairry through for the laird. He gaed into the toon, but, I tell 'ee, he never cam' oot. When the yerls an' the twa lairds, Drum an' Powrie, alang wi' Chaplain Wishart, were enlairged, young Dairsie was still in the toon. He never jined the company : he has not shewed on Clydeside. I tell 'ee he's trappit in the toon. But, gin he's at lairge in the cage, his mistak' in bidin' in may end fine, for the message is to be handed on tae ane wha's in the city. For me tae tak' it—weel, ye ken this face wad land me in the Tolbooth in half an 'oor, an' nae guid dune."

As I glanced at him, he seemed an ugly edition of that Greek, not too well-favoured in feature, Socrates. Since he constantly attended the laird when in Edinburgh, Sim's face was as kenspeckle as the dial of St. Giles. I hesitated.

"Maister Gilbert," Sim struck in, "ye see what a botch has been made o' the business. The lad's uncle, Sir Robert, it was, thocht ye could best get us oot o' it, an' he coonts ye will pass the message, for auld sake's sake."

"What is the letter, anyway?" I asked.

"Letter!" ejaculated he. "There's nae letter. Word o' mou' written on the winds is safer for a' thae days. There's a body ca'ed Gwyn to whom the young laird is tae gie instructions frae Sir Robert. As ye ken, I daurna risk the plainstanes, but the word tae be passed is simple eneuch—juist tae tell Maister John that Captain Gwyn is tae be fund at the White Hart in the Blackfriars. He's passing there as a Dutch herring merchant, an' gaes by the name o' Jansen. Pass the word tae Maister John. That's a'. Can we coont on ye?"

"An' that's a'," I reflected, as I heard this strange request. Henderson's favourite pupil to be a go-between for Malignants! Yet what the Spottiswoodes' servant said was true. There was "auld sake's sake," and it rose very warm round my heart. If any one could with safety to himself get into touch with Dairsie, it was I. And Dairsie I saw not as a Malignant. I saw him in the light of the old happy days, when the laird's house and that of his chief tenant, my father, were on close terms. I had been taught along with Dairsie by the laird's tutor. Dairsie and I flew dragons and guddled trout on many a summer's day together like brothers, and, like brothers, we had quarrelled over such things as our shares of ride-and-tie on his first mount. Till the troubles broke out afresh we were inseparable. Now that the handsome, gallant fellow was drawn by the very name he bore into the camp of the enemy, he was still my very dear friend. I knew that every hour he continued to skulk in Edinburgh, while Montrose and his uncle Sir Robert were on Clydeside or on the march southwards, added to his peril.

It was true, as Sim said, that if any one could pass him a message, it was I. And the strange thing was that, even as Sim argued, I was thinking of the letter from Maister Henderson in my pouch, and how it touched on the matter of Dairsie's safety. I could wellnigh recite from memory the passage :

"I am concerned to gather that John Spottiswoode hath joined himself with the spoilers. As for the older members of his house, my accompt must even stand without alteration, for they will learn no wisdom but their own. But, Gilbert, I am wae for that lad rushing unthinking along the road to ruin. For ruin it will be. It is not for me to mell with the matter at large in a letter, but this much I may tell you. Such a stroke is about to fall on those who are sailing by the gust of success they got at Inverlochy, that they will be put to utter shipwreck. If I had the means to do it, I would fain pass word to young Dairsie and rede him of the deadly peril in which he stands. As an old man who would save the young and foolish from the fate of those whose fathers have eaten sour grapes, my word to your friend, and that in all affection, would be to get him home on the instant to his father's house, and stir not from it. Otherwise, as my name is good for truth, there will be death for him on the field or, if he escapes that, death on the gallows. And from that, though I have all the good will in the world, I could not save him."

Now it was one thing to read this while I thought Dairsie in the camp at Bothwell and out of all chance of access. It was another thing to turn over in my mind the Rector's moving words after Sim's account of his actual situation. It seemed to me a most providential confluence that Sim should come on the very back of the letter to point me the way in which I could carry out Maister Henderson's desire to save him from the peril in which he stood. I seemed to see my friend with the hempen gravatte round his neck, and, considering only that one thing, made up my mind in a rush and said :

" Sim, I'll dae what I can. Nae mair need be said ; sae gang yer ways afore the bailies grip ye."

Sim's leer twisted into his nearest approach to a smile.

"I kent ye, Gilbert, I kent ye," he jerked out. With no more in the way of farewell he slipped out of the room. A moment or two later I saw him, apparently unobserved, making his way down the wynd.

I daresay Sim imagined I had but to skip away on his errand, with nought said to any one. But it behoved me to report the arrival of the books to Maister James Pillans, the only regent then in the town, and to ask whether he had any commissions at the Town's College. There would be, I knew, no question as to getting permission, for, as librarian, seldom a week passed that did not see my horse on the road to Edinburgh.

The regent dwelt in the house of one of the burgesses that lay close by the old Palace and overlooked the loch. As I made my way there, I thought out a plan. I would find Dairsie and get him to pass on the Secretary's message if he cared to and could. But, chief of all, I would give him the purport of his well-wisher's letter and persuade him to take the advice. He would ride that night to the Queen's Ferry on my horse and be safe in Fife ere morning. For me, I would get to the Ferry, recover my horse, and be back in Linlithgow by midday, the whole happening well ended.

So I briskly saw the regent and as briskly went away from him in this mood of assurance. But I had scarce shut the gate of the yard when a waft of reflection came over me. I stood looking towards the loch where the waterhens were bobbing in and out the reeds under the September sunshine. What I really saw was Maister Henderson's manse in its pleasant garden near the

High School at Edinburgh. I saw myself walking in at
its door, when there was some small trouble to report
or some difficulty to be resolved. I saw there the
Master in Israel looking up to greet me from his study
chair, swathed in a plaid because the ague, that gift to
him from the fens of Leuchars, was on him, but busied,
as if a well man, with his papers because the will inside
the man commanded his shaking hand to write. I saw
his great dark eyes, tender as a woman's, dwell on me
with affection when I stumble out that I am in a
perplexity. I saw them still unchanged as he says :
" Well, well, all mere folly is mendable, if so be that
it is not a fault in honour."

That was aye the thing he dwelt on—honour. All
men, even his enemies, bore testimony that he carried
his own unstained.

So I was troubled, as I looked at the loch, the while
I really saw myself reporting my intended expedition of
that day to him. I saw not only my passing on of his
warning to Dairsie, of which I knew he would approve.
I saw also the thing that had been almost buried from
my vision when I decided, the passing on of the Secretary's message. That, to a son of the Covenant and
the protégé of the Covenant's main author, was peril-
ously like treason. It was, at the least, intromitting
with treason.

Oh, these second thoughts ! How often I have
suffered for them. To obey an impulse, and then to
remember other things too late to mend the things done
on impulse !

" Well," I thought, " I have passed my word and I cannot go back on it. The Nestor of the Covenant himself wanted to help my friend, and, if I help him in a somewhat left-handed manner, I think he could make allowance for that rush of impulse from my heart confusing my head, put it down to folly, and say, " Well, well, all mere folly is mendable ! "

And so, having ended the debate with myself thus, I passed down to the West Port, got me my horse, and set out for Edinburgh.

CHAPTER II

DAIRSIE BREAKS FREE

OF all the gifts from England to our country in this
weary time, the likest to the wooden horse of Troy
was the pest. For it the soldiers who sacked Newcastle
in the October bygane took back with them into Scotland. It could not have fallen on us at a more unchancy
time. The harvest had been scanty, so it was a winter
during which many were but poorly fed, that saw the
visitation get its first grips. By April it had spread,
by way of Kelso and the south, to Edinburgh. There,
owing to the concourses of folk for the preachings,
prayings, and fastings, which the perils of State made
almost daily occurrences, the sickness got a mighty hold.
None can marvel that the Council took strict measure
to prevent the passage of folk from infected parts. The
licence the carrier required, ere he could convey my
books, affords a small instance of the fear which possessed the burghs and landward parts where the pest
had not yet appeared. Sad it was to see how hard was
the lot of the sick folk who were kept from contact
with the whole. As I rode into the city by way of the
Colt Bridge, I could see the sorry booths which housed
some of these on the Crosstorphin Hill, and these were

as nothing in number compared to the great gathering of huts at the other end of the town in the King's Park.   Dr. Paulicius and his helpers visited the stricken folk in both these asylums, and bore to them the charity of the churches.   Yet if any died (such was the terror lest men be smit while graves were opened in the town) they were buried within a stone's cast of the booths.

A packman, who led a horse laden with goods, accompanied me from Gogar till his road and mine parted at the West Kirk.   He told me he was going back to Leith with his wares unsold, though he had travelled West Lothian thorough, and that Edinburgh was at the mercy of Montrose if he cared to march into it.   And, indeed, when I saw the city for myself, his statement seemed but the bare truth, for it looked more like a city of the dead than like the brisk town I had seen at the first onset of the plague in April.   The Grassmarket, then so thrang, was a market bare of aught save the grass which grew in the cobbles of its great expanse.   Whereas, from the windows of the tall houses which bordered it, heads of buxom guidwives and bright-eyed lasses would have been popping out in scores at the sound of my horse's passing any afternoon aforetime, not a window was seen open now.   It seemed as if the folk feared the very winds of heaven would blow infection on them.

I was stopped at the West Port, but, on recognizing me as a frequent visitor, the men with the halberts nodded in a spiritless way and let me pass.

It seemed to me that, with danger hanging over

Dairsie, it would be foolish to ride up to the lodging, which sometimes he shared with me, speir for him, and thereby proclaim to all what might be his place of resort still.

First it behoved me to get rid for the time being of the horse. If I put him in a stall at the White Hart Inn, it would give me the opportunity to find whether Gwyn were actually at the hostelry, and so make sure whether the trysting-place named by Sim Cleghorn for his young master could be gone to with the certainty that Dairsie should meet his man. So I made my way by the High Street and the head of the Canongate to St. Mary's Wynd, and so came to the White Hart in the Blackfriars. It was a great and roomy inn, occupying one entire side of a court which you entered by a close. On the other side stood the stables. The yard was empty but for a singular being whom I took to be one of the town caddies, a class of men who exist only in the capital. They run errands, do light carrying, and sometimes clear the way for the chairs when the fine ladies go visiting. Often they begin their occupation as boys and finish as old men, and quite a number of them are oddities. Often, too, they are naturals, and, oftener still, affect to be such, to draw on the compassion of employers. In ordinary times you would see half a dozen caddies lounging in such a yard as the White Hart's on the odd chance of earning a plack or two by running an errand. The sickness had evidently frighted them from their haunts too, except this one who, I thought to myself, must be wellnigh the oddest of them all. He was the kind of creature you had to look at twice. He had a misshaped body, all twisted to one side, and when he moved, as he did on my approach, he moved in a series of jerks which, in spite of their apparent difficulty, sent him over the ground at a strangely quick pace. His head was large, out of all proportion to his slender and shilpit frame. It was crowned by hair the colour of hay, that lay in wisps above eyes which looked as if they had been bleached, and his mouth was open in what I can call only a horrible semblance to a smile. You could not tell what age he was. He might be a grown boy, he might be a man of thirty.

" Wull puir Mungo tak' the horse, yer honner ? " this crab-like creature asked. But " poor Mungo " did not get the chance to do this office, for at that moment a buirdly hostler appeared.

" Oot o' ma gait, ye skellum," he shouted, jostling the half-wit aside. I handed over my mount, ordered a feed, saw in what stall he was disposed, and made my way into the inn.

I called for a small stoup of claret and a matchet of bread, for I had tasted nothing since I broke my fast, and it was now well on to five o'clock.

The landlady herself appeared with the modest refection. " Ye'll tak' yer spunefu' o' Malvoysie first, sir ? " she questioned, pointing to a tiny glass of dark-coloured liquid.

" Why that, gudewife ? " I inquired.

" Hoots," she exclaimed, " it's frae ootbye pairts ye

maun be no to ken o' that. Why *that*? Just because it's the speceefic for the sickness, the receipt o' the great Dr. Burgess. I'se warran' ye there's mair in't than ye wad think. There's reid sage in till't, an' there's lang pepper in till't, and there's ginger an' nutmegs an' Mithridate an' treacle an' Angelic water in till't, forby the guid Malvoysie itsel'. It's sovereign for haddin' the pest aff ye, ay, an' they say, e'en for curin' ye o' the pest itsel' gin ye get smitten."

I was willing enough to get into friendly speech with her, so I cried, "There's nae kennin' what I may come tae, gin I leive aifter takin' yer physic." So, swallowing the draught, I set to at the bread and wine, the while I kept her in chat. By-and-by, after edging the conversation from the inn and the way the plague had affected its custom, I got to my own business and inquired whether by any chance a Dutch merchant had arrived.

"He has so," she said, "a great gaucy man wi' an awfu' likin' tae gab, but gey short in the English an' a fair stot at the uptak' o' oor guid Lallan! An' eh, sirs, I wad raither pey his lawin' for victuals than for drink."

"Ay," I said, "that'll be ma frien'. An' is he no aboot?"

"Aboot? That's juist what he is. He had a breakfast o' rizzored haddie and yale at nine, an' his denner at twal 'oors. Syne he said he wad tak' a *promenade*, and speired the gait tae the Salts o' Preston. He'll be stravaigin' there or thereaboots, unless mebbe he's fa'en

in' wi' thieves at the Figgate Whins.   A tell't him weel
tae tak' tent o' thae gentry ! "

" Then, mistress," I rejoined, " ye may trust tae see
him by supper-time, for he's kent tae be a man o' his
hands."

" Will ye be bidin' the nicht ? " she asked.

" No me," I replied ; " but I may bring a frien' wha
micht, and syne take the use o' my horse the morn's
morn."

" Ah, weel, we'll hae ye an' a twa three mair at supper-
time," says she.   " An' haud ye awa' frae the Coogate,
for the sickness is terrible bad there."   The kindly soul,
having given me this motherly monition, turned to her
kitchen duties, and, as the day was wearing on, I set
out in quest of Dairsie.

In the days before the troubles I had lodged in the
Mureburgh, hard by the spot where the old hermit of
St. John had his cell, before the convent of St. Catherine
of Sienna included its stance and much of the land
round it.   It was a fair suburb, occupied by leisured
persons who mostly lived that self-contained life of which
the Edinburgh folk who have prospered are so jealous.
A better place for one desiring to keep private could
not be, for the high walls of the gardens fronting each
house, like little castle-courtyards, made comings and
goings very unnoticeable ; and, though a feck of folk of
the humbler sort usually thronged the district behind
these houses that ran from the Potter Row to the Bristo
Port, few of these ever seemed to walk by the edge of
the Burghmuir and breathe its freer airs.

It was just after I had walked up by the side of the College, and was slanting down towards this destination by the Potter Row, that a hand was put on my arm. I turned round to see Dairsie himself. I checked my step in astonishment, but he tugged me forward, the while he said in a low voice full of excitement :

"Dinna stop, Gibbie; keep on walking, for the sake o' a' that's guid." His usually care-free face was showing concern. "I'm followed," he muttered; "but they're no just sure it's me. Haud on a wee an' we may gie them the slip. Be ready tae dash when we get tae the end o' the Raw. But pause the noo, innocentlike."

On the word we stopped, while Dairsie gazed about him as if trying to identify a stair-mouth in the street. I took a glisk behind and saw, a hundred yards or so away, two soldiers. They stopped the moment we did, and seemed interested in investigating something, even as we ourselves.

"Ay," said Dairsie, noting my glance, "yon's them. Seemingly they're in nae sort o' hurry ; but we'll sune see what speed they can mak' in jackboots."

Now at the south end of the Potter Row, but separated from it by about fifty yards, stand, all by themselves, a house and a garden. The house is a whitewashed building of modest dimensions. It catches the eye because it has crawstae gables and slabs of chiselled stone round the windows and the door. But the most noticeable feature of it is a very gracious and beautiful pear-tree, which is trained so as to cover almost the whole front of the house. As we sighted the place that evening, a green gate in the side of the garden wall next us stood ajar.

" Noo, Gibbie," cried Dairsie, as the bend of the Potter Row hid us from the two fellows who followed him, " awa' like the deil ! "

Together we dashed for that garden gate at a speed never matched when we played hounds and hare along the howes of Fife. We reached the green gate and closed it before the soldier lads had turned the corner.

" Here," said the panting Dairsie, and dragged me into a little summer-house which stood facing the dwelling on the edge of the lawn. It was a chance, but it worked our way. We heard the rush of feet on the road outside as Dairsie's pursuers ran forward on the line we had been taking.

" They're awa' for the Wells o' Wearie, them an' their jackboots ! " says he gleefully.

" Ay," I responded ; " but will we no hae been seen frae the hoose ? "

" There's naebody in't tae see us," he replied ; " it's forhoo'ed because o' the plague."

We spoke in whispers, but soon there appeared to be little need, for the pursuers did not return our way.

There, in that quiet garden, as the mellow light faded, we swapped news.

Dairsie owned frankly that, though he had the excuse of getting monies, which his father had deposited with a friend, for entering the city, it was mostly in a spirit of bravado that he had ventured in. It appeared he

found difficulties put in his way, so that he could not
rejoin the Master of Napier before the cavalcade rode
off towards Bothwell. After that, though not molested,
there was clearly a design to prevent his passing out at
all. That very afternoon he had indeed got a supply
of money from his father's doer. The doer supplied
him at the same time with the news that the Council,
having first repented of their folly in enlarging the lords
when Montrose was a hundred miles away from the walls,
were now in great heart because he was reported to be
marching south from Clydesdale and had issued an
order to arrest all Royalist suspects, among whom " the
Spottiswoode whelp " had been expressly named.

" I did not let the grass grow under my feet when I
heard that," said Dairsie. " And sure enough the doer
was no speaking without book, for as I passed the Grey-
friars Churchyard I saw the gentry wi' the jackboots,
who were by the gate, gie a signal and begin to follow
me. I led them round by Bristo, and the rest ye ken."

I had to give the lad another gliff. " Then," I came
in, " ye're barely the proper person tae haud a tryst wi'
Captain Gwyn."

" Gwyn ! " cried he. " What dae ye ken o' Gwyn ? "

I told him of Sim Cleghorn's coming and the word I
had promised to pass to him.

" Man, Gibbie," he stuttered out in sheer amazement,
" ye tell me ye took sic a risk for me, an' you a Covenanter, and a canny Fifer forbye."

" Covenanter, ay," I rejoined, " an' canny Fifer nae
less, and it's he that has tae caw gey canny noo."

Then I gave him Maister Henderson's warning, with all the solemnity I could command, and pressed on him my plan for getting clear of dangers to come, and safe to his home.

At first hearing of the name Henderson he barked out, " That auld tod warn me in kindness ! He's mair like tae set the sodgers on me."

But, after I had reasoned with him, and put it that here was a great man going out of his way to be generous and kind, he was manifestly impressed. After thinking a good minute, he cried, " His guidwill I dinna doot, but I dae doot his wisdom. He canna hae heard o' the great mustering o' men at Bothwell Haugh an' the splendid ceremonials when the Marquis gat frae my uncle the King's commission as Governor and Captain-General o' Scotland. His Majesty himself is to join the Marquis on the Borders. It's for that he's marching south. Man, he canna fail. An', even if he could, it's all one. Join the Marquis I must."

His face flushed ; his eyes kindled. I knew my Dairsie, aye the creature of ardours, shutting his eyes to everything except the thing that took his fancy.

" Weel," I said dryly, " if ye're tae join the Marquis, the way is plainly not by the White Hart. Gae there an' ye walk tae the Tolbooth. Ye're kent ; ye're ken-speckle. If yer message is on your conscience, I doot it's e'en the canny Covenanter wha maun cairry it."

At this he cried out, " Gibbie, that's mair than I can alloo ye dae. Me tae gang free and you to tak' a' the risk ! It's no to be thocht on."

" Risk ! " quo' I. " There's nae risk. I'll be weel oot o' that lang traivel tae the Ferry an' get me straicht hame on ma horse the nicht."

" Weel," he said, " there's nae message. There's just this." He pulled a packet out of his doublet. " I dinna ken masel' what's in't," he explained, " but it's my uncle's instructions tae Gwyn."

I took the packet from him. All I said was, " Dairsie lad, it's slippin' awa' I am, an', gin ye're wise, ye'll no tarry."

" Tarry ! " he replied. " As sune as nicht fa's, I'm off hotfit by the Braids tae the Moorfoots. Gibbie, when next I come tae this auld toun, it's no ' that whelp Spottiswoode ' I'll be, but the Secretary's nephew, an' I ken a dour Covenanter wha will share wi' me tae the half o' my kingdom."

He had recovered his spirit and was once more the blythe, care-free Dairsie.

We clasped hands. I left him in the arbour, and, walking boldly out at the gate, turned sharp to the right and made for the Pleasance by that lane running along-side the old Flodden wall that we call the Thieves' Raw.

CHAPTER III

TO be an inn in a plague-stricken city, the White
Hart presented a cheerful appearance that evening.
It was as unlike the deserted place I had visited in the
afternoon as could well be. As I reached the close's
mouth, I saw my hostler leading to stable two horses.
The riders of these were making their way towards the
house, where, in the doorway, a fussy body, habited as
a burgess, stood waiting to welcome them. When they
came opposite him, they swept off their cocked hats and
made a low *congé*. " Hail to the Chief Cockalorum,"
chimed the two as with a single voice.

" Guid e'en an' guid fairin' tae twa Cockylorums,"
responded the fat man, in the solemn and level tone of
a ceremonial. The riders, whom I took to be young
country lairds, straightened themselves, and one of them
said in an easy manner, as if to shew that he had passed
through the formality and was free to be familiar, " Gude
e'en tae ye, Auld Ane. We thocht ye wad be on your
ain midden-heid an' crawin' crouse, pest or nae pest.
But ye'll no tell us ye hae a quorum ? "

" Hae I no ? " replied the worthy. " Hark tae that."
From the house came a cackle of voices.

" Faith, a full meetin'," says the other laird, and the three of them made their way within.

I own I swithered whether to follow them. It was all too plain this was a gathering of one of those convivial societies against which the regents were ever warning us student lads. Things had not fallen well if Gwyn had arrived and I were to have speech of him alone. Yet, for all my faults, I am dour to finish anything I have begun. I crushed down my misgivings and entered the inn. There, in the large room of common entertainment, were disposed over a dozen people, manifestly members of the party that made its howff in the White Hart, and there, too, was my man. There was no mistaking him, the largest and the loudest of the company. He wore a suit of dressed brown leather, surmounted by a flat linen ruff, and his assumed nationality was further proclaimed by the foreign accent of the bellow in which he conversed. I was about to say he poured out talk in broken English, but rather, let me say, he belched it in gulps, like liquor decanted from a bottle held upside down. I should put him as a man of thirty-five, or perhaps a trifle less. I will say he looked his part of Dutch merchant, with his brown hair in close clusters of curls and his beard in the trim fashion whilk we now call after the painter Vandyck. In his manner what he suggested most was just an overgrown boy. Yet there was nothing boyish about his figure. When he turned his head, his short neck shewed sinews like a wrestler's. His neck, indeed, was the only short thing in his frame, for his trunk was long, his legs were long, and his arms great limbs to match both. That first sight of Gwyn made me feel I was looking at a mighty man. Whether he answered also that full phrase out of the Scriptures, " a mighty man of valour," one could not safely say, for at the moment he looked to be only pot-valiant. A great stoup of claret stood at his elbow, and his flushed face argued that it had not been the first to be drained. What gave me greater concern was that he had planted himself at the farthest end of the room, and was launched on his discourse, with the main body of the company between him and the door. I felt, if I was to make my try, I must do it at once. His eye had lighted on me as I entered. It was an eye deep blue, like his own Welsh mountains, and yet with a light in it such as laughs from the sea. Its glance rested on me for a moment and then passed.

"Ah, Jansen," I cried, to give him warning, and made my way to where he sat. A flash of concern crossed his face, but, my certes, he was quick in the uptake.

"Ach! doo, my friendt," he responded, and, as I reached him, held out his great hand jovially. There was no one immediately behind him, so, as I came right opposite, I cried, " Yes, it is me, at long last," and then I added, in a low voice which could reach only his ear, " Take care. I've a message from Spottiswoode for you."

A bellow in what was meant to pass as Dutch followed; but it ended in a soft undertone, " Not now ; wait." Then, in the most natural way, he turned to the

company and, with a face wreathed in smiles, intro-
duced me.

"Dees is my jong friendt Brawan" (he choked over
the name so that it might be anything). "Will you
please me, gentlemen, that you mak' him of your con-
course, even as I am honour?"

"What says the Dean?" somebody asked. The fussy
person, whom I had heard greeted as the "Chief Cockalorum," in public life, as I soon learned, the city's Dean
of Guild, caught up the questioner sharply.

"There's nae deans here. A' distinctions, ho'ever
great, cease when the meetin' is framed. This meetin',
duly framed, has co-opted Maister Jansen as a member,
pro tempore, of the honourable Cockalorums. Is it the
mind o' the cockerels that the new bird's frien', Maister
Broon, be associated for the purposes o' wassail and
wit?"

"*Nem con*," cries a thin little dark fellow, like a
writer's clerk.

"Then Maister Broon is free o' the converse an' con-
veeviality o' this worshipful society," pronounced the
Dean, as if passing a warrant for a new house.

I bowed my thanks, while Gwyn beamed benediction
and took occasion to pledge the company from a fresh
cup of wine.

"An' noo," said the consequential master of cere-
monies, "tae junketin' and jinks."

The junketing meant a supper which showed a very
presentable array of victuals for a plague-stricken town,
and it was evident that the Cockalorums were accus-

tomed to seek an antidote to the melancholy of the times in copious supplies of wine. Certainly the large jars called " tappit hens " were refilled and emptied by the drawer more quickly than I had deemed possible. The air of friendliness, somewhat cautious at the beginning of the repast, soon became cordial.

I was made to feel that my companions of the silly society, with its bairnly play-actings, were in the main good fellows, whose natural high spirits were not to be held down even by the gloom and terror of the time. I could well have enjoyed a merry hour with them, an it were not for my curious situation—all eager to be gone, and yet helpless to go till I had speech of Gwyn. Gwyn, indeed, was my problem, for, if any man of the company seemed anchored for the night, it was he. He sat on the right hand of the Chief Cockalorum, and appeared to find vastly to his mind the little man's converse. He listened to it with an attention which kept his own tongue steady, and his eyes were respectfully bent on his host, except when he turned to his cup to pledge him, and this was often. Gwyn, it seems, had been much impressed by the fact that the little man was a dean. In that brain of his, which must be getting muddled, he was probably trying to settle how deans survived in this barbarous land of ours, and over what chapter of ecclesiastics this particular one presided. His deference would, no doubt, have markedly diminished had he learned that his host's powers found vent in deciding whether the United Incorporation of Hammermen might extend their courtyard, or the auld wives of the High Street put a new haik at their windows for the drying of clothes.

By-and-by the viands were disposed of, and a sedulous application of all to the wine alone gave me the feeling that the wit was about to begin. Nor had I long to wait for the second stage of our entertainment. Three sharp raps from the Dean's mallet brought the buzz of general conversation to an end.

" Birds of the game breed," he began, and, standing, he seemed scarce taller than Gwyn did while sitting, " we have pecked oor pickle wi' oor nebs doun, as a' birds o' the strain hae dune since the pair Noah had wi' him in the Ark. But when we tak' oor wee drap o' moisture, we haud oor nebs up and dinna dip them till the draught's weel ower, likewise following the guid example o' oor namesakes. This nicht, afore we proceed to the continuation of oor ordinary, I command a craw, first, frae ane o' oor new-made brithers o' the roost, Maister Hans Jansen and Maister Broon. Maister Broon is o' oor ain cleckin', an' we may bide tae hear his contribution tae the harmony later. Maister Jansen, hooiver, comes o' the furrin strain ; but o' a maist worthy strain, for the Dutch hae aye been forrad in the true faith an' forrad in tred, ay, an' for that pairt, forrad in war. Maister Jansen is a peaceable merchant, I understand, in the honourable fishing tred ; but, as ye see, he wears his hanger, an', nae doot, can tell us o' ither wark than rippin' haddies, and, feggs, cockies a', I wouldna like tae hae a tuilzie wi' him an' his bare haunds and me wi' my whinger. Seemingly they grow

gey game anes in Holland. Sae chairg yer cuppies and
gie them the auld farin'."

Thereupon, while Gwyn and I remained seated, the
company rose, drained their tankards with great good-
will, and ended by singing a verse of doggerel, inter-
spersed with many cock-crowings, which must have been
their society song. While this childish act was in prog-
ress, I had been praying that Gwyn might be given grace
to refrain from an attempt to reply, in what was supposed to be for him a foreign tongue, and that he
would content himself with a word of thanks. But not
so Gwyn. Apparently the honour had pleased him
mightily, and he was not to be deterred from responding
to it by any thought of the risk to us both. In a moment
he was on his feet, beaming benignly, and perfectly at
his ease. I must say he began well.

" Brudder Cock—cock——" " Cockalorums," half
a dozen voices helped him out. " Brudder Cockalorums, all ov you, and you most of all, shief, vor my
friendt an' self I zank. I better oonderstan' zan I
speak. I com' to zis landt to get ze haerring. Wot you
say ? ' Dess to ze head zat wears no hair ? ' ; bot zer
is no ones to buy, no schip on zee ; all men frighten.
In ze White Hart not zo. For how ? Ze birds zat has
no fright make here zere—fowl-house. Zey show ze
heart. Und in my gontree also is ze heart. Vot you
laike—vine, loof, und goot gompany—I laike. I vood
more say, bot I can sing better zan speak. And zo I
end my zanks by singing ze English song zot I learnt
from an English poet."

Thereupon he lifted his chin, and in a great voice rolled
out these words :

> " I am so fond a lover grown
>   That for my mistress' cause could die,
> Nor would enjoy my love alone,
>   But wish her millions more than I.
>
> I am devoted to her hand,
>   A willing sacrifice could be ;
> If she be pleased but to command,
>   To die is easy unto me."

With that he resumed his seat amid a gabble of " Weel
dune," and " Yer health again in sang," from the company. Some of them must have admired how, like a
man who has a stammer, he sang so much easier than
he spoke. Yet none seemed to mark that equivocal
sentiment in what was given as a love song :

> " Nor would enjoy my love alone,
>   But wish her millions more than I."

Even I learned not, till he could tell me in a safer hour,
what a billie the singer shewed himself to be then. For
this was Gwyn's own song, a song of which he was
inordinate proud, entitled " Upon my inseparable devotion to Loyalty I call'd Mistress." A fine stroke that
of Gwyn's—to throw his Royalist gauntlet down in a
company of Covenanters for any one who had the wit
to see it, and the hardihood to pick up the challenge.
I glanced round apprehensively to see whether Gwyn's
masquerade had really passed off as well as the general
acclamation seemed to argue it did. I saw no trace of

suspicion in the countenance of any, save perhaps in that of one member of the company. The man whom I had put down as a scrivener or doer's clerk was sitting with knitted brows, as if reflecting. An ill-favoured wisp of a man I thought him, with dark skin, oily hair, and but a poor digestion, to judge by the plukey face of him. But, after a moment's consideration, he turned to his neighbour, and I heard him remark, "A sang weel sung, an' no bad verseefication tae, though I think it micht be mended for the better."

"Ay, nae doot, Elshender; but we canna a' be makars like yersel'," the neighbour answered in a tone with some salt in it. For it seems the black-avised gentleman was Alexander Johnstone, who had some repute as a rhymester among the clerks to the judges and the lesser gentry. As I looked him over more closely, trying to recollect how his appearance made me feel I had seen him before, remembrance came to me. Where I placed him was among the attendants at the last contest for the silver arrow that had been held at the archery butts near the lodging which Dairsie and I shared. This man had marked the score, and doubtless wrote a ballad afterwards on the event. Dairsie and I that day had been in attendance on the Master of Napier, who won the arrow. I wondered if by any chance the poet recalled a fact which was a disquieting one to me in that company. I put the thought aside, for the president was on his feet once more.

"The maist honourable company will noo proceed tae the ordinary," he announced, using the expression which must have suggested to Gwyn more viands, but known by me to be taken from the practice some of our preachers have of holding forth for several Lord's Days in sequence, and sometimes for months, on one sappy text of Scripture. This they call their "ordinary."

"The subject proponed is ' The Excellency of Cities,' " went on the Dean. "It has been well opened at previous sederunts, an' this nicht we reach the enlargement on ' The superior excellence of some cities.' I ca' on the bird o' Prestonside tae gie the first craw."

One of the young men, whom I had seen arrive, rose in answer to the summons. He was, sure enough, the laird of a neighbouring property, and, much to my surprise, shewed that he had been furth Scotland and could tell of the excellences of Paris and Geneva. But, though several speakers followed him, it turned out that few of these had been even to Glasgow, and the "enlairgement" resolved itself into an extolling of Edinburgh as *the* city of excellence beyond compare. I had hoped this monotony would exhaust the subject and the meeting take end peaceably; but, alas, I reckoned without Gwyn. As the wine went down his gullet, discretion began to desert his head. He was pricked in his pride at hearing these bumpkins in their complacency give the go-by to his beloved London. Soon his rumbling voice was heard putting in a word for the Hague and Amsterdam. From these he passed, by Frankfort and Cologne, till he began to talk of London. As he talked, the Dutch accent, which he had so well simulated, gradually passed from his utterance.

By the time he was in full blast on the subject of the
lordly Thames and the goodly taverns of London, its
royal palaces and its multitudes of men, he was speaking
English as well as he had formerly sung it. Then he
made the fatal mistake. He reminded his hearers how
William Dunbar, their own poet, had known better than
they, and written one of his best poems to "London,
the flower o' cities all." Where he had picked up this
scrap I know not; but it put the cap on his indis-
cretion. All looked amazed. Maister Johnstone's face
clouded over with suspicion. He turned his head
sharply from Gwyn to me, and then nodded to himself.

Yet, whatever he thought, he could not resist this
double challenge to his knowledge of poetry and his
civic patriotism.

"I can coonter what that auld Papisher, Dunbar,
says," he cried. "Dr. Arthur Johnstone, a distant
cousin o' my ain, a real makar, wrote in the dignified
Lattine tongue a better poem than the profligate priest
on Embro', an' Sir William Drummond o' Hawthorn-
den, nae less, translates it thus:

"For sceptres nowhere stands a town more fit,
   Nor place where town, world's queen, may fairer sit.
   But this thy praise is above all most brave;
   No man did e'er defame thee but a slave."

He gave the last line with great emphasis, and stood
stock still while he bent a sneering glance on Gwyn.
He had not to wait for his answer. Gwyn's face

became like the round sun seen through the fog in
winter. With a heave he was on his feet.

" *Defame*, you scurvy scullion ! " he bellowed. " And
you dare to term me a slave ! "

He made one bound, had the wretched poet by the
throat, shook him as a terrier shakes a rat, and then
cast the shargar creature from him.

How the company would have acted, if left to themselves after the boiling over of Gwyn's temper, is
doubtful ; but they were not given time to consider
the matter calmly. Johnstone had no sooner gathered
enough breath to speak than he screeched out, " Friens,
haud they men. They're Malignants baith. The ane I
ken to be young Spottiswoode, the ither is a Royalist
spy. His tongue bewrayeth him."

In a trice the few who wore swords drew them, and
stood as if in suspense. Gwyn had his hanger bare in a
flash. Pushing me before him in the direction of the
door, he cried, " Out with the horses and shout when
you're ready."

Even as he spoke, three or four of the younger bloods
sprang at him. Gwyn, with a dexterous twist of his
weapon, sent the sword of one flying, while he hit
another a buffet with the flat of his own. I saw he
needed no help. I darted out and dashed across the
yard. The horses of the two young lairds were standing
with headstalls ready for departure. I mounted one,
held the other opposite the door, and shouted. The
guest-room then opened to my sight. Gwyn, who had
worked his way to the exit, was still holding the entire

company at bay. He gave a great roar of triumph, slammed the door, leapt to the saddle, and, before the company had well poured out of the inn, we were through the close and pelting at a hand-gallop down the wynd that leads into the Pleasance.

CHAPTER IV

THE CAVALIER TAKES COMMAND

OUR getting clear of the city so easily that night
was a stroke of rare good fortune. In ordinary
circumstances two men attempting to gallop out would
certainly have been stopped and interrogated at the
point where the old city wall encloses that eastmost side
of the town. But, however strictly the Council had
given instructions regarding comers and goers, its men
in charge of St. Mary's Port that night evidently did
not believe the pestilence walked in the darkness.
They all seemed to be in bed. So we swept up the
incline and cantered along the Pleasance, with nothing
between us and the open country except the long string
of houses which forms that suburb. Indeed, my companion was so easy in mind that he found leisure to
admire that, though the houses were villas, prettily
adorned with parterres of flower-beds and trim with
shrubs, they yet were not roofed with slates or tiles like
those in the city, but thatched with straw.

I said we had to thank the Southerners for this, and
explained how it was a survival of the practice in the
old village which used to stand on that site, bearing
the curious name Dearenough. The villagers found the

English raiders could so seldom resist the temptation to
burn these defenceless dwellings, just beyond the protection of the city walls, that, on the enemy's approach,
it was each householder's custom to carry off the straw
roof of his cottage and leave the invaders free to work
their will on the bare walls.

When we had cleared the suburb there was still no
sign of pursuers. I think my own horse was the only
one left in the inn stable. In any case, I imagined our
friends there would consider it more likely we had gone
by the Cowgate Port, in which case they would follow a
false trail into the city.

Gwyn seemed very sure of his intentions and his
ground. Without a trace of hesitation, he turned his
mount into the King's Park. Soon we were riding
below the great ribs of rock on the south side of Arthur's
Seat, and approaching Duddingston Loch. From the
hamlet that lies just beyond the loch a road leads to
Leith, by way of the Laird of Restalrig's house. It was
the fit moment for parting. I pulled out the packet
Dairsie had given me and handed it to my companion.
Then, if ever, was my chance to say that, the task to
my friend discharged, the Cavalier and I would part for
good and all where the road twinned at the next turning.
But I hesitated to speak, as there was still a little space
to go. The hesitation was made fateful by the precipi-
tate action of Gwyn. We had reached a little rocky
knoll, and he reined up behind it, with it between us and
the line of the road we had taken.

" The soldier had better read his marching orders,

now he is in safety," he said, as he swung himself out of the saddle, with the bridle over one arm. It was a lown autumn night, and, though not dead dark, it beat me to hear a man talk of reading in it. But in a trice Gwyn was striking steel on flint and kindling a candle. I would as soon have expected to see a copy of the Georgics in a bailie's bedroom.

"Ah ha!" he boomed out, as the light shone steady in the calm air, and his glance fell on my astonished face. "You marvel to see a soldier with such a tool. But it is my *vade mecum*, this my little light. 'Tis plain you haven't campaigned much, my friend. Why, I had almost as soon go without a sword as campaign without an honest dip. It helps the Cavalier in many a dark corner, and, when done of service, is the excuse for one drink more. What say the poets? 'Carouse her health in cans and candles' ends.' "

With that he began reading. "See here," he cried, "the old fox Traquair has doubled. The treasure is not to go to his hole or near it. We're to avoid the Peebles Road and go from Morrison's Haven, by Gala Water, to a place Yair, and hand over to a convoy. So, young bird, you've done the army and John Gwyn a good night's work by bearing that message. You recruit the army's chest direct, and you save John Gwyn from playing the fool to dirty old Traquair."

"That may be, Captain Gwyn," I replied, "but you must now hear what I could not tell you before. I am no King's man. I have done the service of messenger only to save my friend John Spottiswoode. And, now that I have delivered my message and helped to get you clear, I will e'en say good-night to you and be going my own gait."

" No King's man ! " he thundered. " Then what in the fiend's name are you ? A Covey ? Do you dare tell me you are a traitor and yet carry for the Secretary ? "

" Less of the traitor will do, sir," I replied, with as much patience as I could muster. " Less of the traitor, seeing on what soil you stand. But, as you are in perplexity, I will give you now the explanation of my position, the same you would have had at my first sight of you to-night but for your own insistence on delay."

So in few words I told him how I came to be in the affair at all, and of my intention to get out of it by riding there and then for Restalrig and the road to the Ferry.

He heard me out. Then he said in a voice which, I declare, carried real regret and not contempt, " You chicken, you absolute chicken, to use the language of our late companions of the cup. The very shell is on your head. You cannot, you cannot turn back now. Consider, you go riding a stolen horse, and you go as one who fled when denounced in mistake for young Spottiswoode. Upon my soul I'm sorry, but your freedom would end with cockcrow. No, my lad, you're on the road with Gwyn till the storm blows over at least ; and, let me tell you, it's no bad fortune to be with Gwyn. Besides, Gwyn cannot afford to part with you now. You know too much. You know there is a treasure, where it is and where it is bound for, and, though I believe that, for a Covey, you're a good Covey, if there be such a thing, your fellow-Coveys might persuade even you to blab under the thumbscrews or whatever they call 'em."

I have ever noted that there are two sorts of men. One sort sees only the best. The other sort sees only the worst. You may call it cowardice if you will, but, though I ever see the best as I think of my friends' fortunes, when I consider my own I see all the black things and none of the bright. In that hour, possibly because of the recoil from the excitement in which I had been living for the last twelve hours, Gwyn's alarming view of my position chimed with my new thoughts on it. I forgot that, though I was in an awkward scrape, a little disagreeable detention was the worst I need anticipate, and that in the end the Rector's strong help would not fail me. But I am telling my own story, and not trying to paint myself as a hero or even a very wise youth. I did think that I was in a parlous state, if I had to answer instanter to the city authorities. On the other hand, it seemed to me that, in a few days, the tangle I had put myself in must unravel and I could return with safety when the trouble had blown by.

"Well, my cockerel, what is the result of all that thinking?" asked Gwyn, who had watched me as I digested his words. "Is it the Tolbooth or a trip with the jolly Cavalier?"

"I don't have to choose," I replied; "but I go unwillingly."

(3,578)   4

" All right," he said. " If it saves your honour, you
go as my prisoner, but a prisoner on parole ; and I tell
you, to be a prisoner on parole with John Gwyn is a
position princes might envy."

He gave a jolly laugh, and in the best of good humour
turned into the road, as if careless whether I followed
or not, so sure was he of me. And, indeed, Gwyn was
never anything but sure. As we made our way east-
wards by a road which runs about two miles from the
sea, he talked to me as if he and I had been companions
for years. The letter from Sir Robert had been Greek
to me, and I did not hesitate to ask him if the treasure
was money from the King for Montrose.

" Money from His Majesty ! " he replied, with a laugh.
" You haven't been with him, or you would know he
has none to send. And if he had, how could he pass it
through the cut-throats who swarm on both sides the
Border, or even send it by sea, seeing they hold the
harbours on the east coast ? Yet His Majesty knew
Montrose's war-chest was empty, and that it must be
filled before his men melted away like snow. He and
the Marquis *must* join forces, and the treasure, in the
care of Jack Gwyn, alone will make the meeting possible
and save the crown. Lad, the treasure never saw
England. It is the proceeds of the sale of the last of
the Queen's jewels in France. It was sent to Dunkirk,
and it has been ferried across by good Jens Gunnersen,
with Jack Gwyn playing supercargo. The original idea
was that it should be put in charge of old Traquair ;
but I was to get final instructions from Sir Robert

Spottiswoode, and that is why I have been risking my skin in that plague-stricken town, passing as a greasy old vendor of stockfish, I who have trained the princes of England to the use of arms from their infancy, I might say."

Gwyn, I was afterwards to learn, was speaking the sober truth in asserting that he had trained the royal children.

" This, and much more, I would do for His Majesty," he went on ; " but conceive you how I long to see these bright boys of my coffers safe in the paymaster's hand, to quit these duds and to be once more the soldier. Why, comrade, till I bought this hanger at the Lucken-booths yesterday, I had nought but a Plymouth cloak to defend my purse against padders in your closes, or mine honour against the gentry who tried to give me a fall to-night. Even this afternoon I was glad of the poor tool in my little journey in this direction."

" Yes," I said, " I heard from the landlady that you had gone by the Figgate Whins to the Pans."

" Ah, that was but dust in her eyes," he rejoined. " I took the road we now take, never looked at the Whins, and never tried to reach the Pans of Preston. The Haven is a snug little place with few about to take notice. I had my conference with the Norwegian there. He is to have all in readiness, and I am in hopes that he will put us on the road forthwith."

Well, here was I not only in up to my ankles, through bearing a letter for my country's enemies, but in to the chin in helping them to convoy the treasure on which,

apparently, the success of their effort hung. I must
be honest, and confess that the thought brought me no
twinge of compunction such as I had felt at Duddingston
Loch. It may have been Gwyn's infectious enjoyment
in the adventure; it may have been just the young
blood in me, which leapt up as it used to do when
Dairsie and I played a game in which one outvied the
other in some mad cantrip, and risked our neck, crying,
"I dare your deed." Certain it is, as we turned into
the coast road beyond Musselburgh, and saw the lights
of the little villages by the Forth twinkle, it was with a
warmth round my heart that I moved on to discover
what Dame Fortune and her present master of mysteries, the mighty Gwyn, had in store for me.

Not a soul did we meet, even when we came to where
the hamlet of the Haven is tucked into the side of the
hill. The tiny harbour itself, with its toy pier of great
stones and berthing room for two or three small ships
at the most, shewed only the black bulk of some fishing
boats, but a dim lantern was burning on the forestay of
a larger vessel which lay alongside the quay.

"That's the sloop," said Gwyn; "and now to rouse
up Jens."

We put the horses into a shed, where I noticed a farm
beast had already been given an extemporized stable,
and sought the sloop. It was then near midnight.
Even Gwyn did not bellow. He found his way famil-
iarly, between kegs and waterbutts, to a little green
scuttle, and hoisted his bulk carefully in. But, if this
caution was out of regard for his friend's slumbers, it

was misspent. A tiny lamp revealed Gunnersen sitting
at a table, apparently ready for bed, for he was undressed to his small-clothes ; but a square bottle of
Schnapps and a rummer showed that the nightcap stage
only had been reached.

" Ah, you here again, and so late, my friend ? "
he began in that excellent English which Norwegians
always seem to command. " And with a companion !
Then it's up stick and away, and no rest yet awhile for
poor Jens."

" Sorry, Jens," responded Gwyn. " But you're right.
We must get the merry boys on the cart. There's need
for us to be miles away before the gossips are astir. We
can manage without rousing your men even, if you will
bear a hand."

" Gladly," answered this imperturbable person, as he
drew on his breeches and slipped into a sea-coat. He
kindled a lantern and led us to the shed on the quay.
The farm horse was harnessed and put into the shafts
of one of those light narrow carts such as hawkers use.
A piece of black oiled-cloth was lifted from a corner
and revealed what seemed to be a pile of fish boxes.
Fish boxes they were, and fish they contained, for I
could see, as well as faintly sniff, the semi-cured haddock
which we call speldings. But heavier fish were never
handled than those in some of the boxes.

" Yes," said Gwyn, noting my interest, as I helped to
lift the first. " They lie on sand, good golden sand."

There were four of these boxes, which it took all the
wit of the three of us to slide into the cart on an inclined

plank. Then two others, which seemed to me to contain fish only, were placed on the top.

"These are our real stock in trade," cried Gwyn; "and see me, serviteur in the royal household, as head of a worshipful company of fishmongers, and you, brave lad, my alderman-in-chief. But let it go at that. There's your quittance, friend Gunnersen," he added, handing the Norwegian a slip of paper, "and with it go my poor thanks for a bit of work finely done. Yet there's one more favour to add to many. You see these horses. They were found grazing on the bents to-morrow morning by your ship-boy, you understand? There's a crown if he leads them to Edinburgh. I have little doubt they will find owners for them there and no harm done, not so much at least as if their masters had themselves come seeking them."

Gunnersen listened to his instructions, and nodded with a comprehending smile. He shook us both by the hand, and wished us good speed. "As for your horse," added Gwyn to me, "by the foot of Pharaoh, it must e'en go to pay my tavern score."

Gwyn had no hesitation as to his route. He led the horse along the road a little way and took the first turn inland. And so, in this monstrously plain fashion, our convoying of the treasure began.

CHAPTER V

ON THE ROAD WITH GWYN

IN that night journey we held round by the east side of the town of Dalkeith, and morning found us beyond the village of Ford. Shortly after passing it, we turned sharp to the right and made for Gala Water by the hill road.

By this time our beast was shewing signs of weariness, and we ourselves, who had trudged all night by his head, were as ready as he for a rest. A mile or two along the track we came on a solitary cottar's house. Here I played the part of fish merchant, and though the gudewife had no desire for our wares, she acceded readily to my request that the horse be turned for an hour or two into the byre while he got a good feed of bog hay.

Desiring to get away before her man returned from the hill, I declared we must reach the Stow well before nightfall to make our sales.

I remember that this shepherd's wife was offended when Gwyn offered her a crown in payment, and that it took me a good deal of talk to excuse him on the ground that he was a foreigner and strange to our ways.

She gave us what she called a chack for the road, and so we parted friends.

By afternoon we crossed the ridge and dropped down on the main road at Middleton Muir. This is the gateway to the Borders from the northern side. The scene presents a fitting introduction to that south country. The wide valley, bordered on the right by grassy slopes which had for their rim the distant Moorfoot Hills, could be seen ahead narrowing into those " dens " which I was to know so well, and, under the September sunshine, gave me my first impression of that pensiveness which has made the natives term even the fairest of their valleys " dowie."

If I desired a corrective to the mood of gentle melancholy which I felt stealing over me, I had but to glance at my companion. Along that bare road he trudged at the horse's head, ever and anon singing the stave of a song. Of rounds and catches he had a great store. A verse of Drayton's seemed to be his favourite however, for he returned to it many times. It runs :

> " Whilst the birds billing,
> Each one with his dilling,
> The thickets still filling
> With amorous notes."

I saw no birds except some peesweeps, and thickets there certainly were none. In my matter-of-fact way I twitted him on the liveliness of his fancy. I drew on me a spate of words.

" Fancy ! 'Odso, and why not, comrade ? Will you tell me how a gentleman, stripped of all outward circumstance, is to bear up, unless he is to draw on the rich mine of fancy, which is just the other name for a quick sensibility, and a well-stored mind? Take an instance. You see me, the second son of the House of Trelydan—a most noble family of Wales which traces its descent direct from Brochwell of Athan, King of Powis—masquerading as a scurvy *vendor of fish!* Would you, because of that, have me trim my spirit to that of a padder or an Abraham-man? No, sirrah! The good Welsh blood in my veins will not suffer it. I see in these mean boxes the treasure that will save an army and perhaps a crown. Therefore I envisage success coming to reward this shabby turn which I have to play.

"Why, when I trained to arms the young princes, there were croakers who used to declare that their sport *fore-halsened* that bitter strife in which the Prince of Wales now bears his part. A fig for them and their croakings! The strife was foré-halsened by the false-ness of disloyal knaves. It was bound to come, and, if Jack Gwyn can turn the dark day into a bright, he of Wales will not forget his preceptor in arms, when we can quote as true my couplet:

" ' So, wheel'd about, each to their proper sphere,
    Princes and peasants, all right as ye were.'

Against that day Jack Gwyn has his gala clothes laid up in lavender. Is he not right, then, by a projection of fancy, to live in what will then be his world, and so to troll his song with a merry heart? I tell you, com-

rade, till I can play the falcon perched on the royal
wrist, I will forage for myself like the sparrow, yet ever
keep the falcon's heart."

The while Gwyn declaimed, I had observed that we
were no longer to have the road to ourselves, for a couple
of riders had come down from the Fountainhall side and
struck southwards behind us.   Gwyn at length observed
my apprehensive glances backward at them, and followed
my eye.

"A gentleman and a lady, I see," he commented.
"No danger from them."

But, not two minutes after his remark, when we turned
the next corner, we saw ahead of us what looked like
danger.   Opposite a house which stood hard by the
thoroughfare, a crowd of people filled the roadway.

"'Sdiens ! " cried Gwyn, "what have we there, a
funeral, or one of your conventicles ? "

"Neither," I replied, when I had myself gathered the
character of the occasion by the merry-andrew movements of one who stood elevated above the crowd and the
answering noddings of heads and lifting of hands from
it.   "What you see is something more serious than a
funeral and more enthralling than a conventicle.   Yon's
a farm roup."

"A farm what ? " he cried.

"A farm sale," I explained.   "The sale of stock, implements, and furniture, which we call the plenishing.   Man,
Captain, toll-bar gates would be easier for us to pass
through than yon crowd in full cry at a roup.   A roup
is the nearest thing to ecstasy the country folk know in

all their lives. Turning drouths off the ale-bench is
child's play to interrupting their pleasure for a minute.
This is like to put a stopper to our easy way with a
vengeance."

" You tell me so ?   Ah ! we will see."

But even Gwyn's confidence evaporated when we
reached the outskirts of the crowd. Stop we had to, if
we were not to commit manslaughter.   The folk whose
shoulders we could have touched did not so much as
turn an eye on us.   Like people in a trance, they gazed
fixedly at the rouper.

In the life of those who are bred on the soil, I regard a
farm roup as one of the saddest events.   It speaks of
dissolution so starkly.   At the tap of the callous mallet,
there go the kindly animals that meant so much more
to those who reared them than they ever can mean to
any buyer.   There go the implements, rendered almost
sacred by the hands that used them, commemorating,
as they do, the alternate fight and partnership with
Nature in every season of the changing year.   There
goes the harness, symbol of the union between man, the
master, and the sleek creatures which were as proud to
give him their strength as he was to make their fetters
as like ornaments as possible.   But it is when the furnishings of the broken-up home are sold off that one
gets the worst grue.   The things the man and woman
gathered at the first, and continued to use as life
mellowed or withered—how can other folk buy these
without feeling they are desecrating a shrine, or a grave,
or both ?

Yet, as Gwyn and I looked on, there was that fellow, the rouper, offering these dear and intimate things with cheap jokes as he stimulated the bidding, and making leering remarks as he named the happy purchasers. Like that of the hangman, no doubt his office is a sad necessity. But what could you say in excuse for the greedy crones whom we call rouping-wives ? They sat on cutty stools as there for the day, and pounced on such things as they saw a chance of re-selling at a usurious rate. Even the neighbours, gathered from ten or twenty miles round, who had known the dead or dyvour tenant of that farm, were, for the time, oblivious to pity or sentiment, and intent only on getting something for next to nothing when the chance came their way.

Gwyn and I stood our enforced wait the more patiently that the lady and gentleman who had overtaken us drew rein and let their horses fidget on the outskirts of the crowd. But after a while the Cavalier's stock of passivity ran done.

At what he deemed a break in the proceedings, though it was only a pause for the rouper to have hoisted into fuller view an article which appeared to be the prize of the day, his great voice began booming in its best Dutch manner.

" Goot peoples, an it please you, a passage for mine carat."

The crowd thereupon took note of us. It would have answered better had I tried them in Scots. They eyed the foreigner stonily, and then turned once more to the centre of attraction, as though he did not exist.

Gwyn caught the horse's bridle and began to edge forward.

"Wha are ye pushin'?" came from one; "You an' yer cairt!" from another; while a third said suspiciously, "What's in yer cairt, an' wha are ye, onywey?"

"Feesh, kind peoples," Gwyn said ingratiatingly, "good feesh that I would sell before sun-going-down. But, if you prefer I go no furder, zen I sell here, if ze master-seller ask you bid a price."

What a scatterbrain! If by any chance the mad challenge were accepted, the gold would inevitably be discovered and disaster fall on us.

No doubt he counted on them taking his suggestion as a joke and giving him passage to get rid of him. But some young farm hinds saw the opportunity for horse-play, and cried :

"Awa' wi' ye; tak' yer fish back tae whaur ye cam' frae. We hae nae trokins wi' Welshmen."

Gwyn did not know that the term was the one in common use among us to designate any foreigners, and he was as proud of his country as a peacock is of its tail. He glared at them angrily and clenched his fists.

"Oh! ye wad, wad ye?" they cried. "Na, we'll no buy yer fish, nor lat ye hurl yer foreign trash. But they'll be hurled a' richt, an' it's yer heid 'll get them."

When they choose to be nasty, none can be coarser than my countrymen. They made a rush for the boxes.

We were done. But were we? Before they could reach the cart, a horse was thrust between them and it. A clear ringing voice cried ·

" Shame on ye ! Would ye fyle the name of the
Borders, ye muck-hacks ? "

The lady had broken from the side of her companion,
who appeared to be just as amazed by her sudden
interposition as we.

" I'll no see that name fyled," she went on. " I pass
here, and if I pass, so do these strangers who have the
liberty of the King's highway."

She struck her mount lightly with her riding-switch
and began to clear a passage.

I believe, if it had been her elderly companion who
had tried to dragoon them, they would have barred the
way, for all his grey hair. But for a woman, and that
a mere girl, thus to rate them seemed to them so unchancy that it fairly left them gasping.

" Follow ! " she cried to us, and on the moment we
obeyed. The girl's guardian closed in behind us, and we
passed clear through the crowd.

As it stood gazing at our deliverance I heard one say,
" The auld ane is Scott o' Menzion ; but wha's the
hellicat he's convoyin' ? "

His neighbour answered, " I'm thinkin' that yanker
maun be the madam they ca' the Laird o' Winterhope,
by the name that same gets for coupin' ither folks'
creels."

A hundred yards on, when the crowd had most evidently returned to its devotions, the gentleman nodded
to us in an amused fashion and rejoined the lady, when
there ensued a lively exchange that ended in a laugh.
Thereupon our rescuer turned in the saddle, gave a bow

and a merry smile to Gwyn, ere the two of them set their horses to an ambling canter. As she gave that parting I thought that her face was the most beautiful I had ever seen. Then, while I watched her lithe form sway to her horse's motion, I found myself wondering whether the old fabulists had never told of a girl Centaur, and if they had, how they might have bettered that conception by imagining such an one as a Narcissus, rescued betimes from the pool of self-admiration, to shew the world how the poetry of motion adds to beauty of form that touch of animation which puts the soul into mere beauty.

Though this lady rode away, even as she came, like a passing glint of light on the road, sighted and lost almost in the same moment, I felt myself for the first time really glad that I had undertaken my strange adventure. What were my gloomy impressions of the city cowering under the plague and that world of greedy passions, from which I could not hope wholly to escape, if the open road held such blinks as had come by a single glimpse of this lady of the beautiful face and the generous heart ?

But, as I rhapsodized thus inwardly, Gwyn grunted, " I' faith, lad, it seems your country has some people of quality. It needs them, to set against the great multitude whose father is Clod."

It did not occur to him to confess that we had come within an ace of disaster through his recklessness, or that it was a singular stroke of luck which sent us a rescuer so timeously. He resumed his jaunty manner and read me a lecture, on the true management of the undisciplined mob, till we passed into the wooded belt that runs along the head-waters of the Gala.

Here our beast again shewed signs of being done out. I told Gwyn of the Stow, and inquired whether he thought we could make the miles.

" I have no intention," he replied. " Even if there is an inn, we should draw on us remark. I desire not to sleep with one eye open on the place where the treasure should be housed. The old campaigner knows how to camp for the night, and the young camarado must learn. See, there is the very place."

He pointed to a haugh on the right side of the road where, by the riverside, there was plenty of grass. It was just such a spot as gypsies or tinkers would select.

Soon we had the horse out of the shafts and tethered, though indeed the poor beast was unlikely to stray, what with tiredness and his keenness for the short, sweet grass. Gwyn and I were as glad as he to see the end of the day, and be at rest. We disposed of the provision the cottar woman had given us, gathered heather enough to form a softer bed than the sward, and soon lay stretched on it.

We were about a mile above the place where the valley narrows just before the road curves round to the Stow. The high wooded hill with bare faces of crag on our left looked sombre as the light stole from the sky, but on our right there were the outlying spurs of the rolling Border hills still shewing bright, while, through the vale, Gala Water ran like a silver thread.

The gentle murmur of the water, the baaing of a few

sheep on the hills, and the occasional whistle of a whaup
only deepened the sense of peace.   Even Gwyn's tongue
ceased.   The troubles behind seemed to me well past.
The troubles ahead might be left to the morrow.   There
was no coldness in the autumn air.   Before I had
thought on the strangeness of my first night with the
whole earth as chamber I had fallen asleep.

When I awakened it was, I suppose, five or six o'clock,
and the valley was full of sunshine.   I saw the huge bulk
of my companion lying like a rock.   Next I saw our
horse.   He had ceased browsing and was standing with
his head up.   Then, to my amazement, I perceived he
was not alone.   A little distance away stood a sheltie,
saddleless but with a halter of grass-rope over its nose.
My eye travelled to the treasure cart.   Bending over
it, and cautiously peering at the boxes, was a man.   I
darted over and seized him.   There looked up at me
the miserable creature who had volunteered to play the
part of hostler to me in the courtyard of the White
Hart.

Under my grip he turned on me with the courage of a
weasel at bay.

" What are ye ? " I shouted.   " Thief or what o't ? "
His snarl changed into a whine.   A look of vacuity
covered his face like a mask.

" Me ! " he whimpered.   " I'm puir Mungo, puir
Mungo, gangin' an errand.   Puir Mungo's hungry.   Gie
puir Mungo a bap, yer honner."

" Did ye think ye wad get baps in herrin' boxes ? "
I challenged.

" Na, na, fish, braw fish, guid kitchen wi' a bap," he mumbled.

Gwyn was now at my elbow.   " A prisoner, comrade ; but a scurvy one," he remarked, rubbing the sleep out of his eyes.   " Where did this innocent spring from ? "

" Hardly so much of the innocent as he looks," I replied, and remarked on the strangeness of the fact that this was the caddie whom I had seen on my arrival at the White Hart.

" Ah ! we must interrogate him, then."

So Gwyn interrogated ; but against all his inquiries " puir Mungo " was proof with his idiot manners.

" Friend," said Gwyn, turning to me, " you have played the good sentinel, for all stragglers should be challenged; but in this case the rouser of the camp is a full-blown ass.   Let him mount his brother and be gone."

" Is puir Mungo no tae get his bap ? " was all the wastrel said.   Indeed he looked a pitiable capture as he stood there, his hay-coloured hair tousled over his shifty eyes.

" Get you gone," growled Gwyn, " before you earn a halter."

The creature shambled up to his pony, threw a leg across its bare back, and made his way to the road.

" A queer world that has room for such as he," was Gwyn's comment.

" I am not sure that he hasn't a greater place in our world than you think," I rejoined.

" Body o' me, he's but a scarecrow, and men should bend their thoughts only on men."

" Mebbe," I said ; " but scarecrows can serve men."

And perhaps Gwyn was more of my opinion when, two hours later, we passed the Stow. There I hailed a thatcher who was busy getting a straw roof ready against the winter, and professing anxiety to know if a well-known cadger, Will Sproul, had passed, got the answer, " Na, there's nae a body gane by this mornin' but the Shauchlin Herd o' Talla, riding a sheltie."

" Wha's the Shauchlin Herd, and what's he aefter herding here ? " I queried, now in a considerable twitter about the half-wit who had passed himself off as a town caddie.

" Wha is he ? Oh, the son of the herd at Winter-hope ; but *what* he does the deil kens. I jalouse it's no *sheep* he herds, onywey."

CHAPTER VI

I MAKE A FRIEND

THERE are worse ways of travelling the country than the way which Gwyn and I had perforce to take. For, though the pace of our horse suffered us to cover no more than two miles or so an hour over the hilly roads, the very slowness let us better take in the face of the country-side. And, if there is a fairer bit than that which we travelled on our second day of pilgrimage, I have yet to hear of it. For we left the Gala valley at the Bow, and, climbing by a country road, crossed the summit into the valley of the Caddon, and so down a precipitous decline to Clovenfords and the valley of the Tweed. As we went leisurely along the stretch by Tweed's banks, from Caddon to Yair, I watched the Welshman. His eye ran along the heights on either bank, mantled with trees, the fields where the earliest crops were cut, but most standing ready for the hook, and the river itself, already majestic, yet retaining still some character of a mountain stream, flowing through a fringe of alders and willows and hawthorn bushes.

" 'Slife ! " he said, " it is a country after all."

It was well on in the afternoon ere we came abreast of Yair. There it stood, the old house of the Pringles who go back to King Robert's time, with its back to high ground crowned by forest trees and its front looking on one of the fairest pools in the long run of Tweed. I saw the trout rising, and doubted not many a lusty salmon lay in its broad expanse. Just a cast beyond the old tower of Fairnalee we could make out the Bridge of Yair, which spans Tweed and suffers travellers to pass along its right bank to Selkirk and the vale of Yarrow.

" Yonder," I said to my companion, " is the place at which you are bidden tryst by your paper. If Dairsie has reached his uncle, the Secretary will judge you should be well on your road. I think you ought not to have long to wait, for you and your boxes will be a sicht for sair een."

Sure enough, as we turned the corner of the road, we sighted a small company of horse round the Rink side of the bridge. Gwyn recognized a pennon that fluttered from a lance. Thereupon he cupped his hand round his mouth and taraed, as if imitating a trumpet, a set of notes like the opening of the old Scottish air, " Up in the morning early."

" That should make them advance in no doubt as to who comes," he remarked, " for that is the air to which we marched when I beat Waller's rear-guard out of Devizes without the loss of a man on our side. It hath been known ever since wherever the King's flag flies as the marching song of Captain Gwyn. Mark you how even here they answer to it like hounds to the hunts-man's horn."

I expect they would have come, call or no call, the moment they sighted us ; but Gwyn took all the credit for his particular signal when two horsemen detached themselves from the troop and trotted to meet us.

" Your names and business? " one of them challenged briskly when they reached us.

" Name, Captain John Gwyn ; business, commanding a convoy for the Governor-General," Gwyn answered.

The troopers smiled to each other as they glanced from the speaker in his leather jerkin to the cart.

" Advance to the post and report," was the word, however, and together we moved to the company by the bridge.

Our meeting was to be delayed by an incident which was just as surprising to the troopers as to us. There came a thudding of hoofs on the steep road that leads down from Rink. A band of some twenty yeomen swung round the corner. They came carelessly and without order ; but they were armed and evidently dashing on a prey they deemed easy to be seized. The sudden sight of the troopers not three hundred yards away brought them an unpleasant shock. They wrenched at their bridles so fiercely that some of them threw the great plough-horses they rode on their haunches. The commander of our convoy gave an order. Almost on the word his men were blowing their matches. No more than that threat of a volley was needed. The cavalcade turned and fled. All but one, who seemed to have difficulty in managing his horse. In a moment or two he humoured it to follow the others, but not before both Gwyn and I had recognized him.

" The Shauchlin Herd," I cried excitedly.

" Yes, by the beard of Aaron, you were in the right about him, comrade," replied Gwyn, " but he's too late. The sheep are in the fold."

And no better credential for his own standing could he have given the commander of the convoy than his explanation of this occurrence—how the farmers of the region must have been hastily gathered by that manifest spy, the Shauchlin Herd, to cut us off and capture the treasure. The commander of the troop picked the situation up with the quickness of one born to the business of accidents or happy escapes by flood or field.

" You and your friend are the ones to have done so finely your two selves, Captain," he said, " and it would have been a poor thing if we had delayed in the coming to meet you."

I noted the Highland accent of the speaker. Here, then, was one of the Highlanders serving in the army of Montrose. I looked at him with interest, and, indeed, in some disappointment, for less of the redshank or cateran we were accustomed to hear about he could not well be. He wore the lowland dress but for a plaid that crossed his breast. Then, too, he rode a horse, which, we understood, the wild men seldom used in their wars. And he spoke soft English, albeit with a certain quaintness of phrase, in a quiet voice. This frank young fellow, with a manner easy yet not familiar, seemed to meet Gwyn's approval.

"I think I have the honour of addressing the Captain-General's Master of Scouts," he said.

"I am not Captain Blackadder, sir. I serve under him. The name that is on me is Evan Mackenzie, but"—here he laughed—"it's seldom or never I get it in camp or on the march. You must understand there were but the twelve scouts of us before Auldearn, and as the commander of twelve is a sergeant, that was the rank put on me. It is a new name in the Gaelic, and the clansmen think it sounds grander than ensign or even captain. Then they would not be forgetting I am the grandson of Eachann Ruadh. So An Séirdsean Ruadh they called me ; and, whatever rank the Captain-General gives me, that will be my name among them that talk the tongue, and, for them that speak the English, it is like now always to be just the Red Sergeant."

He was no more red-headed than I, whose hair my mother, in moments of fondness, used to tell herself was "bonnie brown."

"*Lucus a non lucendo*," came from Gwyn, as he looked into the scout's eyes, which were blue-grey and of an uncommon steadfastness.

"*Forsitan*," responded the soldier, with a smile, in reply to the big man's well-worn tag of which he was shewing his pride ; and, thinks I, "He knows some Latin, too, this young son of Mars."

We spent no more time in taking stock of each other. The scout had all in readiness. The treasure was transferred to a gun-carriage, led horses were handed over to Gwyn and myself, and soon the little troop was proceeding along the road, that follows first the right bank of the Tweed and thereafter the left bank of the Ettrick, towards Montrose's camp on the haugh below the town of Selkirk.

As we passed the ford of Tweed, just before one comes to the fertile haugh of Sunderland, the scout pointed to it. " See there, Captain Gwyn, the danger-point in our defence. I must advise Captain Blackadder to place a picket at that point," he said. " It holds the key to our flank. Let them come along that hillside," pointing to Rink, " cross there to pass along this river bank, and our flank is turned. But I fear the scoutmaster will not heed. Leslie is marching *north* is the word in every mouth. Well, if he is, will he not, like the good commander he is, turn and seek his enemy the moment he learns his whereabouts ? *Mo Dhia !* I never yet knew that a whole army could be *fey*. You and your treasure is the first glint of rightness I've seen since we left the banks of Clyde."

" On my soul," Gwyn responded, " a soldier who has to counter an enemy as strong in cavalry as Leslie is cannot see such a point left like an open gate into his leaguer without uneasiness."

It was, indeed, by the selfsame route to which the young Highlander's finger pointed, that Leslie's army marched, and it was at that very ford, below the Rae Weil on which we looked, that the body which turned Montrose's flank at Philiphaugh crossed.

" A bright lad, with an eye for warfare," was Gwyn's comment to me, as Mackenzie rode forward with a couple of troopers to apprise the camp of our coming. We followed at the slower pace of the treasure wagon.

From the high ground above the haugh of Sunderland I had my first sight of an armed camp. We had left the drumly stream of Tweed, and could see the Ettrick's clearer waters coming to join it. Away on the left the town of Selkirk clung to the hillside like a swallow's nest to the eaves. On the right the hills, purple with heather already toning its fiercer fire, rose steeply. In the valley between both sets of hills, in that fair valley which is the gateway through which Yarrow and Ettrick flow in united stream, rose the smoke from the fires of Montrose's camp.

" A good spot," cried Gwyn; " defended on the south by Nature, and, if this road were held, inexpugnable, I should say."

" Ay," chimed in one of the Irish soldiers of fortune in the convoy. " A nice spot for a camp is Philiphaugh, an it were not that the commons are cursedly short for man and beast—not to say women, therefore all the more welcome is your honour and the fat chests of yellow boys."

The army had moved into quarters only that forenoon, but as we passed the mouth of the Linglie Glen I understood the soldier's reference to women. Numbers of wild, slatternly females, some carrying infants strapped to their backs with shawls, were stravaiging

along the road. One or two I saw held hanging to their
wrist a fowl, and the poorest forager or thief among
them did not fail to carry a meal-poke. I could imagine
how the farmers, cottars, and shepherds cursed these
harpies who came on the heels of the quartermaster to
pick up what he might have spared in his levy. They
were some of the great following of limmers and randies
that accompanied the Irishry.

I believe the hostility of the district to the Captain-
General, and the difficulty which his scouts found in
gathering information of the enemy's movements, were
mainly due to the hatred in which these Irish troops
were held. The memory of the fierce Irish caterans who
accompanied Hertford in his cruel expedition a hundred
years before, and had burned, as an English Borderer
had no stomach to do, abbeys and villages alike, had
been handed down. In our own troubles the Irish were
known never to give quarter, and even to slay for the
pleasure of slaying.

True, when Alasdair, the Marquis's Major-General,
had marched off, he had taken the wilder half of the
Irishry with him, and there remained but five hundred
of the Ulstermen, who were at once better livers and
steadier fighters than those who went with Col ; but
the Irish of the south had left most of their women,
who would not face the wilds of a campaign in the
Argyle country. Women who antagonized the country
folk and numbers of horse-boys who waited to see the
cavalry which did not come, these two elements seemed
to be most in evidence in the environs of the camp, and

in my eyes took mightily away from the imposing sight
it had been in the distance.

Nor was I greatly impressed when we drew up at
the picket placed between the great pool of the River
Ettrick, which flanked the camp on the one side, and
the farmhouse of Philiphaugh, to which it stretched, on
the other. The foot soldiers were busy throwing up
some trenches, but little more than a scraping of the
ground seemed to satisfy them. I saw only three or
four cannons, and these but small pieces, in position,
and there was a mere handful of horses picketed in the
cavalry lines.

Gwyn grunted as he took all this in.

"Leslie had fully five thousand horse when he left
England, not to speak of foot," he grumbled, "and he
will have picked up some more on the way. But
doubtless many of our men are scouting or foraging.
Anyhow here come some."

He pointed to the ford, from which an exceedingly
well-appointed troop of cavalry was approaching. It
was indeed the Marquis's own guard, under Ogilvy of
Powrie, whom he had sent to greet and escort Gwyn to
his quarters in the town on getting the report of the
mighty man's coming from the Red Sergeant. The Red
Sergeant it was who spurred forward from the ford,
returned with Gwyn to effect the introductions, and then
came back to where I halted by the wagon. He greeted
me with a friendly smile.

"They go on to quarters," he said, as Gwyn moved
off with Ogilvy. "You and I will follow when we have

disposed of your precious charge as the Marquis in-
structs. We shall probably be breaking camp to-morrow,
and I am to hold it in readiness against the start, but
not on this side of the river," he added, with a grim
glance at the camp followers who had gathered round
us since we halted. Our little cavalcade then crossed
the river.

Now, on the upper side of the ford, between the great
pool and a bit cliff which rises on the side of the Ettrick
valley, lies a flat piece of shingle studded with patches
of green sward. Here the Red Sergeant placed the
wagon, gave orders that the men of his guard should
pitch their tents round it, and thereafter, having cooked
their evening meal, bivouac for the night.

"I don't know that you have done me altogether a
good service," he remarked, as together we faced the
steep climb that leads to the town. "You have turned
me from being a soldier into being a nurse. The
Marquis, you see, has made me answerable for that
treasure. To-day, while awaiting your coming, I heard
a lass above Fairnalee singing the moss-trooper's lament,
which runs something like this :

"' Oh, how can I tethered on Yarrow's braes abide,
    Wha, far as Trent an' Humber, hae scoured the Sitherns
        wide,
    An' gang nae mair a-rovin' ? '

Well, I have seen Lord Linton desert with his troop to
join his brave daddy at Traquair, and it was wise not to
send the chests to that house. But it's hard on me to

be tethered to the money bags. Precious little is the rovin' I will have, whatever. Yet we'll see."

And we were to see. If Sim Cleghorn was the imp of movement in my life, my coming was to play the same part to my new acquaintance, the Red Sergeant.

CHAPTER VII

WE entered the town by the West Port, just within which the Captain-General had taken up his quarters. Evan, on taking him word of the arrival of the treasure, had found the Marquis in council with Sir Robert Spottiswoode, the Lords Airlie and Crawford, and that fiery gallant, the lame Sir William Rollo. Even as we reached the door, a soldierly man, whom Evan told me was Gordon of Ruthven, passed in to join them. It was clearly no time for such inconsiderables as the young lieutenant of scouts and myself to intrude. In any case I was most desperately hungry, and was glad when my guide led to a largish inn which stood in the market square. This place was occupied entirely by officers, to the exclusion of the citizens ; but even the presence of so many of the masters of the moment could not cow the spirit of the hostess. Most sullenly she stopped in her work of preparing a sheep's head, which some one had bespoken for supper, to take our orders.

The Red Sergeant said pleasantly, " And a fine head it is, too, mistress."

She looked up and, with never a wink of fear, barked

out at him, " Ay, but I wad coont it a finer ane gin it were Montrose's ain."

I could picture Gwyn having such a thing said to him of the Viceroy of Scotland, and how he would have drowned the woman in vituperation.

The young soldier, in a softer voice than he had used before, said, " Yes, mother ; there spoke the spirit which kept this town when all its men stood round their king at Flodden. It's a good spirit, but you and I differ in its application."

Now there are two things these outspoken Borderers love. One is to have their boldness met by a courage which yet shows grace. And another is an understanding reference to that story of heroism which has left the flowers of the Forest unwithering as the asphodel which grows in the fields of the blessed. I am sure the soldier spoke not by craft but of instinct.

" Ay, laddie," she replied, " it's easy seen ye're Hielant, wi' yer smoolyin' weys ; but aiblins ye think it richt tae keep the heid whaur it is. At ony rate it's the hour o' the Prince o' Darkness for hiz. We maun e'en submit ; sae what's yer wull ? "

I had not eaten a real meal for near two days, and did justice to the excellent fare which she quickly set before us. The Red Sergeant did little more than watch me eat. His mind was full of the military situation, and in much concern over it. He told me how, to his thinking, everything had a twist of ill-luck since the day when Alasdair had marched off with half the Irish and all the Highlanders, except a few personal worshippers

of Montrose, to root the Campbells out of Argyle, how
Aboyne had gone off in the sulks with all the Gordon
horse and foot, how the Border earls, Hom and
Roxburgh, were prisoners, willing prisoners, to Middleton and Leslie's advance guard, and how, to fill up the
cup, Lord Linton had just withdrawn with his troop of
horse in obedience to a letter from his father, the Earl
of Traquair, bidding him home.

"You saved the treasure from being at Traquair
before him, anyhow," he ended; "and now there's but
one hope—to break camp, make a dash for the west,
raise as many men as we can muster there, and join the
King. Ah! but here's Captain Blackadder."

The master of the scouts on entering the room made
straight for us.

"Evan," he said, "I have reconnoitred to Melrose
and to Torwoodlee. I have examined the position you
spoke of, and think well to place a picket in the houses
at Sunderland. It will suffice. The enemy could approach the ford you spoke of only by that spot. If the
picket is drawn in, we get warning enough, longer notice
than if I placed them at the ford. Besides, it would
require to be held in force, if at all. I cannot spare men
for that when there's no sign of the enemy within twenty
miles."

So little did he guess, poor man, that, even as he spoke
the words, Leslie was hurrying down the very road
which Gwyn and I had found almost innocent of human
beings when we traversed it at a snail's pace some four
hours ago.

" You can't be spared from your special duty," he added. " I'll send Charteris."

He crossed to an officer, who was refreshing himself with a tankard and a paper of tobacco, and gave him some orders. A few minutes later we saw this officer, Charteris of Amisfield, at the head of a strong picket in the market-place. I say strong, but it was only in numbers. The men were some of the retainers of the young lairds who had joined Montrose from Nithsdale and Upper Clydesdale—a half-hearted crew who knew little of soldiering, and quite useless unless under the leadership of their masters. But these we watched ride off in the direction of Lindean to take up their position in the haugh of Sunderland under the shelter of Rink Hill.

It was now falling dusk, and I had no notion where it was purposed that I should pass the night. The Red Sergeant seemed to have not the slightest concern on the score of my fidelity. He must sleep at the ford with his men, but there was no reason why I should not lie soft at the inn. He would count on me, however, to join him immediately headquarters moved in the morning. He got his horse and rode off, leaving to me the mount I had ridden from the Yair. Ever since the meeting with my new friend I had been thinking much of my old friend whom he in manner greatly resembled. Dairsie, I was told, had been away since noon in the company of young Alexander Ogilvy of Inverquharity on a mission for which the Captain-General had himself instructed him. It was a bit of work most unwelcome to him—to explore the route the army would take on the morrow in its march to the west. Dairsie's thoughts had all run on hunting Leslie down, and even one of those lightning marches for which the Marquis was famed had no attraction for my friend, since it looked so like running with, instead of after, the hare. And so it was a sadly overcast Dairsie who arrived at the inn door, on a very tired beast, at the chap of ten, in company with a mere lad who had a pretty face, like a girl's.

Yet, when he caught sight of me, his expression cleared. The moment he was out of the saddle he ran to me and held me by both hands.

" Gibbie, by all that's wonderful ! Eh, it's lightsome tae see ye, an' on the richt side at last. How came it ? "

I gave him the story of the entanglement with Gwyn, the while the boy Inverquharity listened as to a nursery tale, his great brown eyes alight with interest.

" Well, see here, Gibbie," Dairsie burst out, " this is my friend Sandy Ogilvy. On the moment we must report to Gordon of Ruthven at the Captain-General's, and it may be the Marquis himself will ask for a word with us. You come too. My uncle Robert is sure to be in attendance, and it will be strange if you don't get a sight of our great man. If Gwyn has done you justice, you're sure of a welcome. Come wi' us, thou alchemist who turnest haddies into crowns. Thou art a good portent."

Portents ! I see in my glass of memory to-day these

two—Dairsie in the bloom of young manhood and Ogilvy, a boy who might well still be at school—the one a nephew of the Secretary of Scotland, the other a scion of one of its oldest houses. Then a mist dims the mirror and I am left thinking of two of the cruellest things which happened in our cruel time, and that they happened to just these two.

Together the three of us walked the few hundred yards that separated our inn from the Captain-General's quarters. It was an ordinary citizen's house, not too commodious. When we had passed the sentinel who stood at its doorway, we found the ground floor occupied by the General's council. These were unknown to me, but young Ogilvy got a nod from an old man whom I took to be his kinsman, the Earl of Airlie. Dairsie looked for his uncle, but Sir Robert was with Montrose in a room above. That brisk and soldierly man, Gordon of Ruthven, took Dairsie's report, asked some further questions, and then withdrew upstairs to pass the information to the Captain-General. I had expected to see Gwyn, but it seems the gallant Cavalier, after having explained at great length to Sir William Rollo his standing in the royal house, as no mere " loyal servi-teur " but trusted friend, had been graciously received by the Marquis, thanked for his zeal and discretion in the matter of the treasure chests, and dismissed with an order on the quartermaster for full military equipment. Thereafter, clad in splendour, he had departed with some of Douglas's bonnet-lairds to spend the night in the refreshment of his inner man.

In ten minutes or so after leaving us, Gordon of
Ruthven reappeared. He beckoned us to follow him
upstairs, and led us into a room opposite the landing.
Sir Robert Spottiswoode was seated at a table. At the
head of the table, which was littered with maps and
papers, his back to the window, sat Montrose. His
armour and sword lay on a settle at the side. It was
hard to believe that the man who looked up at our
entrance was but thirty-three years old. He had a
serious look, and impressed by the quiet majesty of his
bearing. Yet his was the face of a man tired by the
perils and ardours of war, and tired yet more by anxious
thought.

So this was the man who had turned his coat and, in
her hour of bitter need, had drawn his sword against
his motherland! I should hate the very sight of him.
Yet, from the first moment my eyes dwelt on his face,
it seemed as if all my thoughts were recast under a
glamour that moved me against my will. I could
understand, as I looked at him, how he was both poet
and man of action, a brilliant leader of handfuls of men,
and the only soldier known as yet who could keep
Saxon and Celt in amity for a common cause. No one
could look on James Graham as on a common man. I
understood how he held Dairsie and his uncle, old Lord
Airlie and the boy Inverquharity, Gordon of Ruthven
and the Red Sergeant on the same string and led them
by a touch. I understood even, I dare to say, how this
man, once a Covenanter, could be as keen now, ay, and
as honest, for the King's Majesty. Whatever he was,

schemer or common turncoat he was not. Here was a man who had suffered a conversion of mind, and, as some men suffer for a conversion of soul, so he was fed by the flame which yet burned him and made his allegiance lead others to follow by the very pureness and high-mindedness of what his faith was to him. The man, in short, was a lover who might have made a blinded choice, but never questioned, or could question, the worthiness of the being he loved.

It was my rare fortune to have a word from one who was hated, not only for his change of faith but also because he was supposed to encourage the barbarities which many of his soldiers undoubtedly practised on our countrymen, more than any man in Scotland.

The Captain-General, with no trace of languor, he was indeed, as he questioned Dairsie and Inverquharity on some points which Gordon's report had left obscure.

" And whom have we here ? " he asked, as he turned on me the head that I have ever since thought of when men used the term Cavalier.

Sir Robert, who had smiled a recognition when I entered the room, now answered for me.

" This is the favourite pupil of that great man, Alexander Henderson, who, as Gwyn told your Excellency, has served His Majesty by passing my instructions to our Welsh friend and by helping him to convoy the treasure."

Montrose's eyes gleamed with whimsicality. His reply was in a low soft voice.

" Alexander Henderson will grudge being overcome

in *this* contest with his King ; but he had against him, as *advocatus diaboli*, that unconquerable ally, the spirit of youth. We who have been young, Sir Robert, understand ; but Henderson was never young. Do not dip too deep in this, young sir. I have enough of youth to answer for already," looking fondly on young Ogilvy. " Keep by the lug of peace and do not draw sword. That's strange advice from one who needs every man. Yet I thank you heartily for a generous deed done on a friend's account, and, if to-morrow sees the army and the treasure on the way to safety, your part of friend to your friend will have been well discharged. You may leave the surly face of Mars to his own scowls, and explore the shades of learning round the shores of Linlithgow Loch till you find the golden bough. And may you carry a pleasant memory of us rude soldiers who say, ' Ave et vale.' "

He nodded brightly to us, and we were dismissed. But, as we went, he stayed us for a moment to speak a word to Gordon. The careworn look sat again on the face beneath its mass of hanging locks.

" Ruthven, I am to be very close engaged with plans and dispatches. See that I be not disturbed, except it be on a matter of real importance. For the others, you deal with them."

Ruthven bowed his acquiescence. His understanding of the Captain-General's instruction was quickly tested. When we reached the ground floor, a horseman was demanding the sentinel to let him report to the General. Gordon went out and we overheard what passed. This

man, with horse gasping after a hard gallop, told how
Charteris of Amisfield had been beaten out his quarters
at Sunderland.

"Beaten by whom ? " cried Gordon.

"By the enemy, I suppose, sir," the trooper replied.

"The enemy! There is no enemy," barked out
Ruthven. "These Clydesdale louts have been at their
cups and had a fracas with the shepherd lads of the
Rink. We know something of these. They can play
at soldiers when it suits them." (I supposed he referred
to the surprising appearance to us on the Rink road.)
"The Captain-General must not be disturbed with clash
like this."

Was it fancy that, as we stood on the high ground
behind the inn, we saw lights, like those which shepherds
use at lambing time, shew here and there on the heights
towards Galashiels ? It was no fancy that we did hear
a great voice trolling from a house where the Kirk Wynd
runs into the market-place :

> "Nepenthe is a drink of sovereign grace
> Devisèd by the gods for to assuage
> Heart's grief, and bitter gall away to chase,
> Which stirs up anguish and contentious rage ;
> Instead thereof sweet peace and quietage
> It doth establish in the troubled mind."

I could not mistake that voice. Gwyn was ending his
day content.

CHAPTER VIII

PHILIPHAUGH

THE night had been as black as the roof of a dog's mouth, and it seemed to me still dark when I woke. It was morning sure enough, however, for the inn was astir. I could hear several of the officers quartered there hailing each other and shouting instructions for a breakfast *quam primum*. Indeed, when I had got me into my clothes and descended to the large public room, I found a little company discussing the landlady's viands to the sauce of her outspoken comments. These were no lie-a-beds. They were Ogilvy of Powrie and two cornets of horse who had been scouting for a couple of hours on Captain Blackadder's instructions. They had ridden as far down the Melrose road as to Faldonside on Tweed, without sight or sound of an enemy. " An' I wad lippen tae ma lugs mair than tae ma een on sic a mornin'," one of the cornets remarked. Scouting, indeed, was mere blind man's buff when candles were needed on the table at seven o'clock on a morning in mid-September. The day before had been byous hot, and, as often happens in autumn, a dense mist lay in the valleys. Wisps of it happed the market square of the town, high though it lay, and swirled it on us even as we sat.

" I think this day will have to be observed as a truce of God," remarked Ogilvy. " It would be a well-led army that could even march."

There was no sign of Dairsie ; but I was minding of my tryst with the Red Sergeant and got ready to go. The landlady pulled me aside. " Whaur's the lad that has the saft tongue for an auld wife ? " she asked. I told her. " Ay," she said, " a' thae gentry hae had my saft beds and my guid vivers, wi' niver a ' by yer leave, mistress.' He'll hae lain on the shingle o' Ettrick, and a wheen Hielan' red-shanks 'll be fechtin' for the mou'fu' o' aitmeal and blood they tell me the critturs live on ; but, gin you're no ower high-minded, you tak' him this pickle of dacent victual frae the auld wife." With that she thrust on me a basket covered with a clean white towel. " Ye can return the naepkin," she added, with a grim smile, " aefter the lairdie at the West Port has gotten his licks."

I had no intention of riding, as an order for general movement had not been issued. So, in anything but soldierly fashion, I slung my bundle on my arm and made for the camp. The few men-folk I met eyed me very sourly, and the women in the close-heads were not at all sparing of their tongues, for, if ever an enemy in occupation was hated, it was the Marquis and all his entourage in that independent, stout-hearted Border town, of which, for its lealness to what it holds to be right in foul as well as fair weather, I should count it an honour to be a citizen.

After I passed the Captain-General's quarters, where,

but for the post round the door, there was no sign of
life, and had gone out at the West Port, there was not
a body met me on the steep winding road down the hill
to the ford. A most fair estate which, they say, con-
tains the spot where Wallace was made Guardian of
Scotland, stretches to the left ; and on the right is a
valley out of the side of which the road is scalloped.
Yet, though I was to see this town and its fair surround-
ings in happier circumstances afterwards, that day all
but a few hundred yards of the landscape was blotted
out by the haar. And a fateful haar it was for Scotland.

I told you that the Red Sergeant had placed his little
encampment under the scaur at the Selkirk side of the
Ettrick. Here I found him with a dozen stout troopers.
The tents were struck. The fire at which they had
cooked their breakfast was already out. The ammuni-
tion boxes which contained the treasure had been placed
on a vehicle with stout wheels and long narrow body,
which I took to be a discarded gun-carriage, and in the
shafts were a couple of horses very different from the
cart-drudge Gwyn and I had. The soldier had evidently
no intention of being in the rear of the march, for he had
laid hands on two mettle beasts, great of bone and full
of spirit. He welcomed me and the old wife's present
with a gay laugh.

" It was her own moss-troopers who set the fashion
of the oatmeal and blood, and they even carried a girdle
at their saddle-bows," he said. " But, if we go among
the Westland folk, I shouldn't wonder if the old mother's
gift were welcome to more than Evan."

With that he gave the package a place among the treasure boxes.

All were not as ready for the route as this little party by the ford. I looked across the great pool and saw groups of the Irishry still by their camp-fires, though other bodies of them were being assembled and thrown into line for their morning exercise by their adjutant, Stewart.

In a moment this quiet scene changed as if by magic. Streaks of fire, followed immediately by the sharp reports of muskets, stabbled the mist which lay on the valley of the Ettrick below the ford. Then out of the mist came a line of horsemen at a hard gallop, and another line and yet another. Leslie's cavalry had effected a complete surprise. When they burst out of the mist, not five hundred yards separated them from the line of shallow trenches. Yet the breathing-space afforded by the time taken to cover even that short distance, shewed me how men schooled to alarms could use it. The adjutant, Stewart, swung his men into line, and, as the drums beat, the groups of dallying soldiers dashed from their bivouac fires, blowing their matches even as they ran. The little body of horse, picketed in rear of the camp, answered to the blare of a trumpet ; men sprang into the saddle and formed line. So it came that, ere the cavalry of the Covenant, which issued like one terrible sword of steel out of the mist, reached the slight rise on which the entrenchments lay, they received a well-directed fire at close quarters. Had I been soldier enough then to understand, I would have known that

their narrowing front as they galloped forward was
against the effectiveness of their effort to carry the camp
at a rush. The line bunched as the space between the
river and the road diminished, and it was a body com-
pact, but somewhat lessened in speed and freedom of
movement, that received the fire which smote them as
Stewart's voice roared out the order. The salvo plainly
staggered them, and, ere they could recover impetus, the
little body of Royalist horse in the most gallant way
dashed into their centre. For a minute or so there
ensued a confused mellay as these troopers hacked into
the leading files and the infantry from both wings of
Montrose's camp poured in a fire on the flanks. A
trumpet sounded, and Leslie's magnificent cavalry slowly
gave way, to re-form down the haugh just out of musket
shot. The first move in the grim game, though it came
within an ace of success, had failed. The men in the
leaguer had got a respite. But it was only to be a
respite. Montrose's few cannons were now getting the
range, and, whether it was their discharge following on
the explosions of the musketry or not, the haar seemed
to lift in great part from the valley. I could see further
masses of cavalry crossing the river from the Dunsdale
side opposite the Linglie Glen. This body, fully two
thousand strong, included Kirkcudbright's Dragoons
under Agnew of Lochnaw, as fine a force of horse as
soldier could wish to command. By the time these
formed behind the original attacking force, there must
have been near four thousand of Leslie's horse massed
for the attack which was to follow. Nor was this all.

His infantry were already across that very ford below the Rae Weil, which the Red Sergeant had indicated as the place specially to be guarded, and, at their slower rate, were advancing along the right bank of the river by the road which Gwyn and I had travelled. You may be sure that this situation, so plain even to me, had not been unmarked by the Red Sergeant.

"*Och! Ochan! Nach 'eil sin tubaisteach! O mo chradhshlat!*" he said to himself in the Gaelic, and then, turning to me, " See these brave lads and hardly an officer. Perdition take the treasure! I'll no longer play its nurse. Will you stand for me here and let me free to use my sword ? "

His eyes were gleaming. I thought I had never seen a man look so like an eagle. For the second time I was to be a stop-gap, and this time for a very new friend.

" Have your will," I replied. " I'll stand by the horses."

" Come then, lads," he called to his troopers ; and the half-dozen of them dashed with him through the ford. A minute after I saw Evan taking command of a group of men along with gallant Douglas, whose own bonnet-lairds were the only members of the little force that had fled at the first shot.

Then, in that fateful pause, I beheld a sight which is fixed by itself in my memory. Down the hill that leads from the town came galloping a single horseman. His hair blew on both sides of his helmet as he urged the horse by spur and the flat of the sword which he held ready drawn. It was the Captain-General. The

rattle of the musketry must have sounded in his ears as
the doom of the King's cause ; but he had flung himself
on the first horse to hand and tarried for none. His eye
swept the valley as he dashed through the ford in a flurry
of spray. He was at the head of the little body of horse
before a clatter on the road turned my eyes thither.
There I saw the Earls Crawford and Airlie, Lord Napier,
Sir William Rollo, Sir Robert Spottiswoode, followed
by Dairsie and the other junior officers who had been
quartered in the town. They were no more than in
time, for hardly had they reached the camp, before the
attack, this time in force, was renewed. Leslie's great
body of horse now advanced against the thin line of foot-
men and the bare hundred riders who held the gateway
of the Border glens. This time the Royalist fire opened
at longer range, and was sustained till the advancing line
had come within a couple of hundred yards of the encampment. Thereupon the defenders' handful of cavalry, with
the Marquis himself leading it, dashed into them. It
seemed madness, but, if ever men proved what can be
done against odds, these did. Apparently swallowed up,
they yet emerged, and Leslie's line got no nearer the
centre. I saw Evan passing in and out like a flash, and
never far from the bridle of the Captain-General, who
himself fought like a trooper. But most of all I admired
Sir Robert. I had ever known him to be a magnificent
horseman, but never expected to see him ride on the
field of battle. Yet now, splendidly managing that horse
of his which was known all through Fife, he played a part
such as Castor and Pollux were fabled to enact. It was,

indeed, like some scatheless ghost that he moved in and out of that vortex of desperate men in conflict, and passed encouragement to them as he moved, yet without himself ever striking a blow. For he carried no sword or weapon of any kind, but only a white riding wand. This man's repute was much blown upon for actions unbecoming a judge when he was President of the Court of Session. I knew also how Argyle and Henderson had secured his release from prison when his fortunes were at the lowest, and how poorly he had behaved to them for all their generosity. But it appears in my poor judgment that, when we sum up his character, we should put a heavy entry on the credit side for his conduct that day.

The two young bloods, Dairsie and Inverquharity, presented very different figures to the Secretary. They were not second to the fiery Sir William Rollo himself in thrusting and hacking with their swords. Yet, while the attack was for the time held in the centre, the Ulstermen in their shallow trenches were being hard beset. Leslie's cavalry charged them, only to be turned more than once by a withering fire. But the advance parties of his foot, who had come from the Rae Weil, were already scattering out along the side of Philiphaugh Hill and galling the Irish by their cross-fire. At length these were beaten out of their poor trenches and forced to take up position in the folds of Philiphaugh farm. There for a time they kept at bay the enemy's horse, but his foot from the Rae Weil worked round the hillside above the farm, and these most gallant Irish found themselves attacked on the rear as well as in the front. More than half of the six hundred of them lay dead before Stewart surrendered, under promise of quarter.

Meanwhile the Royalist cavalry in the centre, after repeated charges, were reduced to less than fifty swords. Even a tyro in the art of war could see that all was over.

Let me pause to relate a curious incident in this engagement which, though to many it would be reckoned only a skirmish and a surprise, was to me, as one who watched his first battle, a very great affair.

There were but few Highlandmen who fought at Philiphaugh, for the men on whom the Marquis relied for his great victories had gone either with Alasdair or home to reap their harvests; but there were a few. Among them was a piper who stood by the far side of the great pool, sounding at times the rally and at times that skirl of defiance which calls to the onset. He never ceased, and, through all the roar of cannon, the sputter of musketry and the clash of steel, still his pipe, which his countrymen count worth a regiment of fresh men to them, rang above the din. It was at this, the very last moment in the fight, that a stray bullet from the opposite hill found him. The air went out of his bagpipe in a wail. His body dropped into the pool like a stone. The piob mohr floated for a moment or two, and then sank. No one said " Well done " to that lone lad from the hills. He went without his wages ; but let this line of remembrance by the Lowlander on the opposite bank, whom he never so much as noticed, be his *requiescat*.

As for the battle, it was over. I saw the little group

round the Captain-General pleading with him. His aspect was that of one who resisted being overborne. At last he yielded and, with some thirty others, rode off the field and took the road to Yarrow. I had no chance to watch what followed, for there burst in on me the Red Sergeant.

" The soldier's part is done for this day, whatever," he cried, " and now I am back to my nurse-work. I was given charge of this treasure, and, by the bones of my fathers, keep it I will for the King's cause, against the day when the cause lifts up its head again. Are you with me, friend ? "

I answered lamely, as appeared to be my mode in such situations, " There seems to be no other choice."

It was not a very gracious answer, but it told the truth. It did not trouble Evan.

" Get you there with the good mother's store, then," he cried, " before the hungry children of the sword are on us."

I placed myself astride the chests. Evan took place in front of me, seized the reins, and started the horses, on the worse than cart-track which serves as a road from the cliff by the riverside, up the broad valley of the Ettrick.

CHAPTER IX

JOURNEY OF A GUN-CARRIAGE

IT may seem strange that we made such an easy, and even unobserved, escape. You must know, then, that the little corner in which I had stood with the horses was like an eddy outside the tide of battle which flowed close to it, yet never touched it, and, further, that, when we moved away, we were most effectively screened from the combatants, who were all engaged on the farther side of the river, by the fringe of willows and alders which grew at the foot of the scaur.

It was not indeed till we had cleared this straggling coppice which ran well into the haugh that we ourselves could clearly see these combatants. Then, at a turn to the right, where a little burn comes in from the heights to the south, we were in clear country and could look back on the field across the lower end of that fair belt of green which is known as the Carter Haugh.

Just where the road bends into Yarrow Vale, we saw the Lord General's little troop turn and beat off a company of Leslie's horse which had been zealous to surround them. But nowhere else were the King's troops able so to resist. Instead we beheld them spread wide in flight on the bare hillsides above Philiphaugh and being hewn down in numbers. My countrymen have often been blamed for giving no quarter on that day; but I have yet to learn that English troops ever gave quarter to the Irish, or even to their camp followers, after the days of the massacres of the English in Ireland.

The Highlanders, Evan assured me, never looked for quarter. Yet it was a piteous sight to see men falling like corn before the sickle; and, from the slaughter we witnessed taking place on one corner of the field, I am not surprised that it has ever since borne the name of Slain Men's Lea.

I think we had left our post about noon, and that it was a bare half-hour thereafter that we looked back on the finish of the battle. Troops we could see crossing the heights in an attempt to cut off Montrose before he got past Newark, and others following on the road he had taken. But, in any case, they were edging away from the line we pursued, and the farther we followed the Ettrick, now flowing below the high bank along which the road winds, the farther we diverged from them.

It was well to be thus free of immediate danger. For myself I had seen enough of battle to last me for the rest of my life. I cannot doubt that my companion was really much more cut in heart than I. For a time he rode very silent and grim. But the spirit of the born soldier must be far different from that of the peaceable citizen. He soon recovered from the sight which sickened me.

"Well," he said, "it's a dog's end for many a brave fellow; but the Marquis is free, and, when the Marquis

is free, he gathers men. He'll live to fight another day.
He is the brain, but here "—kicking the munition boxes
—" are his sinews. It's a poor part for a soldier, again
I say; but a trust's a trust, and it's a long sight safer with
Evan than with his Lordship of Traquair. Still it's an
unchancy thing to trail through the Lowlands ; and, by
that token, we must not trail it far."

Thereupon I asked him what his plans were.
" Plans ! " he ejaculated. " I might well have no plans
at all, at all, had there not been some notion to move
the army by the Moffat road to reach Dumfries or
Annandale. I heard Captain Blackadder's description
of the country, and I opine that, if we secrete ourselves
and the treasure somewhere on the high ground above
the Moffat road, we shall be in touch with anything that
may happen. One thing be sure of, the King's treasure
will be put in safe keeping for the King's cause, though
it may be long before it is claimed."

This was more than I had reckoned on, for I was fain
to think that, if we got off with our heads still on our
shoulders, we did well. But, in the new world into which
I had been so strangely thrown, it was a comfort to have
as a companion one whose mind was so very clear to
himself. Of his resource one could have no doubt. He
seemed to shake free of that nightmare of carnage which
we had witnessed as if it were indeed but an ugly dream,
and as the warm September sunshine, which had broken
long since through the mist, fell on us, he crooned Highland airs which were certainly not coronachs.

In that broad valley the few peasants we saw were

busy winning their bog hay, and generally at too great a distance from the road to mark the strangeness of our vehicle. On the valley lay the stillness of an autumn afternoon, broken only by a mighty baaing of sheep, which told us late spaining was going on in some of the hill farms. It presented almost too sharp a contrast to the scene of sturt we had left.

Fortunately the villagers of Ettrick-bridgend live a good cast beyond the place where the river has to be crossed by those making for the Moffat road, and we swung into the hill track that goes past the old tower of Kirkhope without a human eye to mark us so far as we could see. That entrance, however, ended our ease in going, for, of all roads, I imagine the Swire, as they call it, must be the worst.

It is steep and narrow and sandy, and it climbs to a great height. Yet, though it tried our horses sorely, in its windings by the stream midway, and in the steep ascent just before the summit, it was a delight to us, and Evan agreed the bard had put the heart of such a place into his lines when I quoted to him that couplet which came singing into my mind :

" The soft south of the swyre and sound of the stremes,
    Micht comfort any creature of the Kyn of Adam."

The descent to Yarrow Vale on the far side seemed to me to be even steeper, and we had to pass a chain round the wheels at the cart's tail.

We forded the river near the great pool at the Deuchar Mill (where lately a stone bridge has been built), just below Yarrow Kirk, and held up the vale by a fair good road till we reached the point where the cattle-track from Tweed strikes in.   Fortune, which had shown such a fair face, broke with us here; for down this road came riding two troopers.   At the turn of the little bit of straight where the hill ends they sighted us.   They were brisk lads, clapped spurs to their horses, and bore down on us at a hand-gallop.

" This spills the creel, unless they are alone," cried Evan.

To my surprise, he wheeled the wagon into the road, lashed the horses, and headed straight for the oncomers. I think I never saw men taken aback as were these two gallants.

They were coming from a bootless attempt to cut off Montrose in his retreat at Innerleithen, only to find he had taken the hill-road over Minch Muir.   So they rode carelessly, with their carbines in their holsters.   One of them, indeed, had drawn his sword when they sighted us, but his horse it was that our two galloping beasts crashed into.   The trooper shot from the saddle like a stone out of a sling and landed on his head.   At the selfsame moment, as it seemed to me, Evan discharged his dag at the head of the other's horse almost at arm's-length.

" That has ended not so badly," he remarked calmly as, two minutes afterwards, our enemies were trussed and lying like bales of merchandise on the wagon.

I own I was sorry for them, especially for the lad who had hit the road so hard and lay in a swoon.   The other fellow, to be a son of the Covenant, swore very hard. " *Bi samhach,*" said Evan to him. " Thank your stars it's not into Alasdair's hands you fell. It is your throats he would have cut." Then, turning to me, " This is an awkward capture. We must soon camp for the night, and to let these lads go would be to have a troop of Leslie's horse round us at the dawning and a breakfast of lead. Let us push on." He caught and mounted the sound horse and bade me drive.

Our talkative captive declared vehemently that our triumph was but for a while by reason that half a troop was following. But never a one appeared, and we swung again into Yarrow, leaving any that followed to make what they liked of the poor dead beast lying in the roadway.

A mile or two up we came to the valley of the Douglas Burn. We turned in and proceeded a good way from the main road along the burn's bank, and then camped in much the same fashion as Gwyn and I had done on the Gala. Only we risked not a fire, nor, indeed, did we need one, for the air was kindly. The lad who took a toss on the head had come to himself, and was vastly grateful to be in the land of the living. Even the other thawed when we shared the contents of the guidwife's napkin, and, seeing there was nothing better to be made of it, joined his companion in telling us of their fighting in England under old Leven and the story of their march under young David. We learned of his turning at Gladsmuir to cut off Montrose, and how much they owed to the country folk for the route by Rink and the exact knowledge of the country round Philiphaugh.

They were decent lads, but they had been in the army long enough to jalouse what our boxes contained. I have little doubt that it is to their tale of their hard bed on the wagon that we owe the belief, which holds in the valley to this day, that Montrose's treasure is secreted somewhere in its reaches.

What was of most interest to me, however, was the sight I got of Evan's mind about the war as we lay talking after we had secured our captives for the night. I happened to remark on Alasdair Macdonald, till a short time since the Marquis's major-general, and what a difference he and his men might have made on the day now ending. " Faith, if your fellow-Highlander and chief had been there like you and fought like you——" I was going on—I thought to pay him a compliment ; but he did not even let me finish. He sparked into temper.

" Alasdair ! Alasdair my chief forsooth ! The head of my house would not thank Alasdair to tie his brogues, for all he is the son of an Iona chieflet. And fellow-Highlander ! Troth, it's little he is of that. He has been too long in Ireland and is too fond of its ways for him to claim sib with us. A stirk and the chief of stirks, that's what Alasdair is. Brave ! of course he's that. No one who has seen his front in battle would deny it. At Auldearn he nearly lost the day by his rash courage, and then, by all that's fair, helped to win it by a courage greater still. Give him his due, the great kyloe of beef and brawn ! But fineness, the command and coolness of a chief—no ! Will you tell me how many clansmen, apart from the five hundred Macleans who really drew blade out of hatred to MacCailein Mor, Alasdair gathered, that were not Macdonalds ? I will tell you. Never the one. He rally the Highlands ! There is but one man to draw all of us of the other clans, and him a Lowlander, the Marquis. How he does it ? In the old Highland way, which never a Lowlander before him found the art of—by a *something*. You ask me what it is, and I cannot tell you, except that it's what our own best chiefs have always given us—the sense of being masters and yet our brothers in any lot. The man who felt his own honour touched when the enemy killed the poor drummer he sent to beat a parley at Aberdeen, and mourned as bitterly as any of the young Cavalier's own clansmen as he looked on the dead body of Lord Gordon at Alford, is the man we follow. I tell you, it's not rewards that keep the best of us thirled to him. It's courage and courtesy and, beyond all, honour. Alasdair goes away with his knighthood, the rap of the Marquis's sword still dirling on his shoulder. He goes to settle with the Campbells and glut an old feud. He covers his desertion with fine words, and he leaves the Marquis in the lurch. Let Gillesbeg Gruamach have him and make a hash of his fine fortune, or let him climb the slippery steps over that other self-seeker to success. I care not. He passes. For us who follow honour he ceases to be."

So carried away by his emotions was he that, by the end of this spate of speech, he appeared to have clean forgotten me and to be speaking to himself. Now his eye lighted on me, looking dumbfounded at having drawn on me his displeasure by an innocent remark. He went on in a comrade-like fashion:

"Forgive me, friend, for letting myself be carried away by the hot heart that is in me. You must not think I forget you are not in the galley, or imagine that I would be laying the sins of Sir Alasdair, or Col, as we call him, at your door. And, in sooth, I have the less right to blame him for deserting us in that he has been far longer in the service than myself. For I am only a late-comer to the standard. I had no share in the miracle of Inverlochy, but came in on a dark day just before Auldearn was fought. It was an act of foolishness, Mackenzie of Fairburn told me, and that I was like never to see again the tack in the strath we have held since the days before the Red Harlaw. But, though Fairburn has been as a father to me, a poor cadet of the house, I put the Marquis before him even. To-day's happening seems to make the good man's prophecy seem a true word. Yet I tell you there is but one fate for me—to follow the Marquis, yes, though he should be a setting star. And that," he added with a laugh, " is just the Highland pride of me."

As I settled myself down to sleep that night, I thought of the tragedy of the Douglas Burn enshrined in our old Scots ballad. I wondered whether it was not the same kind of fate which, even in this day, follows man or woman who loves another soul in teeth of consequences when all the rest of the world curdles against that soul in hate. But Evan, who had just given voice to this very philosophy, was asleep long before me ; and it was while reflecting how a quick temperament could yet have such an essential quietness of spirit deep down that I myself joined him and the snoring troopers in slumber.

Next morning we were on the road betimes, and had come to St. Mary's Loch and the mouth of the Megget when the sun was not very far over White Coomb. Had we known the country as we were to know it, I believe Evan would have turned up Megget. As it was, he held on, and, when we were well past the Loch o' the Lowes and in a desolate part of the road, we halted and he set our prisoners at liberty.

" My lads," he said, " that's your direction," pointing back the way we had come. " Get you horses, if you can, at St. Mary's and give the alarm, as your duty bids ; but follow, and, by my fathers, it's Alasdair's treatment you will get from me. Tell Leslie that, if his men catch up on us ere we reach Moffat, I'll let him know the Marquis's way of turning a retreat into a victory before he hands me to his provost marischal."

The troopers looked at the long straight bit of road before us, and the bare hillsides that gave no chance to follow us and be undiscovered by us. They grimaced, and, without further word, began to trudge along in their heavy boots.

" That's the wise men," said Evan to me, " and we are beholden to them for an armoury of weapons, for you see Leslie still follows the old Scots fashion and arms his men with four pistols apiece as well as a carbine and a lance. Yet, just because they're sore at being disarmed, they'll be all the quicker to raise the farm folk. We must not let the grass grow under our feet, but get rid of this tiresome treasure of ours at the first likely spot."

We urged the horses up a long incline and then came to the point from which the road runs along Moffat Water. Some few miles farther on we reached a place where the hillside rises very steeply on the right. We could hear the sound of a waterfall. At a grassy glade Evan stopped. "Here," he said, pointing. Together we lifted the boxes from the wagon. Evan tied the trooper's horse to the tailboard, led those drawing the wagon some way along the road, and then left them. There was no grass to tempt the beasts on that road, cut out of the rocky valley, and we watched them stepping bravely, as if a driver was still guiding them, in the direction of Moffat.

The task of transporting the treasure seemed to me interminable. We emptied box by box and bore such loads of it as we could carry up the steep hillside to the waterfall. It took us hours, and, for all I was handling the coinage of every country from Turkey to the States of the Baltic, and should therefore have felt it to be one of the marvellous experiences of my life, I declare to you I was but utterly weary of the sight of more and ever more of those gold coins. For we worked in feverish haste, and treated them as if they were but chuckie-stones. Last of all we bore the emptied boxes up, replaced the gold therein, and finally sunk these under the shelves of the rocks in the great pool which the cataract makes as it swirls in the pot at its base.

" That's a hidie-hole in a thousand," cried my companion when the task was accomplished, " and its secret is held by only the two of us. I suppose our lives are the more precious because of that. In any case, prudence tells us not to outstay our good fortune in having done this unobserved. We must find harbour. I believe in the unlikely way."

He indicated a mere sheep-walk of a path which lay along the cliffside on the left bank of the stream. We followed it to find that it gave on a wide, open space wherein lay a most sullen lake out of which the stream issued. A little way back from the farther side of the stream stood a rocky knoll with a hollow which could almost be called a cave. To it we betook ourselves, and there kindled a fire at which we did our best to dry the dripping clothes of us, for we were soaked to the skin, and, glistening with wet, we looked more like otters than men.

" It's at the turning dun of the evening," said Evan, when our task was over and we had gathered heaps of heather and bracken to lie on. " We will be putting the world under our heads now. That's a good start for going to the end of Fortune together."

So the Red Sergeant and I took possession of that spot by Loch Skeen which was afterwards to hold in both our hearts a place all its own.

CHAPTER X

JAEL OR ARIADNE ?

IF my eyes had opened to see Leslie's troopers with their swords at our throats, I should at least have felt I had wakened in a world which was real. Instead, it took me some moments to decide whether I was not still a-dreaming, or whether, in passing through the Carter Haugh, I had come under its spell and was now in the land of ferlies and faerie. For there, standing just beyond the whitened embers of the fire we had made in the mouth of our little cave, stood a girl. She remained motionless, her eyes bent on Evan as he lay with his head crooked into the hollow made by his bent arm, like a bairn asleep. A second glance told my half-wakened senses she was no creature compacted of moonlight, like the lady who cast her spell on Tamlin. For one hand held the end of a bridle rein that had been slipped over the head of a galloway, which was nosing for the scanty grass among the clumps of bent at the front of the cave, and her other hand held her riding-habit clear of the ground.

I continued to gaze at her through half-opened lids lest she should mark my waking, and move from that most engaging stance. For here was a maid, unwitting that she was watched, letting her face mirror her emotions as she looked at that strange sight, two outlawed men lying helpless in their sleep, but with weapons by their sides. For all she could tell, they were creatures who, if awakened, would give little law to such as she. Yet she looked. I could trace in her countenance wonder, interest, and compassion. I could not trace in her face the faintest sign of fear. Though that girl had never before consciously bent a glance on me, wonderful to tell, I had seen her before. She was the lady who rescued Gwyn and me from our predicament at Heriot.

It was as pretty a study as ever I had to watch her knit her brows, and I would gladly have waited to see how she would end her reverie; but, as I gazed, Evan stirred out of his sleep. The movement broke the girl's composure. In apprehension lest he should open his eyes to find hers bent on him, she jerked her head right round and looked backward over her shoulder. As she stood, in her long riding-habit, with her three-cornered hat concealing her hair, she must have appeared to one half-awake as the cloaked figure of a man.

My companion had more of the impulsive quickness the wild creatures of the woods and moors possess than any being I ever met. The moment he was out of sleep, he saw the figure in the mouth of the little cave. With him the idea of danger from an intruder and action to meet that danger came in one clap. It seemed to me as if, even as he opened his eyes, he sprang, and was holding the girl pinioned at the elbows in a grip of iron. She turned her head with a start at the rude shock. Her eyes met his.

" My life ! " he gasped, and dropped his arms as if stricken by the palsy. All the fire went out of his face. He looked like a boy caught stealing sugar-plums from his mother's cupboard. Then, with the hang-dog air of such a child begging to escape the paiks he had earned, he went on :

" Ach now, it's your pardon I will be asking, lady. Whatever will you be thinking I am ? "

Colour had come into the girl's face, like the faint red shewing through the pure white of the water-ousel's egg. She drew back and straightened, as the rowan tree does after the gust that bends it passes. Undefended by aught save the cold pride of her, she stood as in a little ring of dignity that set her apart from us and our kind. Then this air of detachment, I had almost said disdain, gave place to one of amusement, self-possessed but not saucy.

" What do I think of you, sir ? " she said. " Just that you're a wull-cat and hae a wull-cat's mainners. I think, tae, that ye're a wandered wull-cat, because we look for them maistly in the Hielans, so we'll e'en forgive you your mainners."

To this Scots which, we were to learn, the girl used when it happened to suit her mood, the Red Sergeant replied in his careful English.

" Yours is the true word, lady. I accept the description and the rebuke, only, whereas the wild-cat of

my hills hunts, the one before you is hunted ; so he has
the habit to treat all whom he meets here as enemies,
till he learns better. Still, it's a new pair of eyes I seem
to be needing, and, if ever I forgive myself for that
rough bit of handling, it will be because I tell myself it
was only a cloak and hat I sprung on ; for, I need not
tell you now, that's all of you I saw. Glad am I there's
one of us who has no excuses to make for bad manners,
except it be for taking a night's lodging on your moor.
Second names do not spell safety for us. My friend
here, by your will, is Gilbert."

The lady had little more than glanced at me till then.
Her eye ran me over. It was as if she was taking an
inventory. Clearly the tame cat was of less interest to
her than the wild.

" Tell me but one thing, sir," she said. " Is your
name Spottiswoode ? "

" It is not, mistress," I answered.

" Weel, that clears my conscience, so far. A maid
maun hae pity on broken men, be they never so mainner-
less "—this with a flash on the Sergeant—" but this
maid winna lee, even for pity. So ye'd better baith
bide wantin' the surnames. Pity ! faith, ye'll need a'
the pity ye can get. Yestreen was a day of blood for
the likes o' you. From Foulshiels tae the head o'
Megget, the sodgers were o'ertakin' an' cuttin' doon
such of your kind as thocht they had escaped. And
you," she broke out in excitement, " you think you're
safe here ; and, though ye're great muckle men an'
awfu' clever, ye're just gowks, and, like the gowk,

crying ' cuckoo,' as much as to say, ' Hey ! Come this way to find me.' "

The Sergeant challenged her with a look in which offence shewed, for he had plumed himself on the cleverness of our escape and the security of our hiding-place.

" Ay," she went on, " even a lassie wad hae kent better than kindle a fire by Loch Skeen. I saw the wisp o' reek yestreen from Winterhope. Ye may be thankfu' the shepherds o' Megget are awa' wi' their sheep tae the low pastures, or it's no a girl by her lane ye wad be collogin' wi' the noo. Ye puir bairns ! There were horse-soldiers beating the braes for you at the heid o' Megget by six o'clock this morning."

" And never a word from a lady about the smoke above Loch Skeen, I can swear," cried the Sergeant, his face aglow.

" Ye need not swear sae rashlike," she rallied. " Five minutes syne ye were terrible like Sisera, captain o' the host o' the king o' Canaan, lying asleep in the tent o' Jael. Ye mind that Jael was expeckit by him tae stand in the door o' the tent and turn aside the pursuers. Instead, Jael took a nail o' the tent and drave it through Sisera's temple. For a' ye ken, I was ettlin' tae serve ye sae wi' yer ain dirk, had ye no slept less sound than Sisera. Ye were helpless eneuch afore ye stirred for even a lassie to play that auld pairt. Then I cud hae cried tae the sodgers when they came, as the woman Jael did, ' Come and I will shew you the man whom thou seekest.' They thocht a heap o' Jael, and for that deed ca'ed her ' blessed above women.' Dae ye no think I'm mebbe a Jael that was jist a wee ower late ?   Div I no resemble her ? "

She looked very engaging as she said this.

Evan, who knew his classics a deal better than his Bible, seemed a wee puzzled to place the lady of the story.   But, after a pause, " I'm thinking you're not like that nasty woman at all, at all," says he solemnly, as if he were a judge trying a case.

" Ah, weel, I'm glad o' that, for I've aye hated the limmer as a cruel randy.   We'll say, then, that the thocht o' her was juist ane o' the things that crossed my mind a whilie syne ; but what mak's ye ony way sure that I micht no be a betrayer o' blood, noo that ye're up and daein' for yoursel's ? "

I felt it high time I should shew I was not just the glaikit lad.

" Mistress," I broke out, " my friend Evan here and I are in your hands, and there is one thing I would say— we never could desire to be in better."

I believe it was then she looked at me seriously for the first time, her previous examination being like that of an onlooker at a feeing market.   I think something tart was on the tip of her tongue, for, indeed, I had edged myself into the conversation which they seemed content to have to their two selves.   Instead, she paused for a moment after her scrutiny to say :

" Ye're gey young at the trade, an' no a hardened man o' blood like your friend here."

She said it in a bantering way, but her voice had a falling accent.

"Young he is," broke in the Sergeant, "but not too young to hang, mistress."

I believe he would have bitten his tongue out before he would have made the plea of pity for himself.

"Hang!" cried the girl. "Who talks of hanging when ye have all broad Scotland before ye? True, ye cannot stir till Leslie's troopers are clear of the valleys. Yet, as long as ye bide here, there's but one body could harm ye—Gideon Amos, my out-by herd. Well for you he was at Broughton with the lambs when ye came on his hill, for Yiddon's a staunch son of the Covenant, and would have had you laid by the heels ere morning. It'll be my business to wear him at Talla Linns and warn him that it's friends of mine are sheltering by Loch Skeen. A sair fecht it will be wi' Yiddon between his conscience and, let us say, his likin' for his mistress; but ye may lippen to Yiddon. He's a lane body, wi'oot kin save a skellum o' a son, wha's aye on the stravaig. See ye shew yourselves not on the hill-line; keep by the loch. And, when Yiddon comes, be guided by Yiddon."

Then in a moment her serious mood changed. "But perhaps I'm Jael, the hizzy Jael. Wha kens?"

"Mistress," said the Sergeant, away down in his throat, "if ye were, I declare I could almost see myself taking my end gladly from such hands."

"Oh, you Hielan' folk for the daft-like compliments!" she cried, making a mou. Yet I could see the wild saying pleased her.

"Mistress," went on the Sergeant, pursuing his advantage, "if ye're not Helen of Troy, or any of the daughters of the world's morning stepped out of the *Seanachas na Finne,* may we not know the name of her to whom we are so beholden ? "

" No mystery about that," she replied. " I'm Alison Laidlaw of Winterhope. Ye'll look in vain for a house on the land that gives us the name. The place is at Cramalt across the Megget Water. Ye should think twice ere ye come chappin' at the door that was Walter Laidlaw's. The very dogs there birstle gin ye but name a Malignant. Yet there's no kennin' but ye might pass a message, if need arise, to one there who is not an unfriend. Ye poor critters ! I declare ye have nothing to eat," she added, for, as she had been speaking, her glance was travelling over our little cave, bare as a bone of food. " Soldiers, too ! An' nae better than callants keen on the day's ploy an' aye despisin' in the mornin' the piece they hunger for at noon. Weel, I maun try to persuade Yiddon tae feed his enemy even ; but, faith, what a tongue I'll need the day ! "

She had hardly finished speaking, when she had gone and was leading her galloway across the hassock-like tufts in the bog which lay between our cave and the firm ground on the ridge of Winterhope. Bunches of cannock dotted the expanse. The white bloom of the wild-cotton and the innocent heart of the girl who carried the life of two outlaws in her keeping and yet made as if it were nothing, brought to me the same thought of freedom and simplicity and cleanness. But, whereas I stood silent, the Red Sergeant gave utterance to his thought, and what he said was this :

" A brave lass, a very brave lass, and it's God gave
her beauty to match the heart of her."

Evan and I had slept the sleep of overwrought men,
and the morning was well advanced when the lady of
Winterhope came on us at the cave. Even so, the wait
till the herd should come seemed long enough in prospect.
We had little fear of being discovered so long as we kept
to the little plateau round the loch and did not shew
ourselves on the slopes of the high hills which fringed
it on the south and west. It was not likely that mounted
men would beat the peat-hags. We were not so resource-
less of food as the maid thought. Evan produced from
his dorlach, the sack the Highland soldier carries on the
march, a small skin bag of oatmeal, which, he explained,
was " hained " against occasions of extremity. A handful of this he mixed with water and made what he called
" fuarach," the poor man's substitute for the " stapag "
that is made when cream is to be had. It staved off
our hunger, and, after the frugal fare was dispatched, we
lay on a bank of dry heather and gazed at our surround-
ings in singular content. It was a windless day and
warm for the season. Nothing broke the silence but the
croaking of a pair of ravens beating lazily above the
ridge of White Coomb. The loch at our feet was unruffled save for tiny rings, made by the small black trout
which abound in it, as they rose to take the midges. I
wonder whether in Scotland there is another loch which
gives such a sense of lonesomeness as Loch Skeen. The
peat-hags which stretch from it to the north look melancholy even under bright sunshine ; but I think it is the

waters of the great tarn itself, lying in the shadow of
those hills which rise above it like walls, and remaining
dark even when the light does its best to penetrate them,
that give an onlooker the sense of an eeriness which
searches his very marrow. I have never heard tell of
any tragic event associated with this loch. Yet it seems
to hold a mystery and to warn the stranger not to inter-
meddle with it.

My companion, who was in the blythest of moods, had,
I was surprised to see, no such impression. Doubtless
he had seen lochans more sinister in his native hills. As
the sun grew hot he declared he must have a bathe.
Yet, when he cast his clothes, swam to one of the heaps
of stones which rise out of the water and boyishly called
on me to follow him, I vow I went into the drumly
water with that fear of a kelpie gripping me that would
have better become him than a lad with the mense of a
Lowland upbringing.

The day wore through. The shafts of light were
shooting from hilltop to hilltop, and missing the cup in
which lay the loch, when a vigorous barking of collies
told us Gideon Amos was coming at long last. As he
breasted the ridge, we saw to our relief that he came
alone. With a word to his dogs that stayed their
clamour, he strode to meet us. He was a tall, spare
man of sixty. Though he had walked that day all the
way from Broughton, he yet advanced with the swing
of a youth. In spite of wisps of grey hair tumbling over
his haffits and an uncouth beard which grew as it liked,
the man had dignity.

" Gude e'en tae ye, sirs," he said, raising his hand to his bonnet in a kind of salute, but not offering it to be grasped. " I hae seen the mistress an' gotten ma orders. I speir nae questions an' carena tae ken yer names. I've been thinkin' a' the wey frae Talla Linns that I'm gey like the beast that cairried the prophet Balaam. But, aiblins the mistress has the richt o't. Ony gate, it's no to be thocht that a Megget man wad hae traivellers sleepin' aneath the breckens. Sae tak' yer wey wi' me tae ma bit."

In the Highlands a peasant would have termed it " my poor house " ; but there was no apology for his biggin' in Amos. With the air which a dweller at court could not have improved on, Yiddon led us across the Tail Burn to a lap of the hills on the east, where, without even the proverbial kailyard, stood a drystane cottage surrounded by sheep fanks. And there, a poor bit indeed, but much kindlier than the little cave by the lakeside, the Red Sergeant and I settled ourselves for the night with the roar of the Greymare's Tail in our ears.

CHAPTER XI

" A MAN'S FOES . . ."

THERE was, in truth, something more affecting than the sound of the waters to sleep on. The cot, little better than a fank with a roof on it, was yet divided into two chambers, the one, and that by much the larger, being the " but " where the shepherd did his simple cooking and where he slept on a box-bed, and the smaller being a tiny " ben " separated from the larger chamber by a partition of deal boards and a rough door. Few and simple were its furnishings, yet, as every Scot knows, the ben is not used by the family except on high occasions. Yiddon was shewing us the honour due to guests of distinction when he insisted on our having it as our sleeping quarters. There was a wooden framework like a bedstead against one wall that seemed to serve as a seat, for it had a cushion stuffed with feathers and a couple of deerskins of a softness which argued more skill in curing than one would have expected in the hills. From a large chest, which spoke of the days when Yiddon had a gudewife, a pair of blankets was forthcoming. And so, after a supper of most excellent collops, washed down with whey, and a conversation which was carefully confined by our host to the weather and to its effect on the welfare of sheep and the prices at Broughton, he remarked we would be tired and would not need the sough of the Greymare's Tail as a lillilu. He handed us the blazing splinter of bog-fir, stuck on a spike in stand, which was to light us to bed.

The Sergeant, who had tried in vain to draw Yiddon into topics which touched our situation, gave over with a good-humoured nod. " A good night to you, friend, and peace lie at your heart," he said, as together we moved into our chamber.

It was soon manifest what had been Yiddon Amos's reason for dispatch. The hour had come for " takin' the buiks." He would not delay the duty, yet as little could he ask us to share in the act of worship, lest his conscience, or ours, should be put to violence. Through the cracks of the deal partition we could not help beholding a sight which affected us greatly. It was undoubtedly the old man's ordinary custom to begin by singing, even tho' his lee lane ; but on this occasion we saw him repeat without sound his portion of metrical psalms, his lips moving slowly at the rate of a person who sings the words. Then, in a low voice, his finger running along the lines, he read a chapter. In public Yiddon would have held it making a show of religion to bow the knee ; but here in his own house, in the secret of God's presence, as he deemed, when he had closed the book, he knelt on the clay floor to end his worship with prayer. The opening words were said very quietly ; but, as he proceeded, the ardour of the engagement caught him. His voice swelled, and, I well believe, he was unconscious of

the fact that we could overhear. For, indeed, part of
his supplication concerned us :

" O Lord, Who in Thy word hast said, ' If thine enemy
hunger, feed him ; if he thirst, give him drink,' enable
Thine unworthy servant to overcome the depravity of
his heart and, for his natural frowardness, give Thou
him compunction of heart. Make him easily to be en-
treated. The lot of all men is in Thy hand, O Lord,
Thou who knowest all hearts. Forbid me from being
the judge of these men who are under my roof. Let
Thine eye be upon us all in mercy and, if theirs be the
wrath of man, O Lord, let even it praise Thee. It is
not in man that walketh to direct his steps. Shew me
a plain path, O Lord, for Thou knowest this path is not
of my seeking. Redeem Thine Israel out of all her
troubles, and let our hands be clean as we compass Thine
altar."

He went on pleading the covenanted mercies of God
and confessing his own unworthiness of the least of
them. From our more dimly-lit chamber we could see,
in the mingled light of the fire and a tallow dip by which
he had been reading, the old man's upraised face and
close-clenched eyes. It was indeed our rough shepherd
transfigured.

" Evan, man," I whispered, " you may doubt our
Argyles, if ye will ; but ye canna doubt that. That's
the voice of the honest peasant folk, and what we hear
is the true spirit of the Covenant."

" It is one good old man, whatever," he replied.
" And the pity is that the Marquis, worlds removed from

him, has just the same spirit. But, tell me, what makes him fall away from the Scots tongue in his praying ? "

" Why," said I, " it is because he's steeped in the language of the Scriptures in King James's English, and does not think it fitting to address his Maker in any other."

" Ah, well," rejoined he, " it's a good sough to fall asleep on."

That is how we did indeed end our day, with the murmur of the water falling and the plaint of a soul ascending to the throne of grace.

And, faith, we were to thank our stars that Yiddon was no Gibeonite in his religion. We had just gotten our first sleep when the collies set up a din of mingled yowling and sharp barks. The shepherd was at once astir. He struck steel on flint, kindled the tallow dip, strode to the door, which was not even barred, and called out into the night, as if sure that a human being approached, " Wha is't ? "

A squeaking voice answered, " Juist me, feyther."

" Whatna ill brings ye, comin' like a howlet ? " cried the old man, and there was more than a shade of fear in his tone.

" Oh, nae ill ava, feyther. Am juist giein' ye a ca' in the by-gaun."

" Weel, if ye maun come in, sae be it."

Then into the circle of the candlelight there sidled the misshapen Mungo whom we knew to be one with the Shauchlin Herd of Talla. From the dogs at all events he got a welcome. The barks gave place to one con-

tinuous whine. By some uncanny power these beasts
had known who was coming, and there is no doubt the
old man had read their signal. No answering gleam of
welcome came from him. He had, indeed, a difficult
part to play.

"Wull ye hae some meat ? " he asked in a level tone.

" Ay, if ye hae ony left, feyther," was the son's spoken
response, but his glance said more as it turned suspiciously to the table.

I could not have credited the shepherd with the guile
he had shewn. One plate only remained, and on it were
some morsels of food. For his son he produced what
remained of the cold collops.

" Braw vivers, feyther," remarked the ne'er-do-weel
as he disposed of them. " I'm gled tae see ye care for
yersel' though a' yer lane, feyther."

" Ay," said the old man gruffly, " I was at Brochton
yestreen."

The Sergeant and I had our belongings in the little
room, and we felt reasonably safe from discovery, provided the shepherd's play could hold out.

Suddenly the eye of the gangrel steadied for a moment.
What arrested its attention was a small metal brooch,
hardly more than a crosspiece and pin, which lay by the
heap of peats at the fireside. It was the fibula by which
Evan fastened his plaid at the shoulder. He had cast off
the plaid before supper and carried it to our room, without observing that the brooch had dropped on the floor.
It was this tell-tale trifle on which the Shauchlin Herd's
eye fell. In that region it betrayed us as completely

as if it had been the red royal ribbon. Yet the old father, who had been watching his son like a gled, also saw the bauble which had escaped his careful attempt to cover up the signs of our presence. He broke his grim silence.

" Whaur hae ye been this lang time in yer walkin' up an' doon the yearth wi' yer maister ? " he asked.

" Oh, tae Embro' an' Salkirk an' a heap o' places."

" What got ye o't ? Tell me that, noo."

" Oh, siller, braw siller, routh o't an' mair tae follow, feyther, vera like, mair tae follow."

It looked as if the creature actually slavered at the thought, like a hungry dog watching a meal being prepared for him.

" Ay," the father responded, " Judas got siller an' ither folk bocht a field wi't. Tak' tent yer siller disna come tae ye in some sic way ; an' ye mak' an end like his."

" Nae fear o' that, feyther," he giggled. " Judas chainged his min'. A winna chainge mine."

The old man dropped his eyelids, as though shutting out something on which he did not desire to look ; and then said, as unconcernedly as he could, " Ye'll be for takin' a sleep ? "

" Na, na, feyther," says he, " nae sleep for me the noo. A gaun fit's aye gettin'. They braw hairst nichts are juist like day. A hae tae be gey early astir ony gait, an' it's maist mornin' a'ready."

As he spoke he sidled towards his bonnet and rung.

" Let me choke him, Evan, ere he stirs," I whispered.

" I could smoor the life oot o' him easy, the betrayer o' blood."

" No," Evan answered, " for the old man's sake he must be scatheless, the dirty foumart ! Let him go. He has warned us by his smell."

The Shauchlin Herd went his ways. Yiddon, left alone, lifted his clenched hands above his head.

" O Lord," he cried passionately, " have pity on me, for Thy hand hath touched me in my very flesh and blood. For whatna transgression hast Thou thus afflicted me ? Yet bane o' my bane he is, an' I'm no' forgettin' it ; but, Lord, grant that his crookit ways be na followed tae ma shame."

He stepped to our makeshift door, opened it, and saw us standing all alert just within it.

" Ye'll hae seen yon, an' mebbe heard tae ? " he queried.

" Seen and heard and understood," replied the Sergeant quietly.

" I thank ye, then, for spairin' tae lift hand," the shepherd added, with downcast eyes.

" Son of yours is safe from us, friend," said Evan, " but we must know the way he takes," and on the word he slipped out.

" Wha can follow Mungo an' him no ken o't ? " Yiddon muttered.

" That one can," I replied.

It was a full hour ere Evan returned. I went out and met him, just beyond earshot of the cottage, as day was breaking.

" All is safe," he reported. " I saw him well set on
the Moffat road and making for Yarrow. He never gave
so much as a look at the falls when he went by the place.
If I know anything of his kind of cattle, it's a thing
he could not have resisted had he known the treasure
was there."

The shepherd, however, was not reassured when he
heard the Sergeant's account of the course the Shauchlin
Herd had taken. Said he, " Gin he has ga'en by the
Lochs, that spiles the plan o' Mistress Ailie, for she
ettled tae hae ye tak' the hill-road oot o' Yarrow that
leads tae Manor Water. But ye dinna ken Mungo.
He's as fu' o' guile as a hill tod. It wad be like him tae
jalouse he micht be followed. It's like eneuch, aefter
mintin' that he was for the Lochs, he wad bend ower by
Birkhill into Megget. At a' events, I canna let ye stir
till we hear what the mistress thinks. Gin I ken her,
it'll no be owerly lang she'll keep us waitin'."

He blew up the gathering peat and set about making
the porridge. Evan and I, like bairns at the school
door, waited the coming of the mistress and the opening
of the school.

CHAPTER XII

THE DISTAFF STIRS ITSELF

SURE enough, betimes in the morning Mistress Alison appeared. She carried a fishing-wand, and a cast of flies on horsehair was wound round her hat.

"Here's what will help to pass the day and give you a good dish of trout if you have the mind," she cried lightly, handing me the rod and then setting herself to untwine the cast from her hat. The wind, stiff though it was, could not blow her hair about, it was so heavy; but the sunlight played on the nut-brown masses.

"There's mair sairious wark nor fushin', Mistress Ailie," said Yiddon.

Her face, a moment since like a sunlit braeside, altered as the same braeside does when a heavy cloud shoots its shadow across it.

"And what serious work may that be, Yiddon?" she cried.

Yiddon told of Mungo's visit in the night. She apparently did not need to have an explanation of what it meant.

"Ay, Mungo," she responded, "noo he sits in at the table we'll need lang spunes. Ye canna gang by Manor, and, of course, this nest is as good as heryit. Gin Yiddon were to hide ye at the back o' White Coomb

itsel', Mungo wad track ye like a whittret. The one
chance is the door nearest. Get down into the Tweed
valley by the Linns o' Talla, as lang as that door is
open."

"But is the road clear, mistress?" asked Yiddon.

"It is that," she replied. "Yestreen Leslie's troopers
passed doun Megget tae Henderland, an' there's not a
hoof on the Tweedsmuir side. I see it," she cried.
"Young Polmood's of your party at heart. I'll pass
you on to him with a token from me. He'll keep you
hid or send you on in disguise."

"And who may young Polmood be?" queried Evan,
with a suspicion of mischief in his tone.

"Oh, just a young laird wha ettles to jine Winterhope
tae his ain lands, if a's true," said Yiddon.

The girl blushed furiously.

"Havers!" she burst out, "an' Yiddon Amos, wha
kens the auld friendship of our houses, micht stop at
that an' no tak' up the country-side clash. Normand
Hunter is mair taen up wi' his blood horses than wi'
lasses. He's just an honest lad and richt eneuch in the
heid, except for notions that some of the present company shares. But I'm no' feared o' your gossip, Yiddon.
See here." She unloosed the ribbon that bound her
hair. "This is all the token I can give you," she cried,
as she held it out to Evan. "Take this. Shew it to
Polmood and tell him your story. For you to wander
without such help as his in Tweedside is to walk straight
to the Tolbooth. It is your one chance. Will you take
it at once, for it's now or never?"

The Sergeant was the picture of whimsicality as he stood regarding this creature of decision and fire.

" Mistress," he said, " I cannot answer for my friend, but for myself I have a charge on my heart which will not let me be leaving this district till I have done my best to carry out my desire."

At this she coloured, misunderstanding the ambiguous word which, I knew, referred to the treasure. He deepened the wrong impression by adding, " I would not be beholden even to a man of my own persuasion, such as the laird of Polmood, lest I should profit by him to his hurt. For myself, I desire only to get out of the danger which threatens us here. Once in the Tweed valley, I should risk lying hid till I accomplish my design. It is for my friend to take what way he pleases."

He turned his look on me and waited. The treasure was next to nothing to me, but to be beholden to this unknown Polmood had no attraction at all. By the pang which shot through me at Yiddon's words, I felt I had for that young laird a most unreasoning dislike. And by that I knew also for the first time clearly that the maid of Winterhope was the one maid in all the world. Have I not shewn you that I am the most illogical of Scots—a slave to impulse and the flash that comes with the moment ? I answered brusquely, " I am with you, Evan."

The girl's eye flashed. She tossed the despised ribbon from her in what I thought was a most delicious fit of temper.

" Well," she said, " since you are for your own hand,

you must let Yiddon shew you how to come ¨down
on Talla. For myself, I bid you good-day and "—she
added, half-relenting—" good faring."

She turned, without so much as another look, and
walked rapidly towards Winterhope.

As the shepherd and the soldier conferred together, I
saw the ribbon resting on the top of a bush of bog-myrtle.
Next moment it was within my doublet, next my heart.

" Mind ye, ye're wrang," Yiddon was saying when I
gathered myself and joined the two. " Ye sud hae fa'en
in wi' her wey. She's got the hert o' a lass, but auld
Winterhope aye held she had a judgment like Solomon's
ain. An', fegs, I never saw her fuff like yon afore. She
must have felt she was dooms richt, tae be in sic a pet.
Gin ye hed lippened tae her, she wad hae weised ye safe
some wey. Noo, ye maun juist trust tae me. An' I
daurna dae mair nor lead you within sicht o' the pass."

" If you do that," the Sergeant answered, " you do all
a friend should. And the sooner we are taking our legs
along with us, the better for the health of all, say I."

Evan had never parted with the pair of pistols which
composed his weapons, along with his sword and the
little knife he carried against his left forearm. Now he
handed me one of the dags taken from the troopers,
loaded and primed.

" They will not stop to parley with us if we are met,"
he remarked, " and that is as good a friend as any to
speak the first word for you."

The shepherd gave me a kind of knapsack he called
a lambing-bag, which contained some simple provisions,

and a stout rung of blackthorn, which Evan declared was
sovereign against water-kelpies, though I was minded it
might serve me as a weapon, similar to what Gwyn had
termed his Plymouth cloak, in the use of which I was
like to be more expert than the pistol. We crossed the
peat-hags, edged to the left, and soon had the head of
the Megget valley lying full in view. Yiddon pointed
to the narrowest part, where the hills on each side
seemed almost to meet.

"Yon's the door Mistress Ailie spak' o'. They'se the
Linns o' Talla. And gudeness grant ye find the door
open. By it ye drap doon on twa-three mile o' bog,
where the saughs gie guid cover, and syne ye haud by
the burn till ye come on Tweed. A'm sweer tae see
ye hunted oot o' ma wee bit, whaur ye cuid hae lain
saft, but for what we ken o'; an', if I can mak' up for
what is ma wite, ye've but tae lat auld Yiddon ken hoo.
Noo, speed ye, speed ye."

We gave the honest old fellow a grip of the hand, and,
almost on the instant, were taking his advice. Then I
got my first lesson in the art of moving unseen across
broken country. Evan, crouching almost double, the
while he used the screen of every rock and patch of
bracken, traversed the hillsides in a zigzag, but with
amazing quickness. I copied his behaviour slavishly.
Soon my breath was coming in gasps. It would have
taken sharp eyes in the valley below to detect a movement, far less to follow our course, in that succession of
crawls and dashes.

At length we came to the jaws of the defile and could

hear the noise of the water in the linn.   On hands and
knees we were creeping past the linn itself when, out of
a patch of heather on the farther bank of the stream,
there started up the figure of a man.   I am sure he saw
us for the first time at that moment.   His face changed
its look of a startled animal into that of a demon on
the instant.   In an eldrich screigh, which rose above
the din of the waterfall, we made out the cry of the
Shauchlin Herd that followed :

"Hey, sodgers, hey !   Here they're ! "

We looked back towards Megget, the airt to which
he turned as he called.   At the same instant a shot
rang out.   We saw three or four troopers, five hundred
yards farther up the valley, advancing on a woman who
held a smoking pistol in her hand.

"My stars," cried Evan, "a diversion !   What a
lass ! "

The diversion was indeed effective.   The shot had
been fired the moment our enemy shewed himself, and
so had drowned for the troopers his cry.   At all events,
if they heard, they heeded not Mungo's screams.   And,
best of all, they had clearly never seen us.   The creature
who had seen realized this.   Once more he shouted,
"Sodgers, haste ye ; noo, noo, ye gomerils, or they're
by wi't ! "

Then, mad with chagrin, he drew a pistol and discharged it.   I question if he ever fired a shot in his life
before ; but fate of some sort winged that shot.   I felt
a shock as of a smith's forehammer, and pitched forward
down into the bed of the stream just beyond the falls.

Evan must have come after me like a mountain goat. I just remember his catching me up and bearing me on his shoulder along the bank of the stream among rowan trees and great rocks tufted with heather and fern. Then the pain in my shoulder struck me as with a dizziness. My head swam, and I knew no more.

When I opened my eyes, it was to find myself lying in a kind of arbour of greenery. Young saughs, growing as they listed in a swampy soil, twined their branches and made a leafy roof which almost shut out the sky. The ground on which I lay was a mass of mint and flowering flags and forget-me-not, for the stream below the Linns of Talla feeds a narrow valley, which at time of flood is almost a lake, and, in the drier seasons, is just a forcing bed for every kind of wild plant that loves water in plenty. Evan, looking weary, had evidently just concluded what was a long carry of my body, for he was in the act of tearing open my shirt, and the pain caused by wrenching it from my wound it was that awakened me. He soused water on my left breast round the shoulder-blade in bonnetfuls from the burn and carefully dighted it with a kerchief. As I glanced squint-eyed at the place, I saw fresh blood welling from a hole which seemed singularly small to have been made by the bullet of a great horse pistol. He slipped his arm below my head, and by a dexterous movement turned me so that he might examine the other side. Then followed a nasty jag as he probed with his finger.

" Thank goodness, Gilbert, it's a clean passage, and

there's no lodger of lead in you. It's a simple job if we had but some linen ; but our old fashion will serve."

He gathered a quantity of the common moss with long shoots that grows in boggy places, teased and washed it, and placed two great wads of it on both openings of my wound. Then, with strips of the lambing bag Yiddon had given us, he bound me over the shoulder and under the oxter and across the breast most cunningly. I felt it little, but had a most desperate thirst. It was a great comfort to Evan that I could move my arm from the elbow, and that, though it was an ugly enough flesh wound, no bone was touched.

"Man," I asked, "how on earth did ye manage it ? You must be strong as a pony and wily as a fox."

"Oh, it was simple," he replied. "I should have settled that vermin Mungo first ; but that would have discovered us to the brisk dogs he had set on us. There was the best of cover, and, I could engage, the shifty lad never saw us after watching you disappear over the bank. We're near a mile from the linns, and his story will have sounded a fairy tale to the troopers, who never set eyes on us."

"Ay," I answered, "thanks to the shot that came before Mungo's."

"Yes," he responded, "and that's a matter we must learn the end of. Did the lady pass it off with safety to herself ? Besides, she maybe saw your wounding, and, if so, will want to get news of you. In any case, Gilbert, she's been proved right in her plan, and it will pleasure her to be told that. *Our* plan is useless now.

We must bide till your wound will let you travel. Who can help us to a new plan but she ?   So I propose to put my pride in my pocket, and, if I can do so without drawing danger on her, have a word with the lady herself at Cramalt to-night. I will try, if you feel you can be so long left alone."

" I would fain know that she has come to no harm by that diversion of hers," I answered. " And as for my condition, I shall e'en lie here as comfortable as if I were in the farmhouse at Dairsie."

So at the gloaming Evan set off. He seemed long gone, and, what with anxiety over my two deliverers, the renewed agony of my wound, and the fantastic shadows and sounds of the swamp, I got into a raging fever. It seemed to me that I was with Gawain Douglas in that scene which he describes at the opening of his *Palace of Honour*. I saw the mouldy trees and rotten runts of his grisly picture, till the pleasant little harbour, in which Evan had left me, became " a fitting den where murderers reft men of life."

CHAPTER XIII

THE BOTHIE

IF it was a bad night for me, it turned out an even worse one for Evan. It seems that he reached Cramalt and got speech of Mistress Alison. He learned that the matter of the pistol shot had gone well. The troopers had taken it to be a prank in which, out of mere mischief, she had her fun by alarming them ; and she had succeeded in laughing it off. As for Mungo's tale of having encountered us at the linns, it seems they had most unwillingly made for the head of the glen from Henderland, where he laid his information, and allowed him to push on to the pass. All the while they doubted him as a natural, and Alison had made such fun of his story in their presence that he simply gibbered and then took his leave, raging mad at being the mock of all.

A hearty refreshment for the men had sent them riding down the valley in great fettle, and, but for the Shauchlin Herd, who had departed muttering, " Ye're no dune wi' puir Mungo," Alison opined we might have returned to Yiddon at Loch Skeen. This of course was impossible, but she told the Sergeant of a hidie-hole she would lead us to on the morrow, were the way clear for

her to reach us unnoticed. Evan thought this time
enough, for he had made her mind easy about my
wound, and said I could lie out on such a fine night
without hurt. He returned to find me out of my senses,
my one idea to fight with everything I touched.

He told me afterwards that I tried hard to strangle
him in my mania, and that he had to hold me down
with his knees on my chest till the frenzy passed.
This started the bleeding again, and I was strong enough
to make a very nasty patient while he redid the work
of the morning. However, there was more than blood-
letting to check my fever. He had counted on a fine
night in that autumn, during which rain had almost
never fallen ; but the hills above Talla are among the
greatest places for rain in broad Scotland.

About midnight there came on a drenching downpour.
It drove up the valley at the spur of a very high wind.
It searched our coppice and soaked us to the skin.
The bed which we had admired for its routh of musk
and forget-me-not became a nasty bog, and there was
no light to shew how Evan could better it. So he
passed what must have been to him a most miserable
night, tending a man whose violence gave place to
passiveness as the water first cooled his fever and then
set him chittering with the cold.

It was noon next day ere Mistress Alison found us.
I was by this time like a log, and as unwitting of what
passed as one ; but it seems they made a kind of litter
for me of saugh and alder branches, and between them
carried me to the hidie-hole Alison had spoken of.

It was a deserted bothie on the hillside which, in the tinchels, or beatings of the forest deer, in the days of Queen Mary and King James, the hunters used. No road led to it. Hidden among the birks, it afforded at least protection from the worst of the wind and rain. It was there, where gallants once gathered, that I had my wakening ; and a right pleasing wakening it was. The lady had brought linen and salve, and it was her fingers discovering my shoulder and the ugly mess of it which made me open my eyes. She bent close over the wound, so that I felt her very breathing like a waft of the myrtle on my face. Her great grey eyes were full of an anxiety that ran through my veins like a cordial.

Then, as she explored, she came on something which had been pushed aside by Evan's dressing, though doubtless noted by him. It was the ribbon, the ribbon stained into ugliness now with blood. There it lay, a gruesome ensign to most eyes. She did not touch it. Her eyelids just widened, and the eyes themselves filled with a look of mystery such as I had marked in Loch Skeen when it seemed to be holding a secret all its own. She remained motionless, gazing and gazing. Then, as if shaking off a mood, she went on, with strong and deft touches, to finish the salving and binding of my wound.

For me, as, unseen by her, I had opened my eyes, so, unseen still, I closed them again. That was a good sight to dream on. Gawain Douglas in his tale passed from the loathly swamp to the Palace of Honour. I, too, had felt dismay like the poet's before the queen came to him ; and, if this hut was but a poor place to pass as a palace, I felt I would not change, for the poet's vision, my own glimpse, in the truth-telling light of common day that fell on Talla, of the lady who had brought me to it.

It was but a short snatch of sleep I had. When I wakened it was to find the fever so abated that I was able to join the others in a discussion they were keen to hold on our situation. Clearly Evan had been considering how much to tell the lady of Winterhope. The whole matter turned on the treasure, and that was his concern. He had made a study of her who had twice come to our help, and I was not surprised that he told her the whole story and where the treasure lay, and how bound he felt to save it for his master and bring it to him, if anything man could do would make this come about. Mistress Ailie listened to him with deep attention. She broke the recital only once at the point where Evan described the journey of Gwyn and myself with the cart. It was to cry in laughing amazement, " Then I've been in this treason almost from the beginning. It was Menzion and I who got the treasure franked through the crowd of angry folk at Heriot. I was sorry for the big Hollander. I barely looked at his companion, for the foreigner was at once pitiable and amusing. Yet I was helping a disguised English officer against my country. It looks either faerie or fate. I wish I knew which."

" It's not anything so hard as predestination I hope to shew you," the Sergeant answered, and went on to finish his tale. Did a shade of disappointment shew when he discovered to her that it was not devotion to a person which chained him to the district till he effected his purpose, and had made him so touchy of being beholden to young Polmood ? I thought her face fell, and, with the thought, the dream I had had over the ribbon did not seem so flattering.

" This lad," he concluded, nodding at me, " will be ready for the road within a week. I feel I have engaged him overdeep in this business already ; but for that there is some small excuse. As he knows well, he is free to make his peace with the Committee of Estates or to follow the venture. But as for you, mistress, I am not telling you my secret to make you art and part in it, and craving help the giving of which would be against your conscience. I just tell you because you have been so much our friend, and because I would hide nothing now of the reason which made me refuse your plan. I was a fool in that, but churl I was not."

" I never thought you a churl," she rejoined, giving him a look which must have repaid him for his candour. " And yet your story puts me in a hank singularly like that our friend here found himself in through "—she halted for a moment before adding—" friendship. Like him, I am of the other side, and, like him, care nothing for its politics, though I do hold with its principles. I ought not to touch your design any more than pitch ; but I take the woman's view that I have touched it in making common cause with you by, I suppose, the same guiding. The treasure you speak of is, after all, your master's. You owe it to yourself to see it reaches him rather than lie in the mint at Edinburgh, or, as is more likely, be found by Mungo Amos or his kind. The notion is most strong that a treasure *was* carried off the field and hidden in Yarrow. They are searching the dens and holmes of the valley for it as with a curry-comb. Find it they will, unless you move it, and that quickly. But for two men, and one of you wounded, the thing is impossible, unless you get help strong and secret ; and where will ye get a man to help you in sic a treasonable ploy in this country-side ? Nae man, not even Yiddon. There's naebody but a lassie wha bids fair tae turn into a renegade."

I noted how, as she became moved, she slid into the Scots.

" Well, mistress," said Evan, " there's nothing for it but me to quest like a kestrel round the Greymare's Tail, putting up such guard as I can, till the other birds come and mob me. Gilbert here can make a cast into Westmoreland and pass over to Wales and safety, or else make for Linlithgow and do his best to get his dominie, Henderson, to clear him with the Committee."

" Is it not a pity to lose the *adventure* of the thing ? " cried the girl. " It would be like one of the old ballads if we could play Kinmont Willie over again and snatch it 'neath their very noses by a bold stroke."

" Yes," the soldier interposed, " but in the old days you had men who cared neither for kings nor covenants and did a man's deed to help a comrade, whether he was king or carle, making of danger a kindly sport."

" Oh ! I see, you want a man as conscienceless as

myself," Alison laughed. "Stop ye, now," she went on; "there is such a man who cares neither for creeds nor crowned heads, and he's—need it seem strange to you—a particular frien' o' mine. Ye'll mebbe hae heard tell o' Jimmuck the Caird?"

The question she addressed to me. "No? Well, he ranges from Carlisle tae Aberdeen, and, surely, must have given Fife a call wi' his string o' horses and ragtag crew of brither cairds. He's horse-couper, smuggler, and suchlike; but, so far, has kept on the safe side o' the law. Jimmuck loves three things—the free life, and good drink, and anither that it's mebbe no for me tae particularize; but, if ye keep him sober, or reasonably so, it's not gold that will tempt him to cry off in an adventure. Jimmuck sold us my first pony. Jimmuck has free grazing at Winterhope whenever he passes up Megget, and never wearies of telling how often my father stood his friend. I heard of him a week syne as being at St. Boswells. I can pass word to Jimmuck by a sure hand. He's the man for your purpose. If ye can waken him up to a sense of the fun of the thing, your treasure is safe, and he'll devise means to take it untouched across broad Scotland. Danger! It is dearer to him than even a good stroke at the horse-couping. And if he were caught, Johnston of Wariston himself could not prove that Jimmuck had not *found* that treasure, just as he would find bog-hay growing at a roadside, and take it without melling with any law of Scotland, much less affairs of State."

"He seems very like some of my countrymen in the

north," the soldier replied in response to this enthusiastic recital. "Your stay-at-homes would not believe
such honour lives among thieves. I greatly like your
description of this gallant of the roads, and, faith, as
you believe in him, that's final for me. See you keep
yourself and your house out of it, mistress ; but if this
gentleman-tinker can have a word with two who are
more truly beggars than he, it will please me mightily."

"Well, then," replied Mistress Alison, "wait his
coming, for come he will if he is within hail. As for
you, Yiddon must keep you in supplies and news. I
dare not venture this way again. The holder of
Gameshope might mark my coming. Though of the
respectable kind, he is fierce for the Covenant, and
would inform as to your whereabouts as readily as
Mungo, though not for the same base desire of reward.

"Mr. Gilbert, you will soon be on your travels again.
You have a nasty memory of the Linns of Talla ; but
you'll never think of them without minding the friend
who got you safe out of them." This with a quick glance
towards Evan. "And now you are to have the same
as companion on your journey, I almost envy you. I
wish I could play the part of Jimmuck the Caird."

The Sergeant stood awkwardly as he digested that
unexpected compliment. Ere he looked up, Alison was
gone.

CHAPTER XIV

EPPIE TAMSON, CHIRURGEON

THESE days in the glen, while we waited the coming of the Caird, will ever abide in my memory. It was then I first realized that I lived in a new world; for love, which had undoubtedly entered my heart before even I snatched Alison's ribbon from the bog-myrtle, was *seen* by me to lie there when I watched Alison's behaviour on her discovering the ribbon.

My wound, which kept me from ranging about at all till the healing had fairly begun, gave me all the leisure lover could desire to dream over the wonder that had come to me.

Though my companion pitied me for being unfit for any sort of tuilzie that might have to be faced by fugitives such as we were, I cannot say I pitied myself. That time in the glen, where I lay and brooded on my new joy, was like my wound, giving me passing stounds of pain, and yet, by the very irritation, speaking of healing. I mind how one day, from the rough track running on the other side of the marsh, I heard a clatter of hoofs and the sound of voices in gay talk and laughter. I felt that Alison Laidlaw was in that company. And, sure enough, when, yielding to an impulse I could not

resist, I had passed, screened by the coppice, to the
lower part of the glen where it is clear of trees, I saw
her. She was riding with a young fellow who bestrode
a chestnut blood-horse and sat it exceedingly well.
Farther down the glen, where it opens on the Tweed
valley, I could see riders, and a lady here and there
among them, converging towards the house of Menzion.
It was plainly the rallying point for some sort of hunting jaunt.

The young gallant, I thought, must be far ben when
he would ride to Megget to convoy Alison. I hardly
needed to remember her remark about his keenness on
blood-horses to know that this was young Polmood.
The gentleman with sympathies for the King's party
had plainly not broken with the lairds and bien farmers
of Upper Tweed over those sympathies. You might
think I am telling this to add that a pang of jealousy
struck me. If so, you would be wrong. I declare it
gave me a thrill of pleasure to see her in his company,
because she was so manifestly happy and care free. On
the four occasions my companion and I had seen her till
then, we had brought to her concern, and in each she
had played the part of the moorland maiden.

As that morning she flashed into the sunshine, riding
her bonny roan, she was the lady of Winterhope, easy
in the company of one of her own rank. I vow they
were a handsome pair, and I wondered not that the
country-side gossip coupled them. Yet, such is the
pride of the lover, that I, a poor landless outlaw in
stained homespun, turned back to my hidie-hole in the

conviction that I would not exchange my chance of winning, by the end of the day, with that well-set-up and eminently suitable match for her, the laird of Polmood. For me, then, it was no great hardship to be tethered to the shieling and a half-mile or so round it.

I seldom tired looking at the great hill opposite, with the clouds curling round its crags and the ravens rouping in the clouds, or to study the dell with its wealth of wild-flowers and tiny creatures following their lives in it with much of the struggle and adventure that men too have to face. I even let my feelings run into rhyme ; but it is a mercy that there were no means to put the results into writing, and the *tabula rasa* of my mind has made a friendly pact with oblivion. Only there remains with me the innocent pleasure of it all, and one impression, which shall never be effaced, that the sights and sounds of the moving world are never so truly understood and cherished as when they be associated with thoughts of one whom we love.

With my companion I believe this time in the Talla glen was one great weariness. He was not, like me, disabled in body, and his mind was as restless as quicksilver. He declared that it behoved him to know the lie of the land, and almost every day he was off on some exploration. You would have thought he risked too much, but he said he would be as invisible as the hill-wind. And I feel sure he conducted his expeditions with great caution.

Amos came with supplies only once, for he, like his mistress, was apprehensive of the farmer at Gameshope discovering our whereabouts. The messenger who, most happily for me, took Yiddon's place was Eppie Tamson, Alison's own maid. Eppie appeared at the gloaming one evening just after Evan had left on one of his prowls. She walked in, unannounced either by the noise of her approach or by knock, stood in the middle of the floor, and said :

"I'm Eppie Tamson frae Cramalt. Hey! There's yer meat," and set down a well-furnished basket on the floor.

There was no grace of manner in Eppie Tamson, and she spoke a Border Scots so broad that it took me all my time to follow her speech. Later, when I knew the Borders well, I should not have had to be told that she hailed from Jeddart-side.

She was a well-favoured lass of about her mistress's age, with great strong hands which had often wrought the graip, and her whole frame had the sturdiness of our peasants who are bred to the hard life of the fields and yet sufficiently nourished. Eppie's complexion reminded me of the apples, reddened by the sun and wind, which grew so surprisingly well without pampering in our garden in the East Neuk. A merrie eye was an offset to her great brusqueness of manner.

"Lod sakes," she went on, giving me no chance to say a word, "what a hoose! Ye're the lad that was hurtit, I see ; but the ither, yer neebor, is a brawer man, an' a rattler, frae a' accoonts. Could he no hae redded up things a wee ? Gin ye hae tae leeve like brocks in a hole, ye sud be like the brocks, wha keep their bit raal trig."

There was, in truth, no furniture in the bothie to
tidy and no fireside to clean up, for we dared not kindle
a fire ; but Eppie, full of purposefulness, and heeding
me no more than if I were a rush, shook up the bracken
beds which the Sergeant had laid, made a broom of
birch branches, and vigorously swept the earthen floor.

When the dust was laid and the contents of her
basket disposed on a white napkin to her satisfaction,
she turned to me. " An' noo, ma mannie," she jerked,
" let's see hoo that naisty cratur Mungo's work is
mending."

" Wi' a' the will in the world," I replied ; " but I
haena had ony say yet. Dinna ye think I ocht tae ken
what gars ye tak Yiddon's place, and how ye hae
managed sae well ? "

" Oh ! Yiddon's an auld, dune body. He's flegged
o' that great hash o' a man at Gameshope. But wha's
he tae haud up Eppie Tamson gaun tae her auntie
at Menzion, whaur there's a hoosefu' of bairns wi' the
kink-hoast, and nae time tae mak' meat for man or
bairns neither ? Oh ! Eppie kens a' about the ongauns,
an' it was Eppie said the mistress cudna be seen
stravaigin' like a basket-woman ; an', whan the mistress
had tae gae doon Tweed on anither daft-like errand,
she says tae me, ' Eppie, ye'll need tae mind thae twa
silly Malignants,' an' mind them I wull. Sae let's see
yer airm or shoother, or whatever it is." I submitted,
and, faith, Alison herself could not have made a more
thorough inspection.

" This'll be the Hielanman's wark," she remarked, as

she undid the bandages with evident approbation. "Gude sen' he's as clivver at mendin' wounds as at his tred o' makin' them. Ah," she went on, as the cicatrix itself was uncovered, "but it's braw balm ye've had here. It's fair knittin' thegither front and back, an' clean. I think that'll be the hinmost dressin' ye'll need," was her comment as she finished. "I'm no a chirurgeon, but there's naething tae hinner ye takin' yer walks abroad noo."

She said this with so much significance that I ventured this remark :

"Your mistress said she could not come to us, and it would ill become me to endanger her by being seen about Cramalt even to thank her."

"Ay," she replied, "if you were raiken roon' Cramalt itsel'; but there's the hill-path in the glen by Cramalt. Mebbe ye dinna ken that's a short cut across the hills Polmood way. At a' events the mistress sud be comin' hame that airt the morn's aefternin. Min' ye," she went on, with a great air of solemnity, "am speikin' only for masel', and the mistress is no ane tae mak' trysts wi' buddies she just meets, an', in ma opeenion, it wad be the Hielanman she wad prefer o' the twa o' ye tae fa' in wi' by chance. But, as your chirurgeon, I wadna say a daunder along this hill o' Muckleside, till ye come doon by the slopes o' Broadlaw on the Cramalt Burn, will be bad for you. Ye'll meet nae crittur but the whaups till ye come on the hill-path—an' I'll no say ye'll meet onybody even then."

"Weel," I said, "ye're no raisin' my hopes dooms

high ; but I ken a kindness when I meet one, an' ye hae dune me mair gude, I think, than ye ken. An deil get me gin I can tell why I am the ane ye help."

" Oh," she rallied, " weemen aye favour the wean wha's got the cuttit finger. But, mind ye, the favour mayna last aefter the finger's better. Fegs, it grows derk, an' I maun get alang Muckleside an' reach the road afore it fa's pick. An' I'm no tae see the bonnie Hielan' lad ? " she added, making a grimace.

" I doubt not to-night, but there are times in store," I answered.

" Ay, an' mair tribbles, nae doobt, wi' them," said she ; " but there's ae text Eppie Tamson tries tae haud in min', ' Sufficient unto the day is the evil thereof.' "

With that the lass, as if applying her motto, nodded to me, and set off along the hillside with the gait we call the heather-step.

CHAPTER XV

A HALCYON HOUR

I GAVE Evan an account of Eppie Tamson's visit, and left him to draw what inference he cared when I ended by saying I would test my strength across the hill on the near side of the Mcgget.

"It's a good airt," he said dryly, "and, if you keep among the four-footed creatures, a safe enough one too."

Soon after midday I was on my way. I had reckoned five or six miles would not fatigue me ; but I did not count on the ground being broken and so steep as it proved, or understand till then how desperately weak loss of blood and fever had left me. I remember that, in trying to breast the last climb before one drops down on the valley, I tried to hurry, and found instead I could not stir a step, being not only breathless but impotent. It was the first time in my life I realized that weakness could lay a finger on you and bring you to a dead stop, whatever you desired to do. I could have cried in sheer vexation. A little rest gave me back poust enough to go on ; but it was a gey forfoughten lad that reached the bridle-track above the burn. Not long had I to wait till I saw her coming. I made no attempt to surprise her, and she doubtless saw me soon enough to let her do some thinking before we actually met.

At all events, as she approached, swinging lightly along in a walking-dress, her face wore a look of distinct displeasure. Then, as she got a closer vizzy, she must have seen how forjeskit I looked. The annoyance passed and gave way to concern.

" How came you here and by your lane ? " she cried. " Has anything misfa'en your frien' ? " I shook my head. " Then is it wise for an ill man tae stravaig sae far ? An', beyond that, is it safe ? "

You may be sure I was not going to betray the good Eppie and her hints ; so I turned the fire on my questioner.

" Me ! " I said. " I'm safe eneuch, for I hae seen nought but twa-three sheep. I'm sound eneuch, tae, an' it's a guid thing for a mending man tae tak' the hill. Gin he war oot o' the sick-hoose ower sune, wha could jalouse he wad run into his nurse an' get his licks like this ? No that the patient wad question his nurse whether *she* is safe," I added banteringly.

She swept the challenge to dalliance aside.

" Oh, me ? Ye want tae ken whaur I've been, though fient the man has any right to interrogate me. Still, I've no desire but to tell, for it's serious. We're in sic a corner o' the land here that, tae get news, we've tae gang for it. Noo there's nane sae like tae ken what's gaun on that concerns your business as Polmood. So I spent last night with the minister's wife at Drumelzier and gave Normand Hunter a call in the passing this morning. By all accounts you're better in the bothie at Talla than anywhere. He tells me the Red Soldier's

Irish friends, O'Cahan and Lachlan, have been hanged,
as a beginning, on the Castle Hill of Edinburgh, and
that the leaders who were captured, Sir William Rollo,
Sir Philip Nisbet, and even the boy Inverquharity, are
marked for death, like bagged foxes, within the next
few days. Also they're holding up Sir Robert Spottiswoode, Lord Ogilvy, young Tullibardine, Nathaniel
Gordon, and the rest for a great trial which will end in
the same way—busy work for the Maiden."

" What of young Dairsie ? " I asked.

" Oh, him ! John Spottiswoode, thanks partly to his
being confused with you, seems to be at large."

" That's one mercy," I cried, " and goes a long way
to repay me for my folly."

" Ay," she replied ; " but I doubt you're not a hair
more safe than he was when you melled with his affairs,
or other folk wouldn't be riding open-eyed to get laired
in the same bog as you're in."

" Does Hunter know aught of the situation of the
Red Soldier and me ? "

" Normand Hunter could ken that only frae one
person, and he's no tell't a' that's in her mind. Ye'll
recollect, tae, that you and the Red Soldier were maist
particeler on ae pint—that ye wad not be beholden to
Polmood."

" That's a *passado* I was askin' for, as Gwyn would
say ; an' Evan fairly agrees ye were in the richt ower
that," I replied.

" Oh, he's generous," she said warmly. " An' he's
loyal, loyal to a fault. I admire this sticklishness of

his over the treasure ; but, weary fa' that treasure, it's
like to be the undoin' of ye baith by keepin' ye rooted
here. So the sooner we get Jimmuck the Caird on
terms wi' yer braw sodger the better. If my messenger
finds him, it's no the messenger that will be chappin'
at my door, but Jimmuck. I think I'll break my own
rule, and take him to the bothie myself."

"Will Eppie not serve for that and be safer ? " I
inquired. I told her of Eppie, and how she had taken
charge of house and householder, with much liveliness.

"Young Mr. Gilbert," she responded, with a mock
severity, " it's easy seen how you thrive under a real
housewife and nurse."

Then I knew I had not fallen in the estimation of the
mistress through taking so much pains to convey to her
what a treasure I considered she had in her handmaiden.
But when I used the chance to tell her it was well
worth being hurt to be touched by her own hand, I
found that this lady loved not to be thanked. Indeed
I never knew, till I learned it from her, that a woman
could have such a lively and sensible imagination, and
such a way of doing things without fuss in herself
or annoyance to others. That afternoon in the glen,
while the burn bickered at our feet, there was no attempt
on my part to make love to her. I knew not how her
mind moved, for all she had done could be explained
by mere kindness. I felt she had compassion for me,
but I was too proud to accept even the flower of her
regard if grown only on that root.

Further, there was something so disarming in that

frank friendship of hers, friendship as of a sister, innocent and trustful, that my good angel told me not to
ask more than it now and to be content. So I was
content when, in just that mood, she felt constrained to
tell me more of her story than I yet knew—how as an
only child she had passed her girlhood since her seventh
year motherless, how her father, Walter Laidlaw, had
taught her book-learning and the guiding of affairs so
that, when he died a year since, she was left as that
singular thing, a lady laird, with no guardian to call her
in question.

"And that, perhaps," she added, as she drew to an
end, "is not considered a'thegither as it sud by the
douce folk round by the lochs and doon by Tweed.
They think there's something uncanny in a lass gettin'
top price at market for yowes or lambs. I'm said tae
be magerful. I shoodna wunner but ther's a grain o'
truth there. Take this meddlin' wi' your affairs. My
father was sterk for the Covenant, and sma' wunner.
The Covenant was a great thought, and it bred great
men. The nation was behind it, and the nation will
be behind it again. But to-day the fortunes of the
Covenant are mainly in the hands of wild talkers or
plotters, set on their own advancement, and they have
shown themselves cruel men. I dinna think Adam
Laidlaw wad hae approved o' this cruel shedding of
blood that's like to become the one argument. Be that
as it may, his own schooling has made me what I am.
For the moment I'm of no party, unless, indeed, there is
a party that mingles mercy to one's countrymen in the

fulfilling of the law. But here am I talking like a
dominie, and it's waste o' the bonnie hairst day. They'll
be almost ready for the headsheaf in the carse lands,
and that minds me. Are ye no hamesick for yer ain
folk ? "

I paused a little ere I replied. " I wad be that, gin I
had a hame ; but that's what I haena. There's neither
kith nor kin o' mine in the auld hoose at the Mains o'
Dairsie these three years past. My father was aye set
on me bein' a scholar—I think in his hert he devoted me
tae the Kirk. A' he left me, aside frae his blessing, was
just siller eneuch tae see me through my course. An'
noo I've broken his hopes into blads an' wounded the
hert of my father's friend an' mine, or will dae sae when
he hears o' my defection, for a base desertion it must
appear to him, wanting any explanation. An', God
forgie me ! I do not repent of my folly. Yet, you see,
I cannot think of my old life or the place I once called
home without pain."

" Regrets will not mend the past," said she. " The
thing is to be up and doing now, and make what you
can out of your very mischances."

So then, if I looked for a soft condonation of my case,
I was not to get it from this strange girl. My face must
have told her that a sick man had not expected to be
bidden pick up his armour and put it on again.

" Ah ! " she cried in a little confusion, while her face
lost its resolute set and softened bewitchingly. " You
can understand now how some of them term me
' magerful.' I've had to think for myself and act for

myself since the days when I learned my first letters. I drive myself hard, and spend but little time on self-pity. Yet that's not to say I cannot pity others. Believe me, if my father spoke first in me just now, my mother had whispered even before that. Only I cared not to speak her whisper loud in words. I see it's not every one that takes the kindlier thought for granted. But, if I seem to be like giving you orders, you may conceive that it is because I am ordering myself. Eh, Gilbert Halkett! It is strange to think you and I are under the same cloud through venturing far afield on other people's troubles. Maybe, in like case, our fathers would have taken the hill-wind on their faces to help folk in need, and so would not be ashamed of us. For me, I think the skies are brightening and bid fair even to be altogether clear ere we are much older and much wiser."

On this happier note she ended. Insisting that I was not yet sufficiently rested for my journey back to the bothie, she stayed with me one brief hour longer. We talked of the things we both prized—the sights and sounds of the quick world, and how we made pictures of the one and laid up the others in memory, so that they might come back freshly to delight us when days were dull or nights were long. I confess I do not remember much of what was actually said. I found my fancy distracted in watching how her cheek flushed with the excitement of a thought, and how her great grey eyes mirrored her moods, now flashing into merriment, anon changing in a moment to a pensiveness which seemed to withdraw her far from me into that region which old Boëthius calls " the centre of quiet," whenever something with a touch of pity in it was spoken of.

I wondered whether she read the mute signal of that gaze. She gave no sign that she did ; but, if feelings can pass through the common sunshine and air, she could have known that all the beauty and all the wisdom I cared to have out of this great round world were symbolized for me in the lovely head of her.

In some of the lonelier streams of that district the kingfisher is to be found. It so happened that one of these birds flashed to and fro along that stretch of the burn while we sat on the heather above its bank. To-day I can see again the glitter of its azure, as I recall, out of the troubled days, that blink of sunshine which I call my halcyon hour. It ended, as all such hours must end. We took good-bye. Alison went her way, down the burn, towards Cramalt. I set myself to my stiff walk.

As I drew near the bothie I mused whether Evan would ask how I had fared, and so touch that hour in the valley, which I would gladly keep as a little sanctuary in all the lands whither I should come. I need not have troubled myself with these speculations. Because, when I reached the bothie, tired indeed, but not in too exalted a frame to be sorry to contemplate supper and bed, it was to find, waiting my arrival, Jimmuck the Caird.

CHAPTER XVI

THE COMING OF THE CAIRD

IT came like a shock to pass from that snatch of peace in the glen and be confronted with the sight of those sons of the storm, the Caird and the Soldier. Surprising, too, it was to think that Ailie's world not only had room for such a being as the Caird, but also that she had chosen him to be a partner with her in our deliverance. For Jimmuck, as he looked up at me on my entrance, appeared to me one of the ugliest and most villainous-like creatures I ever set eyes on.

In body he was not ill-formed, being indeed of good stature, with well-proportioned limbs and a chest like a barrel, which argued great strength; but his face was dreadfully marked with the pits of the smallpox, and there were at least three seams in it which could only be the scars of old wounds. He wore that kind of dress which most all the wandering folk follow, something of the horse-boy's, gaitered about the legs in a neat fashion, but loose in the jerkin. The jerkin, cut away just above the elbow, was open at the throat and shewed his hairy chest. But while his neck was thus open, he yet wore, in a twist round it, a neckcloth in which the colours cried out against one another.

Jimmuck could not have held a chain of gold in more regard than that neckcloth. I cannot even think of the Caird without seeing that twist of red and yellow. It distinguished him from any of his followers, if, indeed, he needed a distinction other than his unforgettable face.

It was a sinister face but for a twinkle in the deep-set eyes of him. He wore a great knife in a sheath openly at his belt, and, for all one could see, carried nothing else in the shape of arms.

He was swarthy to a degree, though I fear grime had deepened his natural blackness of visage. He wore no hair on his face; perhaps the pox had eradicated it. This made it difficult to guess his age, but I put him down as a man of forty-five.

Jimmuck and the Soldier were already chief, and the Caird very much at his ease. It was ever my luck to seem to be the interloper, and it looked as if I had broken in on two men well on with their plans. In this I did them wrong. They had not opened the matter, by Evan's request, against my return, and had passed the time in getting on friendly terms, the which was made easier by a case-bottle of brandy which the Caird had brought as first-foot, and by the fact that he had been encouraged to use his tobacco. This he did, blowing great clouds of blue smoke from a blackened pipe which lay very close to his nose.

The Red Sergeant did not follow the habit, which was strange, for it came in mainly through his soldier countrymen, who had learned it while campaigning in

the Low Countries ; and I have often thought it a pity
he did not, for it might have calmed his restlessness in
many an hour when he did nothing but chafe, and that
to no purpose. He had, however, a sup of the brandy
in his cup, though the bottle bode all that evening
singular close to Jimmuck's elbow.

" Oho ! " cried Evan, as I appeared, " here's the
tongue of the trump. Now we can have the music.
Our friend Jimmuck and I have just been swapping
opinions on the goodness or badness of the Highland
line, but we've kept the business that brought him till
your coming."

If I judged the Caird to be a wild barbarian creature,
who could scarcely be expected to understand such
language to converse with us intelligently, I was unduly
prejudiced by his uncouth exterior.

Jimmuck, as it turned out, had no great vocabulary,
except in the jargon of his own folk ; but he possessed a
quick mind. He was in constant touch with men, at
market if not at kirk, in all the Lowlands, and was
anything but dull in the uptake on any subject that
came within his experience. Often afterwards, when
the Caird brightened what would have been a dull day
for Evan and myself by a lively tale, maybe garnished
with sculdudry a wee bit, or shrewd observes on some
practical difficulty, I had reason to think how foolish
my first impression of him was. For in truth that
night in the bothie I could not get over the thought
that some of the ancient Picts must have lived on by
strange hap in the hills through the centuries, wearing

the human form, but only half human, and that this was one of them.

" Say on, friend, now," cried the Sergeant; " let's have your side of the story."

" There's naething muckle tae say," replied Jimmuck. " I wis on Leader-side wi' a curn horse I got at Bossels, a twa-three no bad yins amo' the feck that needed a month's gress afore they could move. Auld Yiddon Amos cam' wi' word frae the mistress at Cramalt tae tryst ye at the bothie here on the quaet, and be tellt o' a ploy that micht need a man or twa. So I e'en saddled Barefit an' cam' straicht. Twa-three o' the lads are following, an' ocht tae be at the haugh fornenst Menzion by nicht tae be ready gin they're needed. A ca' frae Mistress Alison is eneuch tae be gaein' on wi' for Jimmuck, but I'm a' in the derk. Barefit's stabled wi' Dauvid Douglas, the herd at the Menzion, nae questions speired, an' I'm here. Sae what's yer wull ? "

By what instinct do men of the open air understand who can be trusted and who not ? I should have thought that the last person to whom one would confide the story of the treasure and, above all, the proposal to make him its guardian, was Jimmuck. Yet Evan, who had used the time of waiting for my arrival to read his man, had not the slightest hesitation in making the Caird his confidant. True, he did not at the moment tell him where the treasure lay ; but he related everything, even to its amount, and ended by making his proposal that Jimmuck should aid us to recover it from the secret place and, in our company, transport it to

Montrose himself, or to some sure hand, if it were not feasible actually to reach the Marquis. I was vastly surprised when he ended by saying that, if it were delivered safe at any spot on this side of the Highland line, the Caird would receive a hundred pounds ; while, if we had to follow the Marquis into the mountains, fifty more would be given. Afterwards, when I remarked to Evan on the strangeness of trusting such an unlikely agent with a great sum, which might be all his if his honesty failed, and offering him such a miserable moiety of it as reward for being its custodian, he explained it was his thought-out policy.

" You see, we were risking everything on Mistress Ailie's belief that the Caird would jump for the adventure, if he jumped at all. Doubtless, if the spell of it broke, there would be the plain temptation to slit our weasands and have all the gold. I risked his holding staunch. He would not do us the service for money alone ; but recompense he must expect, for he's not exactly a Wallace wight. Now, if you consider on it, the great sum would draw suspicion on the Caird, and, if he dared to take it, he could not, in his narrow life, find means to spend it, whereas a hundred or two hundred pieces of gold mean wealth to a man like Jimmuck, and put the honey on the good oatcake of the adventure."

I know that many will not credit this part of my tale, and will take Jimmuck's decision then and his doings after it as a fabulous narration, impossible as it is foolish. And who am I to blame such, seeing I was so much of a sceptic as I listened to the Soldier unfolding his seemingly ridiculous proposal to the Caird ?

Jimmuck heard him out without word or motion. He suffered his tobacco pipe to go out, and even left the case-bottle undisturbed. When the Red Sergeant had ended, he sat silent for a space, the while he nursed his chaps with his left hand. Then, with the right, he pulled from its sheath the great knife, which he called " his wee Eskdale souple," and birled it in the air. When it fell he looked to see which side was uppermost, and towards what airt the weapon's point lay. What he saw evidently satisfied him. He spat on the knife, replaced it, and said, " I'm wi' ye, maisters. It's a bargain, an' may ma throat be cuttit by my grandda's gully there, as I've sworn on't, if I dinna haud by ma bargain. An' noo, whaur's yer bit treasure ? "

Evan, who had felt the suspense more than I, gave a grunt of relief. He drew his skean dhu and pressed the naked steel to his lips. " That's for you, brother," he cried, " and Gilbert here is with Evan in it."

My misgivings largely passed at the sight of the solemn way in which the Caird took this response to his ritual. Indeed, it would have been folly to entertain them unduly, for we were now fully committed.

Evan told how the treasure lay in the pool at the Greymare's Tail, how it would be men's work to retrieve it, and a puzzle for wits better than his to pass it unbeknown through the Lowlands.

" It's lyin' in a naisty bit for han'lin'," Jimmuck said in response, taking the disclosure of the place very easily. " I cud dae wi' twa-three o' ma fallows. Guid fallows, I alloo they are, for a' in the ordinar' wey o' the horse-coupin' ; but the tribble is that, tho' ye trust Jimmuck in this kind o' ploy, Jimmuck canna trust them. The three o's are fit tae get it on the road. But what aefter ? Weel, there's muckle Joseph, a half-Egyptian lad, has a kind o' covered-in cairt he uses when he gangs tentin'. I'll hae it sent frae Leaderfit tae Birkhill by a laddie, for Joseph himsel' wad be wantin' tae ken mair gin he drove it. I'll gie him chairge o' the company and gang wi' you masel'. We'se hae a sma' string o' horse, tae gie colour tae the coupin' business, and, gin Jimmuck the Caird disna throw sand eneuch in folks' een tae mak' ye twa pass as twa 'prentices at the gaun-about business, he's been cleckit ower late in the day. Min' ye, the sesson's wairin' late for horse-coupin', but mebbe I cud get ye as far as Stirling or Angus afore it'll seem strange for us tae be on the road."

We discussed the plan up and down. It seemed good. It was two men feeling the new venture had opened better than they had had reason to expect, who saw Jimmuck start on his way down the coppice-side towards Menzion where his tatterdemalion followers lay.

CHAPTER XVII

A CAPTIVE OF THE COMMITTEE

JIMMUCK made things move briskly. Within three days, during which we elaborated our plans and stirred with more sense of security as we accustomed ourselves to the dress, somewhat resembling that he himself wore, which the Caird brought us the better to play our part later, he had his lad with the covered cart at Birkhill. There Jimmuck himself joined him on Barefit with a few led horses, and, to cover the intended departure, spent the nights in a rough shelter of sacking, stretched on hoops of willow, with a small camp-fire burning at his feet. Evan had decided that it would be unfair to ask Yiddon to take any active part in the raising of the treasure, and that we should carry out the work our three selves. But the old man knew we were on the point of moving, and we ourselves had settled upon the night of the day, which I am now to describe, as giving us just enough moonlight for us to see, and yet not enough to let our movements be too easily seen in our enterprise, when there came an interruption that connached our plan.

Just about noon Jimmuck appeared in what was for him somewhat of a fluster.

" Ye'll mebbe hae tae tak' tae the hill a wee," he cried. " Joseph and ane o' the laddies hae been takin' a cast roon' by Drumelzier, and, juist as they crossed the ford and cam' on the road frae Brochton, they rode into a sma' company o' sodgers and twa buddies—gey like the kind that cairt ye awa tae the Tolbooth, the Egyptian thocht. At a' events he kin' o' dawdled and cam' cannily on ahint them, an', whan he saw them turn aff at Tweed for Talla, he galloped on an' lat me ken. I've come bareback, an' ye haena meenutes till they're here."

" It looks like we are the hare they hunt," said Evan, " but we'll not break cover till we see. If we have to take the hill, near the foot of the fall on the Moffat road you'll find us at the mouth of night, Jimmuck."

The two of us stole down to where the thinning of the coppice let us see the rough track they called the road. Sure enough, there appeared a sergeant's guard of soldiers, such as Leslie would not have owned as his, poor sweepings of the Edinburgh garrison, I should deem, and with them two men in rusty black, who seemed sorry that their seat was a saddle and not an alehouse bench by the Tron. Two led horses accompanied the troop. Though there was no mirth among the company, they certainly did not suggest that they were trying to effect a surprise on men in hiding. The soldiers paid no heed to the country on either side, but looked steadily to the road at their feet and held on up the glen. We kept pace with them in parallel, to make sure this was no feint, till we saw them turn to ascend the hill at the jaws of the pass into Megget.

"So the riderless horses are not for us after all," remarked Evan, as the cavalcade struggled up the rocky road. "I wonder whom they are meant to carry to the Tolbooth."

We were to learn that before long. Burst in on us, late that afternoon, the old man Yiddon.

"Eh, sirs, sirs," he cried, "an awfu' thing has happened! The mistress!"

"What of her?" we both called out, as the old man gasped for breath.

"Oh, dule tae me that I should have to tell it," he half sobbed. "The sodgers hae come tae Cramalt tae tak' awa' the mistress. It seems that child o' Beelzebub, wha's nae true child o' mine, Mungo, swore a declaration at Embro' that she had been in arms against the Estates, and had tried tae compass the death o' its sodgers. The sodger lads cudna deny that the lady had fired a shot, but said it was in daffin'. Mungo threepit that it was o' fell intent tae wound, for she was in league wi' twae Malignants wha were even at the moment escaping by her connivance. The Committee is searching for blood like slouth-hunds, an' e'en lippened tae the false loon. Eh, wae's me! It's like tae gae ill wi' her faither's bairn. Gin it does, my grey hairs will be laid i' the mools wi' shame."

"Hoots, man," I said. "It's a ill tale ye bring, but there were waur losses at Flodden, an' the battle's no lost for us yet. But haste ye on tae Menzion and gie Jimmuck word o' this, and bid him join us."

For once it was I and not Evan who did the ordering. Indeed the thought came to me that, in that narrow valley, we, with the aid of Jimmuck and his men, could effect a rescue. But it was not so to be. Jimmuck could not be found by Yiddon at Menzion. So it came that, an hour later, the Soldier and I, powerless to help, had to cower there in the bushes and watch a procession the sight of which made our blood hot. The company was as we had seen it before, except that the led horses now had riders. On one sat a figure, at the sight of which, in a less sad setting, we could well have laughed, the faithful lass Eppie Tamson. Her hands were free, and both she used to clutch the forepart of the saddle, while the reins were let lie as they pleased on her horse's neck.

It was otherwise with her mistress. They had the cruelty—and stupidity—to bind her arms crossed in front of her, and to guide her mount by a rein stretched to a trooper who rode alongside. As if in fear that even then she might escape, the poor trash crowded round her as much as the narrow way would permit. Yet, if Alison was convoyed out of her estate with every mark of outward contempt, she went with unruffled dignity.

"Oh, my love, my love," I whispered to myself, calling her this for the first time, as the pitifulness of her plight and our part in it rent my heart. "Would God you had not saved one of us at least, since this is the cost."

She must have known we were near by in the brake,
yet, so wise was she, that never a look towards it she
gave. But it was almost as if my warm thought had
reached her, for the moment after it had caught me
round the heart, her pale face flushed. A sad little
smile played round her lips, and she lifted her head with
a stately movement, such as you have seen the swan
make when she rears herself up in courage to defend her
nest. Then the cavalcade turned a corner out of sight.

"By the dust of my dear ones," muttered the Soldier, "but that was the worst minute Evan ever lived
through. To think we had our eyes on that, like
two frogs in the marsh, able to do nothing but croak
over it!"

"Bide you, Evan," I replied; "the minute has
passed, but the day is not done yet."

"True for you," says he. "Let's follow, for they
cannot travel much farther, and sleep we will not till
we have had a try at a rescue. I tell you she's in the
toils. It would be almost a laughing matter had it not
fallen out in this day of the inquisition of blood. Once
let her fall into the hands of the crew who can link up
that fateful shot with her doings for us, and she's in a
net from which there is no escape. I fear Mistress
Alison, like yourself, must throw in her lot with the
Malignants. It'll be for us to give her the choice,
whatever. So let's find Jimmuck."

We made our way down the glen without concern for
our safety, for the folks in the clachan of Tweedsmuir
were all at their doors watching the cavalcade go by.

If there had been any to observe us as we passed up the right bank of Tweed to Menzion, he would need to have sharp eyes to take us for other than two of the Caird's ragged company, so well did our duds mask the soldier and the student. Certainly we passed easily as two members of the band when we inquired at Jimmuck's crony, the Menzion shepherd, for the whereabouts of the Caird.

" A'body's speirin' for Jimmuck the day seemingly," he replied. " An hour sin' auld Yiddon cam' seekin' him, like a hen that's clecked duke's eggs an' sees her little anes tak' the water. He gaed awa' pechin', puir body, as if he cud owertak' Jimmuck when he's muntit on Barefit. An' sma' wunner. What wi' the sodgers liftin' Winterhope's dochter, an' his ain foul-farren geit hae'n the wite o' that ill deed, auld Yiddon micht weel gang wud. But it's no for the likes o' him tae try runnin' like a maukin. Eh but, certes, look at yon. Gin ma een dinna deceive me, Yiddon's baith fund him an' gotten up in the warld."

He pointed across the Tweed to a little bit of haugh below Menzion, where the Caird's men were encamped. Coming into it from the Tweedsmuir side was Yiddon, mounted on Barefit, and Jimmuck leading the horse cannily across the hillocks of turf.

We did not wait for more, but, crossing Tweed by the rocks and stepping-stones which were shewing at the foot of the pool below Menzion because of the lowness of the water, made haste to the tinker's camp. To our outburst of impatience over Yiddon's failure to get word to Jimmuck and so effect the rescue we had hoped for, the Caird had his answer ready.

" Rescue ! " he cried. " What kin' o' a rescue cud we hae cairrit oot in broad daylicht ? We micht wi' luck hae flegged the sodgers into confusion an' got awa' wi' the lass ; but we wad hae been followed, an' worse, we wad hae been seen an' kent as Jimmuck an' Jimmuck's folk. Na, na," he went on, with a slight show of temper, " ye were no the only folk tae think o' a rescue. Jimmuck didna need puir auld Yiddon's message. He jaloused wha was tae be ta'en, the moment the sodgers passed yer hidie-hole, an' Jimmuck was awa'. Awa' whaur ? Oh, juist doon Tweed as fast as Barefit cud cairry him. Weel, there's a lad noo hingin' aboot the Bield, an' he'll hing on tae that braw company till it settles for the nicht. Then he'll tell Jimmuck whaur, an' syne Jimmuck will, gin ye're still minded for a rescue, gie ye the benefit o' a wee plan he made as he led that puir spent body back on his horse. An', Sodger," he concluded, turning to Evan, "it's no the liftin' o' the lass only that's on my mind ; there's what we ken o' to be cairried oot as weel. Noo nae time's being lost. Nicht's the ae chance for Jimmuck's plan, and, till nicht fa's, deil a fit or hoof can better it by stirrin'."

" Jimmuck," Evan said, his face now clear of vexation, " you have the right of it all through. You're the chief of this creagh. We'll drive off the cattle and get the booty under one bidding, and that yours. Isn't that so, Gilbert ? "

" It is indeed," I responded heartily.

Jimmuck looked more than a trifle pleased. So we settled down, a reasonably contented company, to await the fall of evening and the coming of Jimmuck's spy.

Near a dozen of the Caird's following were gathered there, ostensibly to tend the score or so of horses which grazed along the haugh. A curious lot they looked, odds and ends of the wandering folk whom Jimmuck had picked up. One or two were clearly of the Egyptian strain, though not of the pure stock ; for its members consort only with their own kind. Some were of the class which has long joined the tinker's trade to horse-couping, with a greater fondness for the latter. The company was completed by one or two of the people called " broken men," who had found life in towns dangerous to their necks or distasteful to their restless habits. They were at once a villainous and a merry crew. You should have seen us round the supper-pot when the Soldier and I broke bread with the company, and so set up a comradeship closer than our mimicry of their clothes or even our friendship with their chief had yet established, by taking our portion. Let no one say cairds do not fare well when the land they camp on suits the lanky grews that sneak at the horses' heels. Mutton came out of that pot, but also came out hare and coney and partridge ; and, whether one supped the soup from the wooden bowl, or parted the solids with one's fingers, it was a meal such as the new-comers to the band had not tasted for long. And to see Jimmuck, like some ugly heathen idol surrounded by worshippers in the incense, when the tobacco was lit, with a look of content on his wound-scarred face, was to understand how, in such a republic, the president is the man who can most strongly act and most unconcernedly rest.

The light had begun to fade on the grassy uplands which hang above that fair stretch of Tweed, when a halflin lad entered the camp on a sorely blown horse. He walked straight to Jimmuck and gave his report. The Caird raised his great voice, that was like the belling of a stag.

" Here's a fair hunt," he cried. " The quarry we're aefter is couched for the nicht at Polmood. Things cudna hae fa'en better. An' noo, ane an' a' gaither roon' an' cock yer lugs for the plan o' the ploy."

CHAPTER XVIII

THE GUISERS

WHEN Jimmuck explained the plan, which will become clear as I describe its carrying out, he looked round his motley crew. "Are ye wi' us or no, billies?" he asked.

Then that free company responded, manifestly tickled, "Ay, we're wi' ye a' the way, Jimmuck."

"Dod, it's a gran' baar tae get a rise oot o' the sodgers, an' a better ane tae hae a batter at thae naisty rottans frae the To'booth," one lusty lad put it, and doubtless voiced the sentiment of all.

"Weel, get a'thing in order," the Caird went on; "we stert at mirk, and that's no far off noo." Then he turned to Evan and me. "There's twa things, aefter the lads hae their frisk, that only hiz maun ken o'. Tane is the treasure and the tither is the lass. Ye've doobtless thocht on baith maitters, an' it's clear we maun divide if we are tae save baith. Noo, frien' Sodger, ye've made it plain that ye hae the chairge o' the treasure, so it seems you and me must dae oor best by it, gin the nicht's ploy succeeds. That still leaves the lass. The young lad here maun convoy her tae a place o' safety, an' than jine hiz at a named spot."

I saw Evan wince. " It seems to be the way the duties fall," he replied quietly.

" Weel, hae ye thocht o' a hidin'-place for the lass ? " asked Jimmuck.

I own there fell gratefully on my ear this proposal to give me charge of the precious person and not the mere precious thing ; but it was Evan who answered.

" It will of course be for Mistress Alison to say whether she thinks herself in danger great enough to need hiding. For myself, I think she is. And, if she decides to hide, the question is where. Now, I say, run to the point of danger. Get her to Edinburgh. It is the last place in Scotland they will expect her to seek to. Gilbert, can you bestow her in some asylum there till this storm blows by, think you ? "

" Ay, a braw jape on them that, Sodger," Jimmuck interrupted. " The doe runnin' tae the hounds' kennel."

" It's better than a jape," I remarked, " it's sound strategy. Anyway, I'll take in hand the convoy and how I can have it bestowed."

" Well, for rendezvous," went on Evan, " where and when should you and I be able to tryst him at a place within easy cast of Edinburgh ? "

" Weel," said the Caird, considering, " there'll be an awfu' fracas in this valley aefter the nicht's wark, and, if me and you can slip quaetly doon, as I expec', by Yarra an' the Slacks tae Traquair, we should be anaith Caerketton, even if we hae tae traivil maistly in the mirk, on the second nicht frae noo. There's a real

quaet bit, on the toon side o' Swanston, whaur hiz cairds
aften gaither. Frae there ye can drap doon on the
roads that gae west or north whan ye ken whaur yer
bit boxies are tae be ta'en. We can tryst him there."

" You know the bit, Gilbert ? " asked Evan.

" Fine," said I.

" That's resolved then," says he. " An' here's to our
happy meeting there, with both the treasures safe."

While we talked, the rest of the company were busy
making preparations, which would have made a spec-
tator, who had not heard their chief's plan, think he had
landed on an assemblage of mad folk. Most of them
had been daubing their faces and hands with the black
dyes used in the tricks of the couping trade. Others
contented themselves with powdered charcoal from the
wood fire. And all were now putting splatches round
each other's eyes with the white ash. Those who wore
shirts the least resembling in colour this adornment had
stripped and put these garments on above their jerkins.
The halflin lad had slipped up to Menzion and returned,
from a stealthy visit to the herd's killing-shed, with
half a sackful of sheep's horns. These the tinker members of the company were now bending on to strips
of tin so that these might be slipped on to complete
their head adornment. Jimmuck's men resembled a
company of guisers at Hogmanay, only, with their
blackened faces and Satanic horns, I declare they looked
in the half-light more like denizens of the nether world.

" Here's the brunstane," said one wizened old fellow,
producing phosphorus. When it was applied the black-

ened faces began to gleam with a horrid wavering light, and the company looked more Satanic still.

" Keep a lick o' that tae freshen ye up at the gates of Polmood," said Jimmuck.

He himself was not above taking the precaution to slip on a black visor, which no doubt was a common disguise with him, for he was able to supply Evan and myself with one.

He would be a hard swearer who would stand to the identification of any one there in a court of justice. As I looked, the craft of the Caird's plan, as well as the well-calculated buffoonery of it which had appealed to his men, struck me as singularly well conceived.

Suppose the night's work were tracked to Jimmuck, there was a fair chance of his escaping serious consequence, for, in spite of the grimness of the times, Scotland had not quite forgotten how to laugh.

There was a wee bit of moon as we moved off, just enough to make the company appear the more ghostly. And, like ghosts of the old prickers of the Borders, we passed down Tweed, the horses treading noiselessly on the grassy edge of the road. The house of Polmood lies in the mouth of a timbered glen, which opens on Tweed, some five miles down-stream from the haugh we left.

It was indeed a wily stroke of the Estates' officers to ask from the laird who was suspect of disaffection quarters for them and their prisoner.

Jimmuck's spy had wit enough not only to learn that young Hunter had received the posse of the Committee, but also to note how they and their charges had been bestowed. The soldiers were assigned the kitchen quarters of the house, while the two apparitors of justice and the sergeant of the guard were disposed in the dining-hall on the ground floor. The prisoner and her maid were under Polmood's seal of safety in the upper apartments of the house. The offices stood at a little distance from the mansion, and there the horses of the company were stabled.

Jimmuck halted us a little distance from the gates, and we tethered our horses lest their whinnying should give the alarm. Sign of sentinel we could see none. So it was an unobserved troop that glided noiselessly into the policies surrounding the house. Half a dozen figures made for the stables, and in five minutes all the beasts there, including even poor Polmood's precious blood-horses, were led out, to be turned loose in the woods.

The soldiers were our first and chief concern. We stole towards the longish wing that formed the kitchen premises. It was, I judge, about ten o'clock, and we had hoped that we should surprise the men, who had gone a hard day on the roads, asleep. As I had guessed, however, those fellows were not the seasoned troopers of the Covenant, but valiants of the trained bands. Not often did such a jaunt as this come their way ; and, if they had to endure its hard riding, they were determined not to miss the little pleasures that waited at the end of the day. Through the shutters we watched them for a little taking their ease, and truly these

burghers had little to learn in the art. There they
sprawled before a great wood fire which they had had
kindled for their comfort, though it was still early
October.

Truly they shewed but little of the soldier in them,
for their bits of accoutrements lay scattered about the
room, their boots had been kicked off, and they pointed
feet, set in home-made hose, towards the fire. A
dresser, which, judging by the fragments that remained,
had groaned with good cheer, was set to the side of the
room ; but a smaller table, placed within easy reach of
all, held two great flagons of wine, so that from these
each man might with ease replenish his goblet. Young
Polmood plainly desired to be considered no churl to
the Covenant when he felt constrained to give its queasy
soldiers the free run of his cellar. Upon their highnesses
a couple of Polmood's serving-maids attended. It was
evident that these country lassies did not relish the
badinage the fellows were accustomed to pass with the
joes of the plainstones.

"Sing, lassie, sing," one of heavy face and hanging
chaps was crying, with little suggestion of being a
precisian. "Sing a gay, bauld ballat, and ye'se hae yer
supper, ay, an' on this knee tae."

"I've nae mind tae sing," the lass said ; "there's
naething tae sing aboot the nicht."

"Oh, I ken brawly," replied the swashbuckler, "ye're
thinkin' o' that prood hellicat that ye thocht was tae be
yer mistress. Eh, the mim mou' o' her ! We'll see
what it hiz tae say tae the Cooncil ; or, gin she winna

answer the Cooncil, what she'll say when the thumikins are on her heigh han' or the boot on that fit of hers whilk wad tramp through the bluid o' honest sodgers like oorsel's."

Glad was I it was not Eppie Tamson of the tart tongue that had to answer for her mistress. But the lass did well enough.

" Stite and havers," she sparked out, " Mistress Laidlaw disna shed the blood o' *sclaters*, gin it's bluid they beasties hae."

" Ye impident limmer ! " the fellow cried, jumping up. " Aefter that, it's no sing ye sall, but dance ; for ye're a true limb o' this treasonable hoose, an' it's me that'll gar ye."

" Ay, ay," came in chorus from the troopers round the fire. " Clear the ring ; let her kilt her coats an' dance."

Fegs, the ring was cleared in another way than they thought on.

" Noo," whispered Jimmuck. He heaved his great bulk against the door. Into the room dashed the horde of us. One threw a cloth over the two sconces that stood on the side-table, so that but the rushlights on either side the chimney and the fire itself remained to give light. A dozen demons, with black visages gleaming horridly above garments like grave-cloths and crowned with curling horns, did another kind of dancing from that called for.

" O Lord preserve us," cried the fellow, so valiant but a moment since. " Auld Cloutie an' his deevils— an' me red in ma sins ! "

His fellows were like men turned into stone with terror. Only the two maids gave voice, and they, poor lassies, only in screeches. Jimmuck uttered not a word. We had his instructions, and, before the wretches had time to recover their sense, they were bound and blind-folded, and lying huddled on the floor like sheaves of corn.

Heavy feet clattered along the stone passage connecting with the house. Jimmuck flung the door open. The sergeant and the two officers of the law who followed him fell into our waiting hands, to be smoored in table-cloths before they well saw us, who straightway bound them. There was still young Polmood. As we passed along the trance, Jimmuck spoke for the first time. "Mind, even he is no tae ken us." We came on a little entrance hall, from which a flight of stairs rose. At the top of them, in the light that streamed from the room behind him, stood young Polmood. I could spare a thought of consideration for that man. There was he, roused by the noise of some sort of attack on his house. How was he to know we were friends? I thought he looked very gallant as, in his ignorance, he stood with sword drawn to stand guard over defenceless women. Though he must have got the surprise of his life when our strange throng burst on his sight, there was in him no sign of superstitious terror, such as had made our work so easy with the others.

"Stop!" he shouted. "I'll run the first man who mounts through!" and advanced his blade.

"Nae time for mainners," growled Jimmuck to us.

He bounded up the stairs, struck the blade from Hunter's grip with his cudgel, and then served him such a buffet on the side of the head that the young laird fell like a log.

"Bide ye there," cried Jimmuck to the rest, while to us he added, "Gang in yer twa sel's."

Evan and I darted into the supper-room in our tattered clothes, but with our masks removed.

Mistress Ailie was just within the door, and, by her, Eppie, both in amazement.

"Mistress," said Evan, "it's a rescue. You can escape, with scaith to no person concerned; but it is for you to decide. Will you be rescued?"

"Will I not indeed?" she answered, for hers was a mind that jumped to face a new situation in a moment. "But you, Eppie?" she queried.

"Dis a rescue mean bein' free o' they tykes o' sodgers an' aiblins haein' a dad at them aefter?"

"Ay," said Ailie; "but mebbe wi'oot the dad."

"Oh! A rescue, by a' means," was Eppie's stolid reply.

"There is your guardian, then," said Evan, nodding towards me. "Your plans you must concert with him outside. Don't be alarmed at the sight of your other rescuers. They are Jimmuck and his men. But haste you, for it's not healthy to linger here."

We passed out at the main door. I was wae to leave Polmood lying senseless on his own landing. We left the house of folk helpless, if, indeed, we except the servant lasses. That they would set the soldiers free after a little was like enough. But there was time and more for all that now remained to be done. We bade farewell to Evan and Jimmuck at the gates of Polmood. Then, with Ailie and Eppie Tamson well mounted on two of Jimmuck's horses, and I on the beast I had ridden thither, we turned towards Broughton and the Edinburgh road on what I took to be the best adventure I had happened on yet.

CHAPTER XIX

A SQUIRE OF DAMES

IF there was to be any pursuit of the party which left Polmood, it would be hard for the pursuers to determine whom to follow and whither. For the tinkers, the likeliest people to be suspected of the rude guising which had succeeded so well, were to ride across the hills by bridle-tracks known to them, and be found in camp at Leaderfoot by daybreak. Jimmuck and the Red Sergeant were making straight for the lad with the covered cart at Birkhill, whence they were to get the treasure on the road, after passing the word to the old herd to guide things as best he could at Winterhope till his mistress should return. And we, Mistress Ailie and Eppie and I, were going, in yet a third direction, by Broughton and the Leadburn Muir, to Edinburgh. Yes, that was the great thought which seemed too good to be true, as I remembered my despair at seeing Ailie so fast in the toils. Yet there, in the soft moonlight on the deserted road, was the clink of the horses' feet beating time to a song of freedom that sang in the heart, and a little laugh now and again from the rescued lady to tell me she was past the terrors of the night. This was surely contentful enough for a knight-errant, who was not even asked by the damsel what was to be the next chapter in the adventure.

We pushed on at a brisk trot, for I was concerned to put distance between us and Polmood by daylight and was happy enough to do without conversation, till a groan from Eppie made me think for the first time of that staunch lass. I beheld her holding hard by the pommel with both hands, the while her face wore a look of mingled agony and fear. Poor Eppie! she had never ridden any horse kind but a great soft-backed farm beast, going to the watering. Now she was risking her neck and being flayed, like some early Christian martyr, at one and the same time, for the sake of her mistress, and yet never a cheep from her till the groan which she could no longer repress. I drew rein and steadied her mount to a walk.

"What's the maitter, Eppie?" I asked. "Is it the seddle?"

"No, it's me masel'," the poor lass replied.

"Bide you," said I.

I made her dismount, slipped off the saddle, which I slung across my own horse's back, got a couple of the grass-ropes, by which they tie the ricks, from a hay-field by the roadside, twisted them into stirrups, with generous loops at the ends of them for her feet, and hoisted her again on the beast's back.

"Can ye gang cannily wi' that?" I asked.

"Ay, brawly," she replied. "It's maist like sittin' in an airmchair."

We went on at an easy shamble, and she kept her

balance to admiration. But I saw by this little set-back, which would never be thought of as likely to happen in one of the old romances, that my plan must be altered. At the best pace Eppie could command, we could not hope to reach Edinburgh by a brisk ride through the night. We should have to make two bites of the cake, and, with a pause on the road, there came the chance of our being discovered or overtaken.

"My lass," I said, "when the licht comes, ye'll hae tae tak' tae yer seddle aince mair."

"Oh, mebbe I'll be a wee better by then," says she, and her mistress gave a little gurgle which set us all a-laughing, so that very merrily we rode on at a curious ambling trot, strangely like the gait of the Shauchlin Herd. For myself, I would not have shortened a minute of that journey in the night. For the first time since I set out from Linlithgow, I had the sense of being free and my own master. Not only so, but the lady who had looked on me with indifference by the shore of Loch Skeen was now trusting me to take her somehow out of her troubles, as if I were an old friend and of tried judgment. Was she the same that had been called " a magerful maid " ?

The break of day found us no nearer Edinburgh than Leadburn. I dared not venture resting for a meal at the little inn by the roadside there, for we were an ill-assorted company, and it would be hard to explain how a dainty lady came to be raking through the night with a horsewoman of such comical equipment as Eppie and a travelling caird like myself. So we rode

on, before the folks were astir, to the great moor beyond
the inn, turned our horses into a place which a hillock
screened from the road, tethered the beasts and let
them have their will of the grass, the while we ourselves
rested and refreshed ourselves with the provisions which
Muckle Joseph had, with gypsy foresight, stowed in my
saddle-bags. Right glad was I then that I had not
thrust my plans on the lady in the darkness, for I should
have missed the sight of her face under the light of
morning as I broke them to her. Then, for the first
time, I saw it like that of a child who listens at the
nursery fire to an older child, and waits for wonder to
follow wonder till the story ends. I cannot tell whether
my narration answered her hopes, for, indeed, I had
little wonderful to propose. I think that, if Eppie's
discomfort had not slowed down our pace, we might
have gotten within the city before daybreak, and so
escaped notice. I said nought of this, but went on
with the plan which I had devised, since it became plain
the quick journey was not possible. This was that,
after recruiting ourselves and the horses, we should
make cannily for the place where Evan and Jimmuck
were to tryst me below Swanston. We could avoid
Penicuik and slip down to the north slopes of the
Pentlands. I should there camp, leaving the horses as
part of the string which would give face to subsequent
play-acting as coupers. Mistress Alison and Eppie I
would then conduct quietly into the town at dusk, and
seek asylum for them in my own former quarters.
There they would lie in safety till the storm blew past.

Eppie broke in, " An' wha's in chairge o' yer quarters, young maister ? "

" Oh, a Mistress Cowieson, Eppie. She mithered me
a' my student days, for, when a lass, she was in chairge
o' the kye at Dairsie. I can trust her wi' a wee bit o'
the story, an' Mistress Cowieson can be maist con-
veniently deif where folk speir. Ye'll be as safe wi' her
as at Cramalt, Eppie."

" Ay, mebbe," says she, " but I wish she wis a
Jeddart wumman, or even frae Ha'ick ; an' wha's tae
pey the lawin', young sir ? " went on this sturdy
sceptic.

I produced a sporran. " Here's twenty gold pieces
to be ga'en on wi'," I said, " an' mair tae follow, gin
there's need."

" It's the Hielanman's purse, isn't it ? " she pursued.

" Ay, an' the Hielanman's lining tae," I laughed.

" Deed, it wad be. He's the lad," she retorted.

Alison, who had watched Eppie's tilt at me with
amusement, broke silence.

" I think your plan's the best we can devise," she
said. " I own I am glad to lie hid as long as Mungo is
moving, an' once settled in the city, Eppie an' I can
brave it out an' yet not be altogether nuns neither. If
Mistress Cowieson is feared tae tak' us, I should e'en
just try going openly to a hostelry. I have the where-
withal," producing a little leather bag. " They didn't
fleg me oot o' mindin' it when I thought it wad be used
only on the turnkeys o' the Tolbooth. But I am
grateful to your friend's forethought for all that. You'll

thank him for me, and tell him he'll need all his
siller for his big adventure and no tae heed my little
one."

"Ay," chimed in Eppie, "an' wha kens but the
naisty sodger critturs are aefter him at this verra
moment ! "

"Oh, he can give them a hunt worth following," her
mistress assured her. "And I'm clear he would be the
last not to have us enjoy the present," she added.

"And indeed why not ? " I said to myself.

You would have seen little sign of fugitives from
justice in Ailie and me as we busied ourselves in weav-
ing cocked hats out of the rushes, playing soldiers with
the dusty-headed flowers we call carl-doddies, and,
when tired of such bairnly play, lazily watched the
great bumble bees patiently trying for the last sip of
honey from the few tufts of the sweet-scented thistle
with the purple tops that still had a bloom or two.
Eppie, decent lass, who had started knitting grasses
into a cockscomb, fell fast asleep over it. But her
mistress seemed to have no weariness, and noon went
by in peace on that moorland, with never a soul passing
along the road that ran through its waste of heather.
Indeed, I do not know that I altogether pleased her
when, on seeing the sun turning towards the Pentlands,
I got us to horse again.

"Oh," she said, looking round, "for this quiet after
all our stramash, I think I will always have a kind
thought of the wee howe in the muir."

And, though I said nothing in word, I resolved within

myself that if Fortune in the end showed the smiling face, of which we had had a glisk that morning, Mistress Ailie would not think kindly only of that place, but visit it, and that I should be there to see.

We had no encounter of any kind upon the road ; and, before evening fell, we reached the camping-ground which Jimmuck had described. It lies on the west side of a little wood on the ridge across from Swanston, and looking down on Comiston. Mistress Ailie had never been in Edinburgh, and, when I pointed her the Castle rock, which we could just see beyond the edge of the hills of Braid, and then the blue Firth and the kingdom of Fife in its mantle of greens and yellows, so clear in the evening light that it looked as if one could step across the one to the other, she held her breath at the sight.

" And yonder are the spurs of the Highland hills," I said, pointing to where at the west of the Ochils rise the dim blue masses of Ben Ledi and its sisters.

" Is yon whaur the braw lad bides whan he's at hame ? " asked Eppie.

" Oh, far farrer nor yon," said I ; " but he'll feel a hantle safer when yon wall is atween him an' the sooth."

" He hes nae need tae misdoot the sooth," snipped she. " I that sey it ken ; an', min' ye, the farrer sooth in Scotlan' ye gang, the lealer the herts—o' the wimmen, onywey. But nae doot he disna hae tae be tellt that."

She tossed her head and looked towards her mistress.

The patch of sward along the edge of the wood had black bits where tinkers' fires had burned, but there were none of these gentry encamped there then. So I tethered our beasts that they might graze, hid the saddles in the wood, and then we three set off on foot towards the city. We came in by the Burghmuir, Eppie being much moved when I explained how it was on its great expanse that the Scottish army gathered before marching to Flodden. There was no city gate, with its interrogation by the guard, to face, and glad was I that my old quarters lay in the little suburb which clusters round the old convent of St. Catherine of Siena. We saw only a few folk finishing their game of gowf in the gathering dusk, and some others clustered round the tavern at the north side of the Links.

I led my companions boldly up to Luckie Cowieson's door, and, to pass as friends of her with any onlookers in case she made a fracas at the door, marched right in on the dame. She sat her lonesome and was spinning at the fire, as I could almost have prophesied the eident housewife she was would be. She looked up, to see me and the two cloaked figures close behind. I had counted on the change my caird-like dress would make on my appearance ; but I own I had not realized how my face, unshaven since the day I set out on my adventure, was transformed by the fluff of beard which now clothed it.

" Mercy me, robbers ! " she cried, and was like to swoon in terror.

" Na, na, Mistress Cowieson," I said reassuringly,
" there's nae robbers here. There's just yer runagate
Gilbert Halkett come back."

I would have gone on, but the poor body could not
believe her ears. She threw her apron over her head
as if to hide us from her sight.

" Maister Gilbert," she sobbed, " fell into the hands
of violent and bloody men. Ye've murthered him
atween ye, that's what ye've done, an' on yer mur-
therin' errand ye raise yer evil han' against a puir,
defenceless wumman."

I do not know how I should have fared had not a
gentler hand than mine touched her and removed the
apron, to let her see a girl's eyes looking into hers.
And, indeed, my plan fell so badly out that it was Ailie
who told the story, and told it very much more to my
credit than I could have, and it was Ailie who threw
herself and Eppie on the old woman's compassion.
And it was Ailie who succeeded so well that, before the
recital was done, Ailie was " my dear bairn," and Eppie
" my fine, strappin' lass," and Gilbert " my laddie,
though ye're an awfu' tyke ; " and Mistress Cowieson's
word was passed that hostelry there should be none, but
bed and board for the refugees and a quiet sough till
the way should be opened up for a clear quittance out
of all our troubles.

It was a happy Gilbert who, an hour later, left for his
night in the open on the windy ridge below the Seven
Scars. The thought he had to sleep on was the last
sight of the lady of Winterhope with shining eyes, who

had said, " Friend, you have guided all well, and, in
spite of the beard coming near to wreck an otherwise
well-laid scheme, there's one doesn't think even the
beard distinguishes you to your disadvantage, and that
one's—Eppie."

CHAPTER XX

I WANDERED at my will in the city while I waited for Evan and Jimmuck. Apart from the completeness of my disguise, there was surprisingly little danger of being even suspected as a runagate. The first spate of excitement that followed the fight at Philiphaugh had died down. Indeed, Edinburgh did not for long continue the centre of interest. The dragoons had combed the Border valleys and hills for fugitives. Such stragglers as they came on, hiding like Evan and myself among the heather, they had in general themselves shot down without further parley. Apart from the two Irish officers who suffered, as Polmood had told Ailie, on the Castle Hill, but few of the humbler among the captives had been taken to Edinburgh. The notables among them were waiting trial in Glasgow, whither Leslie had moved with the greater part of his army. The clash even of the alehouses was that Rollo and Nisbet and young Inverquharity were marked for a trial, sure to end in their immediate death there, and that the others, Sir Robert Spottiswoode, Lord Ogilvy, and young Tullibardine, would soon thereafter follow them the same road.

I took some risk, indeed, by loitering about the Bristo
Port ; but I was well rewarded, for about noon I learned
that, late the night before, a sergeant's guard of soldiers
had ridden in from the Border country with a great
tale of how the Malignants had risen there, attacked
them in force, and, after a severe resistance on their
part, carried off their prisoner. It seemed they had no
wounds to shew, but were very bitter men. This was
laughable matter, but I got what stanched my joy later
in the day. For, as I mingled with a little throng that
gathered in the space between St. Giles' Kirk and the
new Parliament House, where some excitement was
forward, who should be the centre of it but one of the
officers of the law whom I had last seen trussed like a
fowl in Polmood ? There had evidently been an examination held within on their strange story of the
rescue, and an indignant participant was venting his
grievance to his cronies.

"Na, sirs," he was declaring vehemently, as I came
up, " I tell ye they didna credit honest men on the
evidence o' their plain senses, an' teeheed at the hale
tale. The tap at Polmood was ower guid, they tellt us,
or we wadna hae lain doon tae a wheen Border Jock
Ellots. They lauched tae scorn the notion o' them
bein' broken Malignants gaithered frae the hills ; but
there's ae satisfaction," he added, with venom in his
voice, " that lang-legged jaud was held tae be airt
an' pairt wi' them. The delation is confirmed by this
ongaun, an' she's to be proclaimed an active agent
o' the black traitor, Montrose. An', fegs, it's me

that will get giff-gaff when I hear her pit tae the horn."

" An' wull there be a reward for her takin' or for layin' saut on her ? " a squeaky voice inquired.

It gave me a grue to see with the tail of my eye Mungo Amos hanging on the answer the penny-dog of the law gave.

" Ay, there's eneuch to be offered for the apprehension o' that hizzie to keep ye bien a while, ye moudiewart," he barked out; "but ye'll need tae hae mair success nor has attended yer burrowing up till noo."

With that he began to move off, and, as I had no wish to be subjected to notice from the ferret-like eyes of the Shauchlin Herd, I edged under the shadow of the Luckenbooths, and thence slipped into the tide of folk in the Lawnmarket.

This was bad hearing. The bridges were cut behind Ailie even as they had been cut behind me. I only, however, suspected I had been outlawed. Poor lass ! there was no such dubiety about her case. She was faster than I in the toils. I must warn her of the ill turn affairs had taken. It was a great excuse as well for setting eyes on her once more.

I found the threesome in great fettle at Luckie Cowieson's. Alison had got far ben with the good dame, and they were having ongoings at a looking-glass. She had wisely discarded her riding-dress and was attired in a gown of humble stuff, much like that which Eppie wore. The old lady had completed the toilet by

producing from a chest, where it had long lain, a silk
screen of dark blue, which the maiden now wore upon
her head and shoulders. This bit of finery, genteel but
not conspicuous, gave the lady of Winterhope a singular
demureness. Concealing, as it did, those masses of hair
which hung almost to her waist, it made her look not
so much a girl as a young matron.

" Isn' that a braw weedaw, noo ? " cries Eppie, after
she had delivered a preliminary admonishment to me as
an " unmainnerly tyke, birsting in on leddies at their
ceerimonies, wi'oot e'en chappin'."

" Ay," I said, " she's safe tae pass the sodgers an'
inqueesitor bodies on the plainstanes ; but what o' the
een o' the Shauchlin Herd o' Talla ? "

I told what I had overheard at the Parliament House.

" His een ! " cried Eppie. " I cud scart the gleyed
een o' him oot wi' thae ten commandments "—holding
up her crooked fingers. " Ay, an' syne I cud thraw
his neck like a chuckie's, gin I encoontered him."

" Wheesht, Eppie," Alison said quietly. " Mungo
will no bide here, but seek back to the Border for traces
of us ; an', by the morn, we may walk abroad. I'm no
fremyt o' the proclamation. The Estates hae grander
folk nor Alison Laidlaw tae mell wi' the noo, an' there's
something tells me this will a' blow by an' be a lauchin'
maitter ere lang. I'm content tae bide an' brave it
oot."

With that little toss of the head, which I had come to
associate with her quick decisions, the lady ended the
discussion of her present fortunes. And it was then

that for the first time she called me by my Christian name. "What matters most is, have you learned anything of how your own case stands, Gilbert ? "

I told her no. I had not dared to make inquiries lest they should just rouse suspicion.

"I think, if it was me," she rejoined, "I would know the best or the worst ; but I understand. You're under the glamour of the Red Soldier. You would rather be at large and in danger with him than give yourself up and explain how the confusion of you with John Spottiswoode led you into this web, seeing the explanation would maybe mean disaster to the Red Soldier's plans or even the Red Soldier's self."

"You've put your finger on it, so far as I understand my own mind," I owned.

"Well," she said, "there's nothing for it but faring on and seeing whether my second-sight about a good ending will come true."

"I am prepared to trust to it," I responded. "For good or for ill my old way of life is broke ; and, though I cannot yet fully tell you why, the new way gies a heise tae the hert an' leaves me aye, and at the worst of it, a hantle happier than ever I was before."

"Oh, if that's the fashion of it, you're indeed pixie-led an' beyond the reason of a mere woman," she said, laughing. "You don't altogether look a True Tammas ; but there's no accounting for the fairy folk's tastes, and, like enough, in the Rhymer's manner, you'll come back to peace and men's dwellings in the end."

This was our parting, and no more sentiment to it.

Yet her half-jocular dismissal of me had more consolation than if she had grat on saying farewell. I felt it was a strong heart that gave a friend gaiety instead of groans, and sent him out with a quip for the road, where he would have at least the interest of events, whereas it had to expect nothing but dullness at the best or danger at the worst, and yet made nothing of either. And so, as I made my way across the Burgh-muir, that look on her face was framed in the silver of the moonlight. Better still, within me I seemed to carry her very spirit, and I knew that, as long as I did that, I could never be either comfortless or craven.

"Hey, billie, whaur awa'?" a voice challenged at the bend of the road above Comiston, and I found myself confronted with Jimmuck. "Fegs, it's himsel'," he rumbled out, "himsel', comin' hame like Napper Tandy, wi' deil a thocht for ither folk. An' hiz thinkin' we wad hae tae gie a ca' at the Tolbooth for the lad that left the horse short-tethered and naething tae eat but the win'. I doot Jockie's been at the fair, an' mair ta'en up with lasses an' ribbons than mindin' the toom wames o' the Sodger and the Caird."

"So you're in, Jimmuck," said I, jinking his reproaches.

"In, ay, they twa hoors, an' bidin' on you to be suppered an' bedded, for we've a laverock's stairt the morn's morn."

"Were ye really feared for me?" I asked.

"Ay wis I," says he. "I'm aye feared for ane of

my company wha stravaigs in the wynds o' that auld
cutty, Embro'. The bield o' the dykeside in the muir
an' the road afore ye for me an' my kind. But come
yer weys."

A cheery wood fire was twinkling beyond the belt of
trees. By it sat Evan. The horses grazed on the sward
beyond. Within the light stood a round-backed vehicle
which must be the covered wagon. So the Sergeant's
plan had succeeded.

"Are we not the complete coupers now ? " cried
Evan, starting up to greet me in response to Jimmuck's
bellow, " Here he's, like the coo's tail."

" Look, man. A string of horses, a brisket of mutton
brandering at the fire, and Jimmuck's chariot with the
boxes as Gwyn and you took them over first. My
heart ! I would not change places with Alasdair at the
head of his tail of kerns. But, tell me, how has the
other convoy fared ? "

I gave them my tale. " It might have been worse,"
was the Red Sergeant's verdict ; " but, my faith, it's
the lion's heart the lady has in her, and those who live
shall see how it will bear her up. I should feel reasonably sure if we could but run that fox Mungo to his
earth."

" Bide you," broke in Jimmuck. " I hae my ain
weys o' passin' a message among oor folk ; an', if
Muckle Joseph canna lay saut on the tail o' that skellum
afore the mune changes her horn mony times, the
Egyptian 'll be coonted a puir leader o' ma wee
band."

The assurance seemed to satisfy Evan, who, I could
see, had established the close *camaraderie* of the open
air with Jimmuck. I myself, with the evidence of his
lealness that the presence of the treasure wagon gave
before my eyes, felt strangely confident. I gave myself
over to the enjoyment of that first night by the camp-
fire on the ridge that looks down on the old grey city,
within which, I trusted, the lady who took a greater
venture than any of us in security slept.

It was indeed good hearing to learn how the twosome
carried through their adventure, after they took over
the horses and the covered wagon from the lad at
Birkhill. The Soldier gave the garland to Jimmuck,
and made me alternately shiver and laugh as he described how the Caird, like a great water-rat, took to
the pool in the darkness that lay on it and heaved up
the treasure, using language the like of which Evan had
never heard matched in violence even among Col's
Irishry, and how his mighty strength made the task of
transporting it to the wagon appear easy, even under
the poor light the moon shed on the hillside track from
the waterfall to the road. After that there remained
but to make all the speed they could before the country
folk wakened. Yet it was a notable achievement that,
by the time morning broke, they were at the summit of
the Slacks, the pass between Yarrow and Tweed, and,
for all that any chance passer-by could tell, had been
camped there all night after a day's journey on their
trade of couping. And as coupers they passed on, at
a more leisurely pace than that at which they had to

make their moonlight flitting, Evan driving the cart, and Jimmuck riding Barefit and leading the string of horses.

The scheme had succeeded indeed marvellously, and all the success of it went back to that wonderful work of Jimmuck and Evan in the night at the Greymare's Tail, for, had they not got clear of the Yarrow valley by daylight, they had resolved to take the long roundabout way by Moffat, which would have made our tryst to time impossible.

This was the first of the nights I often go back to, as I lie in what most folks regard as the only comfortable fashion—on a soft bed within the shuttered house. But, though in wild weather the tinker's way of passing the night is dreich enough, believe me, when you have once accustomed yourself to the strangeness of sleeping under the sky, there is, in reasonably fair weather, no cause for the cadger to envy the king. He has his bit bield of tent-cloth stretched on hoops of withes, and there he lies upon bracken or heather, his feet towards the blaze of a fire, if it is chilly. Through the opening he sees the stars blink in the sky, or the clouds go scouring the face of the moon. The steady crop-crop of the horses, as they graze, is broken only once in a while by the cry of the peesweep, the cheep of the field-mouse, or the sough of the wind. He is body-tired and ready for slumber ; but these sounds gently push sleep away again and again, yet ever with less insistence. When, lo, in a moment, there are the grey ashes of the fire, and, beyond, the green grass with the dew twinkling on it, the birds, not as frightened and crying, but in song, and the light filling his blinking but no longer tired eyes. It is morning and another day, to be like its fellow that has gone, lying fresh for him, who wanders the world thorough, and is free of it all.

CHAPTER XXI

THE HORSE-COUPERS

SO now you are to imagine us as we kept the road for days, Evan riding alongside the wagon, which I drove, and Jimmuck coming on behind, leading a string of horses, and himself mounted on Barefit. Barefit was a great, raw-boned brute that had little comeliness. He owned a ridiculous white face of the sort which we country folk call bawsand. The pink-coloured nose of him gave him a look which somehow always suggested that he would take a bite of you in preference to his proper provender. Though in general of a blae colour, he had the near foreleg white as his face, and, as he moved with a fine action, raising this adornment as if to shew it off, the white leg of him was even more noticeable at first view than the face. Most would have called him white-stocking, but to Jimmuck a white foot was apparently a wonderful sight, and he named the horse to mark such a phenomenon. The Caird thought the world of Barefit, and would stand better a word against any of his consorts than one in disparagement of that horse.

It was by falling in with a cattle-drover of his acquaintance, coming from the Carse of Stirling with

kyloes for Edinburgh, that, amid the other clash that
passed as tidings of the day, we got our first news of
Montrose's whereabouts. The drover had it that the
Marquis was in Athole raising men. It was said that
four hundred of them, leaving their harvests standing,
had rallied to the call. On the drover moving on,
Jimmuck was for planning the route to Blair, and began
bewailing the likelihood of the weather breaking before
we had travelled so far, yet inwardly glad, no doubt,
that it was well beyond the Highland line, and would,
therefore, earn him his fifty extra pieces of gold. But
Evan broke in:

" If the Marquis is raising men in Athole, it's not for
using them in Athole he will be. The Marquis makes
for his enemy, and none can do the quick dart over the
hills like he. Where is the enemy ? At Glasgow, says
Gilbert here, and there, too, are the Marquis's friends
like to be hurried to the gibbet. The Marquis will make
for Glasgow, or I am no soldier. He'll try a foray at the
least, in the hope of putting off the evil day for the
prisoners, if not rescuing them by a happy stroke. The
Marquis will make towards Glasgow, then ; but he'll go
by his own country, to pick up those of his tenants who
have returned to the Lennox. So, if we would be saved
a chase of the swiftest marcher in the world, let us cut
the corner and come in by the Braes of Balloch. If he
has not passed them, we can take a cast to the west,
for it's like he'll come down Loch Lomondside."

Jimmuck and I were not to put our opinion against
the Soldier's, and so we moved on the westward road

14

towards Falkirk. Evan cast his eyes on the wagon, and muttered to the boxes :

" Oh, my grief ! much as I hate the sight of ye, ye'll be a salve to the Captain-General. The brave lads of Athole can give him their claymores and their lives, leaving bodachs to gather the harvest, but gold is what they cannot give, gold to feed the willing and to hire those who will not fight for love. Ye have tethered Evan like a cow, when he would liefer have lived on stappach in the camp ; but it's soon he'll be free of you, and you doing for him what Evan's one blade could not.

" Hech, sirs," he ended, laughing with me at his own apostrophe, " am I not a trifle too high on my horse to-day, and overlooking the lad that's been like a foster brother with me in nursing this same nasty treasure ?   Gilbert, my dear, for all its irksomeness, it's fairy gold.   It's brought you and me, and another we know of, together ; yes, and Jimmuck too.   I tell you, it's fairy gold to him also, him that will not so much as touch what must be in his eyes as a king's ransom. I've cursed it deeply and often ; but I'm a spoiled child, with my impatience and my pride.   I begin to see that, like some one in the holy books, I've been kicking against the pricks.   This treasure is a touchstone.   It has brought out to my sight the gold in three I know of."

The saying held very true of Alison and himself, and it was true of Jimmuck to a remarkable degree.   I believed the Caird found in the Soldier a man after his heart, and that Jimmuck never for a moment went back

on his solemn oath to play fair.   But that did not make
him less of the caird.   He could not see that it was a
danger to us for him to indulge in trokings on the road ;
yet this temptation he would not resist.   He sold some
of the beasts and bought others, and, what was his
favourite enjoyment of all, " niffered " indifferent cattle,
docked and clipped and brandered into smartness, for
others which his eye told him were better.   These
ongoings, I allow, may have served to pass us off as
genuine coupers ; but the real danger lay in his inordinate love of drink.   Again Jimmuck was but following his practice here also, and could not understand
how, with the best intention to keep faith with us, a
careless word dropped by him, or a tuilzie in which he
might become involved while in drink, might ruin both
our mission and us, as surely as if he had sold us to our
enemies.

A gliff of this kind we got.   We were camped for the
night on Stenhousemuir.   Evan and I, had we but
thought, might have known that the centre of the cattle
trysts was the one place through which we should have
weised the Caird with special care.   As it was, he
slipped away unnoticed into the town.   Evan and I
were on his track without loss of time, determined to
find him before liquor had loosened his tongue.   We
might have spared ourselves concern on this occasion.
Just beyond the out-by houses there was a wee plantation of scroggy firs and whin bushes.   Bands of school
bairns were dancing in and out of it, and shouting with
glee at the top of their shrill voices :

" Jimmuck the Caird, Jimmuck the Caird, he's selt his horse and tint his cairt."

The imps darted in and out, tousled Jimmuck's hair, jerked out his beloved neckerchief even ; and all the while Jimmuck sat like a stone image.   His one interest was in trying to raise a jar to his lips ; but it was beyond his power to do this.

" *O mo chràdh!* " cries Evan.   " It's usquebaugh, and he's been swallowing it as if it was water from the brook."

There had, indeed, been no danger of talk.   Jimmuck went straight to the first change-house and purchased there a jar of strong waters, with hospitable intentions, for the camp.   But at the plantation he had preed the jar, and for Jimmuck that meant a deep drain, and then another as soon as he recovered breath from the first draught.   The Soldier took the situation coolly. He told me he had seen men in a well-disciplined army behave in the same way at the taking of a town, when they came on casks of liquor after weeks of frugal living. But to see Jimmuck helpless and the sport of bairns, with an inane smile on his ugly face, was to me a most disgusting spectacle.   Nor did the feeling of disgust lessen when Evan and I had to carry that great bulk of a man, as if he were a corpse, back to our encampment. Jimmuck had neither apologies nor explanations forth-coming next morning ; but the incident made us wary lest it should be repeated.   Whether he saw our guile or not, Jimmuck made no remark on the fact that we shepherded our shepherd past all the danger points, by

Kirkintilloch and Dumbarton, till we came to the Vale
of Leven and the eastern end of Loch Lomond at
Balloch. Then, indeed, we reckoned ourselves safe to
allow the Caird to do some business, for there we were
in young Drummond's country. We ourselves hoped,
ere the day ended, we would learn something definite of
the Captain-General's whereabouts. Jimmuck proved
to be in great fettle. Though he began more in the way
of pretence, haggling about " swappings," as the day
wore on it saw him with most of his string disposed of,
for horses of any sort were being sought for far and
wide by the Stewarts of Balquhidder, whom it was
suiting to take Leslie's side. A fateful day's work it
was to turn out for me.

Our camp was to the westmost side of Balloch, on the
flat where the Leven, a purposeful river, for all the short-
ness of its course, runs out of the loch. If there is one
place safe from prying peasants, it is a tinker's encampment. And if you have a treasure to guard in such
a place, the best way to guard it, as we had already
learned, was to behave as if there were nothing to guard.
Should a curious passer-by happen to peep into the
wagon, he would see but a confusion of tinker's duds
and broken bits of horse harness and our sleeping shelter,
all piled carelessly above the precious boxes. He would
indeed be curious who was tempted to search, even if he
did cross the boggy land that stretched between us and
the road which lay two hundred yards from the willows
screening us. We had had a marvellously easy passage
so far ; but I noted that, the nearer we seemed to come

to our goal, the more anxious Evan became lest any chance should dash the cup of success from his hands when it was almost at the lip. He elected that we should stand guard over the treasure that day, though he would fain have been with the Caird keeping that worthy's tongue in check. So we stood in the light of the afternoon looking at a scene which enchanted me, who had hitherto seen the gold and green mantle of the kingdom of Fife, and the kindly curves of the Border hills, but nothing of the majestic look on old Scotland's face. The great loch was like a mirror, its islands floating double in it. The bracken glowed golden on the hills above Rossdhu, and, beyond, towered Ben Lomond, wearing its mantle of blue and crowned with a white wisp of cloud. I heaved a great sigh.

" Ay," answered Evan, responding to my unspoken thought, " Albainn is good at the tamest of it ; but oh ! the bens and the glens and the mighty moors. Seven of them, as the old stories have it. There's ten times that, anyway, and you are fairly looking at the gate into them all. Ay, it's there we'll soon be faring if the Marquis has still his old way."

He ended by shouting something in the Gaelic. I imagined it was a capping of the high mood into which he had wrought himself. Yet, when I turned towards him, I saw he was gazing, not at the ben, but at the fringe of willows round our encampment. I followed his gaze and looked right into the mouth of a levelled pistol. The dag was not five yards from us, and the eye that trained it on Evan's heart belonged to a wild High-

landman. He stood like a carven image, motionless ;
but no image could have made my backbone seem to
melt as did that figure. He was of no inordinate height,
yet such a concentrated piece of danger, for the stature
of him, I had never looked on. He wore the kilt in the
belted plaid form, the brogues of deerskin, with pelt
undressed, of the real cateran, claymore at his belt, a
dirk at his knee. Head-dress he had none ; but in his
matted locks he looked more fearsome than if he had
worn a morion. His eyes, in a fixed stare of remorseless
calm, behind that levelled dag of his, told me that in a
moment the image might be a death-dealer, and that
the dealing of death would give him no concern.

" Stand still ; move not so much as a muscle," whispered Evan to me, and then continued to pour out an
almost breathless stream of Gaelic. All at once it had
its effect. The cateran's features relaxed into a kind
of grin. He lowered his weapon and gabbled quickly.

" Ach," sighed Evan, in manifest relief, " I knew it.
I saw by his tartan he was a Farquharson from the
Forest of Mar, and therefore bound to be of the right
side ; but he had difficulty in believing me a loyal Celt
in this disguise and in an enemy country. He has the
best of news. The Marquis is in leaguer at Buchanan,
and this lad is one of the scouts sent out to see whether
the road by the Braes of Balloch is reasonably open.
His surprise of us was his way of asking questions.
Now all's clear."

He engaged in conversation again with the cateran,
who now looked singularly awkward in his passiveness.

But the Soldier had some way of convincing him that he
had a right to command a service, for, with a grunt, he
turned from us and betook himself through the bog
westwards.

"He's to pass the word that we're coming," Evan
explained. "Now to recover Jimmuck and get on the
road. Gibbie, my dear, though yon lad is not just the
bonniest wearer of it I've looked on, it's me that's glad
to see the tartan again. Ach, it's the wearing of these
clothes is near over, and I'll be having a soldier's dress
for a soldier's work and be done with you, you old
spliucan."

He shook his fist at the wagon. So it had really
ended, our dangerous adventure, without any danger to
it. We had but to rejoin Jimmuck and be done. So
simple it was.

CHAPTER XXII

WHERE CELT AND SAXON MEET

THERE is no part of Scotland so interesting, either for the happening of events or for the study of men's character, as the broad fringe where the Highlands and the Lowlands touch. For there, when there happen to be straths which conduce to the easy passage to and fro of men, the people of the clans remain for the most part in the places in which their fathers dwelt, and yet, these being places of a more or less settled nature, where some sort of common law is honoured, the Lowland population has flowed in. We have therefore in such places a mixed populace which seems to present the elements of what may yet become a common nationality of Saxon and Celt in this land of ours.

Such a region is the Vale of Leven, where we sought the Caird that day at the clachan called Balloch.

I think it will be found that, in most of such centres where the two races mingle in more or less of an amity, each race has been altered. The Celt generally is seen to have a kind of cleverness in business which is not so engaging as the simplicity he shews for ordinary when under the direct rule of his chief. On the other hand the Saxon often has a distasteful sort of plausibility,

which is a left-handed compliment to Highland courtesy,
and not so attractive as the honest, if somewhat bluff,
outspokenness which he affects when his manners are
not tempered to conciliate his neighbours. I would
lay a good deal of the blame for this on the regions
respectful to law, but actually liable to be subjected to
the caprice of the clan-force, which may at any moment
sweep away the bulwarks of that public order in which
the cannier south abides. At all events the result of
this artificial mingling of the two bloods is not altogether
pleasing. I dare to say that you see Highlander and
Lowlander at their worst where it is difficult for you to
tell at first encountering whether you are dealing with
a southern man who has tried to take on something of
the northern manner, or with a clansman in some degree
habituated to our southern customs.

I do opine that the borrowed clothes are in general a
misfit.

My first lesson in what I have been trying to teach
was given me that afternoon in the change-house at
Balloch. For there, as we expected, it was we found
Jimmuck birling the bawbees with the men to whom he
had sold his horses. I have little doubt he had cheated
them handsomely and that the luck penny was no trifle.
When we arrived, it was plain Jimmuck had invited all
and sundry to wet the bargains at his expense. And,
judging by the brisk passing of the cans, his victims
had the best of will to drink with the Caird.

Nor, indeed, when I looked at them, did I put them
down as in any way the superiors of Jimmuck in station.

They were, as I have hinted, collecting what beasts they could in a country singularly bare of mounts by the drain Montrose's army had put on it before the fight at Kilsyth. These they were gathering, not for cavalry, but for the wagons of the force which was afterwards to join that of Campbell of Ardkinglass, already preparing to raid the Menteith Lands, in what he supposed their defenceless condition, from his own country of Lorn. The buyers were mere underlings, spending the money of their masters, but, even as such, I thought little of them.

Three were Stewarts from Balquhidder. These wore Lowlander dress, and, though they spoke mostly in the Gaelic, Evan grued at the badness of it. The others, men of the Menzies name, who hailed from Rannoch, were more personable to the eye, being sturdy fellows who set off their Highland dress not so badly. But, when I thought me of the fiery lad who had held us so unflinchingly in the bushes, I felt they were but oddments of men by comparison. And, withal, I liked not the sly eyes of them.

"Seven own brothers of the Shifty Lad, I doubt," Evan muttered to me when he had run his eye over them.

Jimmuck seemingly made no question of his company. Here were men to drink with, and drink with them he would. So, when the Soldier and I entered the one considerable room of the change-house, as his two lads come to tell him the hour appointed for breaking camp had chapped, it was not the more-or-less guidable Jimmuck we encountered, but a jovial, roaring master-couper, who bellowed out :

" Hoots awa' wi' you an' the camp. Fill yer jougs, lads, an' see the boddom o' them as aften as ye like. Tae the mischief wi' camps ! Here's a braw doon-sittin'. Sae rest yer hunkers. For me, I dinna move frae a bit whaur ye hae but tae sey, ' Draw,' an' ye fair soom in the guid liquor. There's some of hiz ken what happened tae ma last jorum."

Alas that the unemptied jar at Falkirk should have so rankled in his memory ! There was a trace of nastiness in this remark of Jimmuck's ; but Evan tried to mend the situation. Dropping into the Scots, which he had come to understand, but never of choice spoke, and using the cant term that might be expected from a young caird when addressing his chief, he said :

" Ay, Dad, but ye'll be mindin' the wee paircel o' goods yer frien's up the loch are expectin'. Ye'll surely no disappoint them."

Jimmuck's wits were still to the fore, for he cried :

"Disappint them !   Na, kimmer, na ; Jimmuck 'll sure eneuch gie the bit lasses their fairins ; but time for that, and time tae spare, and Jimmuck 'll be a' the blyther veesitor for haein' preed a wee sook o' the barley bree."

It was usquebaugh he was drinking, not indeed in the shameful fashion of the Falkirk sally, but as one sure of a long night before him. The Soldier evidently deemed that more harm would come of insistence than a cheerful acceptance of the delay. So he called for two flagons

of ale, as a more suitable drink to our supposed character
than claret would have been, and he and I settled ourselves within easy earshot of Jimmuck.

It was a dreary enough trial to our patience. Jimmuck, his great slab of a face kindled into animation,
conversed mainly with the Stewarts, who had fair English; but his stories, of master-strokes in couping and
brawls at this tavern and that, grew tiresome to us.
One lanky, gley-eyed Stewart kept up the interchange,
and seemed to be preparing for the time when he could
with safety take his fun off Jimmuck. He was clearly,
as we say, running on ice. The Menzies four, who had
almost no English, said little even to each other in the
tongue, but most steadily replenished their cans.

By-and-by the Stewart fellow evidently judged that
the Caird was far enough gone in liquor to be a safe
object for quizzing. He had the temerity to question
the credibility of a tale of Jimmuck's in which Barefit,
according to its master, had shewed an amazing turn of
endurance and speed. Jimmuck thereupon remarked
that he was prepared to mount Barefit, take him, or
any other dirty man who bore a king's name because he
had none of his own, and swim him to Balmaha, dropping his passenger half-way that he might get water
enough to wash himself. The Stewart was the man
who lost his temper, and, perhaps, small wonder. His
hand went to his dirk. Then he thought better of it
and checked himself. There was no more quizzing, only
he looked uglily out of his squinting eyes at Jimmuck.

I nudged Evan and murmured to him we should be

gone. Then it was the Soldier did one of the few
thoughtless things I can put to his account. I have
told you that he and the Caird drew greatly to each
other. Well, one night at the camp-fire Evan chanced
to use some Gaelic expression and Jimmuck surprised
him by remarking, " I ken what that means."

This led him to try Evan with a lingo which, it seems,
the wandering folk talk among themselves and will not
even own to others exists at all. Again and again on
our march Jimmuck tried it on Evan, and Evan was
quite as keen in trying to get a hold of it. In time
Evan could follow Jimmuck, for the lingo has many
Gaelic words in it pure, and others with an added
syllable, and some with the sounds reversed, and a good
many, Evan said, out of old Gaelic. Jimmuck declared
Muckle Joseph, who was half an Egyptian, had assured
him it was *not* the Egyptian tongue. For me I could
make nothing of it, but Evan used to practise his Gaelic,
with what he picked up of this language of the roads, on
Jimmuck, and they could converse haltingly. It was
another bond between them. A dangerous bond it
proved now. For the Soldier, in a fret to be gone, tried
by this lingo to convey to Jimmuck that Montrose was
up the loch, and that it behoved us to be getting forward
with the wagon. The few Gaelic words fell on the ear
of the already offended Stewart.

" Ach," he cried, " and you have the Gaelic. Strange
is it to me that a tinkler bodach and his gillie should
have the Gaelic."

Who could ever guess where Jimmuck's pride lay ?

" Me have the Gaelic ? " he roared, as a herd does at a badly behaved collie. " Ye spewin' o' the pit ! I dinna speak *yer* lingo. What me and my son spak' in was the language Adam and Eve talked thegither whan they gaed wannerin'. There were cairds afore there were cattle-thiefs. You chaw on that till yer teeth braks. Syne rin hame an' tell yer minnie ye hae seen Jimmuck the Caird, an' the hail claikin' o' yer whaups amo' the heather 'll be cheepin' ower the news."

" It was the Gaelic, whatever, that the young caird had," the squint-eyed one insisted, and a ready chorus came from the other Stewarts, " It wass ; it wass indeed, indeed."

Evan bit his lip ; but, if he had made a mistake, he did not make the further one of trying to mend it. There ensued a sulky silence, broken after a little by the Caird's hearty :

" Kimmers, nae black looks ower Jimmuck's daffin'. Sen' roond the ewie wi' the cruikit horn."

The shifty man from Balquhidder rose, as if in a huff, and left the room, to return in a little and sit among the Rannoch redshanks. To these he mumbled a word or two, as if asseverating how right he had been.

All this time we had been served by a lass who, in my mood of impatience, annoyed me by the way she dragged her feet along the hard earthen floor. She had, indeed, bauchles that were too large for her, and these, being scant of ties, flopped about as she moved. Now it so happened that, turning quickly on a call from Jimmuck, she lifted one foot clear out of its shoe. In a moment the Soldier had picked up the bauchle and was standing with it ready in his hand to fit it on again with a " By your leave, mistress."

The lass let him slip it on, and, as she steadied herself, with head turned on shoulder towards Evan, whispered :

" A queer caird, you ! Man, tak' tent ; the muckle gleyed man hes steikit the hoose door." Then she passed with a loud-spoken, " Thank ye kindly."

" It looks like as if some bad Stewart blood will be let before the door's unbarred," Evan muttered to me.

But the house door was to be opened in a more peaceable way. On it there sounded a continuous rat-tat-tat, and a wheezy voice was heard from the far side of it :

" Are the folk a' gane wud hereawa' tae ? Is there nae asylum tae be had the day, even in a hoose o' public entertainment ? "

" Deed ay, Maister Crombie," came the voice of the luckie, summoned by the new-comer from her place of barrels and bottles. " Deed ay. But, ah ! yer beastie's fair smored in sweat. Here, lassie,"—this to the maid of the bauchles—" awa' an' gie Maister Crombie's meere a rub doon in the stable an' a pail o' meal-water afore she touch aits. An' come you yer weys, Maister Crombie. Ye'll no min' the company, some honest lads wha hae been buying horse for the richt cause."

" I'll mind the company o' no *honest* men," says a little pursy man, for all the world like a white mealy pudding, making his way into the room, " for honest men is what I've no seen the day."

" Dae ye tell me sae, Maister Crombie ? " The landlady was determined to mollify the testy one. " This," says she to the company at large, " is Maister Crombie, doer tae Sir George Buchanan an' factor o' his lands."

" Wha *was* doer, say, mistress," cried the wee fat man, who was sore out of breath and took what he got in gulps.

" Ye say, sir ? Dinna tell me onything ill has happened to you or tae Sir George."

" Ill ; the warst o' ill. Ye may say Sir George at the moment present hes nae estates for me tae factor. This day at twal hours, when we wis in peace yokin' tae oor denner, doon comes the hale crew of the Hielan caterans under bandoune o' the so-called Marquis o' Montrose, if ye please. They're roond Buchanan in their thousands, like the plague in the days of Joel—' that which the palmer worm hath left hath the locust eaten.' Deed, there's naething left for the cankerworm and the caterpillar. They've eaten a'thing up a'ready. An' wha was tae tak' wurd o' the desolation ? Wha but me ? Sae I e'en escaped out o' the whirlwind of destruction an' hae galloped ma meere Queenie in a mainner unheard o'. An' noo, mistress, if ye'll gie me a bit chack an' a stoup, I'll rest a wee an' syne on tae Dumbritton tae gie the alairim, that this tide of ungodliness an' wastrie may be stayed."

" Wae's me, Maister Crombie," ejaculated the goodwife. " Tae think o' a' the guid lands o' Buchanan bein' gi'en ower tae the Prince o' the Power o' Darkness !

But here's soldiers o' the Covenant tae stan' by ye,"
says she, pointing to the Stewarts and Menzieses.

The sight of them did not seem to carry much comfort
to the baron-bailie, or whatever he was.

" An' wha's this ? " asked the little man, fixing his
eyes on Jimmuck. " Will some ane tell me wha's
this ? "

The Caird steadied himself into a drunken gravity.

" Dae ye ken, frien's," says he, " I hae a notion I've
seen that wee cock-sparra afore."

" Ye sorner ! Sae ye've seen me afore, hae ye ? "
The little man trembled with anger, more than, I think,
he could have trembled with fear as he pelted away from
the invading army at noon. " An' I've seen you, seen
you tae my cost an' shame. You are the black to whom
I sold my meere Queenie at Dumbritton a twalmonth
last June. She was white, with a lang tail and mane.
An' ye are the same cheat-the-widdie wha sold me a
new horse, brown, with docked mane and rumped tail,
at Luss, a month thereafter, for thrice the price ye paid
me. A new horse it was till the Lammas floods washed
out its bonnie brown ; an', behold, it was my auld
Queenie ! For a notour rogue an' thief, I'll hae the law
o' ye. An' wha are yer frien's, ye muckle limb o'
Sathan ? "

" They speak the Gaelic," cried the Stewart, " an' I
am thinkin' they're found ower near the false Marquis
for their healths at the hour that now is."

" Ah ! " cries Crombie. " A Malignant nest ! Weel,
lads," turning to the Stewart and his crew, " gin ye

stand by me, we'll tak' a prize oot o' the very jaws o'
the enemy wi' us tae Dumbritton Rock, and we'll see
gin they can change their colour there."

" Oh, it will be the first use we'll make o' the horses
tae take such pretty fairings tae our frien's," said the
squinting Stewart with evident enjoyment.

"Wull it, then ? " shouted Jimmuck. " Tae me,
billies."

I think the caterans possessed ancient firearms ; but
into the room they had taken only their swords. They
were between us and the door, but the space was much
contracted by the trestle-like tables, at which we had
been drinking, and the chairs. So they held not so much
advantage as might seem, though they were seven
against three. I say seven, for Maister Crombie, ere a
blow was struck, received a kick from Jimmuck's great
foot in the most portly part of his front, sank under a
table, and there remained. I had the mighty rung I
told you of, and both Evan and I carried our pistols
disposed in the long pockets of the loose coats we wore.
But Jimmuck despised firearms, though he was not
without respect for his grandda's gully. Apparently,
on this occasion, like Samson, he was bent on victory
through a simple weapon. He picked up a stout oaken
stool, and I never in my experience saw a more bull-like
charge than Jimmuck made, as he plunged straight at
his opponents, with the Soldier and me on either side
of him. I know Jimmuck both dashed aside the claymore in the lanky Stewart's hand and cracked the lanky
Stewart's skull. My cudgel at least warded by a blow

from one of the Rannoch lads that was aimed in no play-acting spirit. Evan caught a cut on a chair which he used as target, and, before the fellow who directed it could extricate his blade, gave him his fist—for he had no intention of using his pistol—straight in the face, so that it left him spitting teeth.

But most we owed to the lass of the inn. Bauchles or no bauchles, she was singularly happy in opening the outer door at this very moment, and, thanks to her, we dashed out into the road.

" Barefit, I maun hae Barefit," that strange mixture of grossness and sentiment, Jimmuck, cried.

What height of folly he would have gone to in an attempt to recover his beast I cannot say, for down the road came pelting a half squadron of horse. They seemed to understand that we were pressed, and, as the caterans poured out of the change-house, scattered them with a clout or two in the passing. In a minute they were back opposite the change-house. The officer leading them was Dairsie. Apparently he had not dreamt whom he was rescuing, for, as he gazed at Evan and me in our outlandish clothes, he shouted :

" By all the powers, the Red Sergeant and Gilbert Halkett ! "

So it was a happy company, with Jimmuck on his recovered Barefit, that rode up the loch-side convoying the treasure.

But one individual we had forgotten—Maister Crombie; Maister Crombie, recovered of his cramp in the stomach, Maister Crombie, to whom, in his joy, Dairsie had

betrayed the Soldier's identity and mine. I believe
that, up till that moment, there was some doubt as to
whether I were prisoner of the Malignants or myself a
Malignant. I owe it to the doer of Buchanan that,
from then on, there was no doubt in the public mind.
And so, if I rode westwards towards Montrose's camp
happy, because, in helping one friend, I had been
helped by another older still, it would have tempered
my joy to know that I should be proclaimed through
broad Scotland as a traitor and an open companion of
traitors.

CHAPTER XXIII

A GREAT MAN AND HIS SERVANTS

IT has often been a source of wonder that even so great a master of the art of war as the Marquis was able to hold out against overwhelming numbers for full three-quarters of a year after that day at Buchanan. According full credit to the gallant little band, bound to him by no other tie than personal devotion, we must attach great importance to the treasure which the Red Sergeant saved from the field of Philiphaugh, and brought to his master as an unexpected windfall that October day on Loch Lomondside. Whether it was a good gift that fell into the Marquis's lap, I leave you to judge. The gold it was that rendered possible the great attempts the Captain-General made to raise such an army as he knew he must have if his campaign was to be no mere series of raids and diversions but a serious effort to save his King's cause. The treasure indeed arrived in his camp at a fateful time. At Lochearnside he had learned how Lord Digby, having with Nithsdale and Carnwath penetrated the south of Scotland as far as to Dumfries, in an attempt to join hands with him, was in full retreat. But he was steady, in spite of this

disheartening news, to harass Leslie round Glasgow, so
as to prevent further executions of his followers who
were in captivity there. He had his handful of men
quartered round the seat of that pillar of the Covenant,
Sir George Buchanan. From his camp there it was but
a step to his own lands, already transferred by the
Parliament to his great enemy Argyle. But there must
have been strange misgivings in his mind, despite the
boldness of this throwing down of the gauntlet. Conceive, then, how it must have affected the Captain-
General, alone and even then weighing how far he could
hazard even to save his friends, when young Dairsie
burst in on him to tell how the Red Sergeant was in
camp with the chests of gold which he had carried
untouched across broad Scotland.

In other days, when surrounded by a hedge of high
officers, the Captain-General would have received the
news, and passed out a message to the convoyers of the
treasure, or commanded them to his presence. But
there was little state, or even the usual formality of a
camp, in the small force that lay round Buchanan.
The Marquis himself came out with Dairsie to greet us.
He wore a plain suit of brown leather, the doublet well-
worn at the places where the cuirass had rubbed it. He
carried no star or ribbon to distinguish him from any
simple leader of a troop of horse. He came, too, bareheaded, as if he had been caught in the waft of Dairsie's
boyish excitement. And, indeed, as a gleam of amusement passed over his face when his glance fell on the
treasure wagon, and beside it the three nondescripts,

Evan, Jimmuck, and myself, he looked for the moment scarcely older than Dairsie.

"Ah Eoghainn," he cried, striding forward to greet the Soldier in a comrade-like fashion, which made Evan flush with pleasure. "You scout of scouts! Spottiswoode has been telling me of this exploit of yours. It is indeed a notable creagh you have driven. The sough of it will reach the Queen herself. You are a second Jason! A golden fleece was never more welcome, for this company is shorn to the very skin."

He turned to me. "I perceive," he went on, smiling a little wistfully, "that you are a recruit in spite of all warnings. Well, we shall have to do our best to protect one so gallant against damage for taking the old road of adventure. And you, friend," bending a look on the now sobered Jimmuck, "you've kept faith in a way that shames some older friends of mine. But," went on this man, who was great enough to be mindful of the danger that might fall on even an irresponsible caird, "I rede you now to forget that you've even so much as seen me or this camp, and to take a long cast round ere you return to your people."

Jimmuck was not a hair abashed.

"Ay, sir," says he, "I wis ettlin' tae winter in the Angus, an' I hae some braw frien's tae keep me company."

He gave the Marquis a leer and tapped a leather bag fat with the gold pieces which Evan had already handed him as fee for bringing the wagon across the Highland line.

The Captain-General nodded, as one who understood the Caird's view of life as well as the Captain's. He addressed himself to Dairsie. " John, see to quarters for the two dragons of our garden of Hesperides, and get them relief from their garments of scales, though we shall not forget they've worn them for our sakes."

A slight cast of melancholy made him once more grave and dignified. He bowed slightly and returned to his quarters. As for Jimmuck, he wasted no time. He shook us both up to the elbows, the while he was taking his farewells.

" It's been a grand ploy a'thegither, tho' it's ended enow. But min' ye, if ye need Jimmuck for anither sic-like, ye'll fin' him gallivantin' throw the lan' as free as a laverock, for a' the baron-bailie bodies in Menteith." He mounted Barefit and rode on his way. And so parted from us a very true friend in need.

Let your eye rest on us for a moment or two that evening on Loch Lomondside, as Dairsie sat with us, rehabited and refreshed by the sense of having accomplished what we had set out to do, in the quarters the camp-marischal assigned us. Conceive Dairsie listening to our story and then regaling us with a great gust of high spirit, ignoring the dangers of the last six weeks and brushing aside the difficulties Evan and I saw filling the future. On the morrow, according to him, we should make our dash on Glasgow and rescue his uncle and the other prisoners. Huntly would swing down from the north with his splendid cavalry, the Lowlands would rise ; we should sweep Leslie out of Scotland, then invade England and rescue the King.

In the softness of that hairst twilight, when the great mountains round us were golden, and the stooks, in that bit of fertile strath where we lay, shone golden too, the small but exceedingly fit body of men seemed like a real army, spread out widely as they were round the house of Buchanan. Dairsie's talk seemed to me not too flattering to be possible. But to Evan it was plainly a fairy tale told by a confiding child. True, he listened to the friend of my boyhood with patience and courtesy ; but he chafed Dairsie by that very silence, so that at last he broke out on the Highlander : " Man, you're a soldier. Does this touch you not ? "

" It touches me much," he answered, " but not as you would wish. God knows I have no desire to put the hawk into your sky ; but facts are facts. Leslie has three thousand troops in Glasgow alone, seasoned men ; and finer horse than Lord Kirkcudbright's regiment proved themselves on the field at Philiphaugh no man would wish to see. We have here twelve hundred Athole men and Farquharsons, and three hundred horse. A good little company for courage, I grant, but some of them very new to the trade of continuous warfare. A fair beginning, you say. Well, my answer is it's as big a force as the Captain-General will command, and it's my belief the Marquis, God save him, but fears too well it will be so. I never saw the eagle eye of him so hooded as it was to-day. Colkitto will come with his thousands of redshanks, as you call them. Will he just? Alasdair has but one thought in all the big bulk of him, and that is to feather his own nest. Give him booty where he is, and the Marquis will not whistle him nearer a yard for what is merely the King's cause. Huntly and the Gordons will come, whatever, you say. I know the Gordons; and, horse or foot, there's no prettier men, tho' I say it to the slighting of my own blood. But what are men with such a chief? Do you know old Huntly? It's there you have, in one human skin, all the child's whims in the world. He's a clever creature, but as full of pride as a peacock, and jealous of the Captain-General to a degree. Pride and jealousy would push him at a pinch to cold treason itself. Aboyne, the one son, would do the soldier's part always; but, then, he's at the end of the old man's tether, and has to shift his ground every time he tugs. Lord Lewis, the other son, will, like enough, bring his single sword, for he has nothing to lose; but he will also bring his tongue, and it will loose all his sword might solder, for it's a weaver of plots he is. As for the Lowlanders, the strength of the rising is sitting there in Gilbert's boots. True, we have sympathy from many who do not love MacCailein Mor, who would be king of Scotland; but rising there will be none. The Marquis is a wizard. Give him but the wizard's wand, and he will do things no general but he could do in this Scotland. But, if every staff he leans a little weight on proves a rotten runt, can you see any end but one to all his magic?"

"Well, I think it still a most strange view for a soldier to take," mumbled Dairsie; "and would you

have us give over in time to save our skins ?   Is that
the part of a soldier ? "

Evan flushed a little, but answered in a slow,
monotonous voice, which was the more impressive con-
trasted with his usual vivacious fashion in speaking :

" I give the opinion because I am a soldier.   As for
giving over, it is the thought that has not entered my
head.   I am for trying everything you drew in your
picture—the rescue of our friends ; using every art with
the Gordons and even with Alasdair ; making yet another
attempt to mend the expedition from England that has
gone to pieces ; anything, everything, in the hope that
the wand may be put into the wizard's hand.   And
then," he added, " if the worse comes, there is always
the dying for him left, and that will perhaps be the
easiest thing to do."

I leave with you, then, this impression of that night,
and the talk of my two friends as a kind of forecast of
the months which followed.   For if I were to give the
detail of them in diurnal fashion, it would make too
long a story.   Not but that there were passages of sur-
passing interest which shall ever dwell in my memory,
but because I should be telling what is, in the main,
known to most of us now living.   We did, as all men
are aware, make such dashes at Glasgow that, while we
failed to save our friends, their enemies were frightened
at that thrust of the Marquis with his handful, and
removed them to St. Andrews, where, alas, the tragedy
of vengeance fell on Sir Robert Spottiswoode and most
of his fellow-prisoners.   There followed the terrible

journey our little army made in midwinter across the
mountains of the Esk and the Dee, when the Marquis
sought to effect a junction with the elusive Huntly.   It
was done in the season of that killing frost, which men
speak of with horror still.   This was my first taste of
those terrors of war that precede or follow the less
dreadful trials of the foughten field.   I mind of the
Athole men, their brogues worn through the soles,
threading those corries and scrambling along those
rocky summits sprinkled with ice-spears, staining the
snow as they doggedly planted in it their bleeding feet.
I am haunted by remembrances of our poor horses, up
to the belly in half-frozen bogs, or crashing through the
ice that gave way under them in the greater pools of
the mountain streams.   And, when I saw men follow
him through purgatoria with dog-like devotion, I learned
something of what Evan meant when he spoke of the
Marquis as a wizard leader of men.

As for how the rest of the time was filled up, I must
not forget to mention two journeys, one with each of
my friends, which took me away from those weary
dashes hither and thither in the north country that
constituted so much of what I can scarce dignify by
terming " the campaign."   One was a mission with
Dairsie, as bearers of letters from the Marquis to the
Earl of Huntly at the old Bog of Gight.   Then I saw
much of that delightsome land, the Laich of Moray,
though it was in a cruel season when its great rivers
were heavy with blocks of floating ice and its fir forests
mantled in snow.   The other was a journey, through

the country of Glengarry and Clanranald, to the island
of Coll, as the companion of Evan, who bore letters
from the Captain-General to the chieftains there. I
have, indeed, more than mere memories of these two
months—for so long it took us to go and to return—I
possess a short account which I wrote afterwards; for
this first experience of the real Highlands so caught
my imagination that our days on the windy moors or
storm-tossed lochs, and our nights, sometimes spent in
the house of some friendly tacksman, but oftener in
the shieling of the lonely cottar, seemed to demand a
chronicle. But most of all, I think, I wrote the account
because my heart was full of admiration for the Red
Soldier as he moved among the folk of his own blood
and language. What daring, ever cleared of mere
foolhardiness, he evinced in all those days in wild places,
often among suspicious folk to whom his bearing was
his only introduction, what quenchless courtesy to the
humblest as to the highest of them, and, above all,
what rare and almost woman-like consideration for me.
It was then I picked up what I know of the Gaelic; it
was then I could listen to the soldier's *sgeulachdan*,
enriched ever and anon by a phrase of the tongue, which
gave them a tang such as they never had, even when he
amused me with them during the healing of my wound
at Talla Linns. It was then I saw deep into that heart
of his, so strong in the rush of impulse, yet so well
controlled by the delicacy of his feelings, that gave the
Red Soldier his power to charm. Often in those days I
counted everything well lost to hear his light footfall by

my side, and to catch on occasion, in that silence of
consent which is the deepest proof of friendship, the flash
of his understanding eye.

So winter passed into spring, and there was nought
to shew for all the Marquis's clever checkmating the
Parliament's commander, Middleton. Then, in the end
of May, Huntly fairly fled from his Bog of Gight rather
than consort aught with the Marquis. The Gordons
were, indeed, a prop that tottered and gave way. But
our mission to the west had prospered. The Macleans
of Coll were coming, and so too were Clanranald and
Glengarry. Evan at last believed his hero could do
what he had done a year before, and flash through the
south country like a blazing comet. Then the blow
fell. The King had surrendered to the Scots early in
May, and, on the last day of that month, came Robin
Ker with the King's fatal letter to the Captain-General.
It contained the explicit command : " You must disband your forces and go into France, where you shall
receive my further direction."

There was no arguing against the clear word. That
day on Speyside saw the eclipse of all our hopes. The
one thought of the Marquis thereafter was for the
protection of us, his followers. Assurance of this he
asked when he replied submitting to his King's command. It was waiting for this assurance that kept him
in arms till mid-July. Meantime Seaforth and Huntly
were making their own terms with Middleton. Alasdair,
with that pretended King's general of the Isles and the
Highlands, Antrim, was in the thick of his private feud

in Argyle. In the end of the month Montrose and Middleton met on the banks of the Isla and arranged terms. The Marquis wrung out of his soldierly opponent a free pardon and restoration of forfeited estates for all the Royalists, except a few of whom the principals were himself, Lord Crawford, and Sir John Hurry. Those exempted were to leave the country by the first day of September in a vessel to be provided for them by the Estates.

The Captain-General took farewell of his army, the interests of which he had thus saved, amid a scene of such lamentation as I have never seen. Thereafter he set off to keep his tryst with the Estates, and it is at this point I take up my story in some detail again.

CHAPTER XXIV

A GREAT MAN AND HIS MASTER

I WAS now free, if there was trust to be put in the assurance of the Estates, through the terms made by the Marquis with Middleton. I could return to my interrupted studies or to any vocation that opened to me ; and the odd thing was I could do this simply because I was classed an avowed follower of Montrose. More curiously still, the lady of Winterhope was sure of her safety because she was in the same case. The pardon, which the great man had so chivalrously secured for the rank and file of his followers, would cover any charge the Estates laid at her door for her supposed attempt on the soldiers at Talla Linns and the rescue by force of her from the Estates' officers at the house of Polmood. You may be sure that, through the long months since last I saw her face, I had not endured to be without news of her. We had our secret emissaries as well as the Estates, and once and again sure word came to me that, so far as her enemies were concerned, Alison Laidlaw had disappeared, and that none recognized her in one of those humble lasses, the nieces of douce Mistress Cowieson in the north side of the Burghmuir. You may wonder, then, why, after that day at Rattray, when I saw even the Athole men steal sorrowfully away

from the standard and make for their homes, I did not
haste me to Edinburgh and Mistress Alison with the
good news that she was free to return to Megget, and
that we two young folks, pulled almost against our
wills to follow the fortunes of the Marquis, were to
benefit in such a ferlie fashion by his misfortune.   The
reason why I contented myself with a bit of a letter
to her, and continued with the little band round the
Marquis to see the end, was this.   We were not at all
easy in our minds as to what that end would be.
True, Middleton was both a man of his word and a man
who would not brook that word being overridden by his
masters.   But the truth is, the Estates were fuming
over the generous terms which Middleton had agreed to.
The first day of September had been fixed as the date
by which the Marquis, and the others for whom there
was no pardon, must leave Scotland.   If that date were
passed, he and they would be outlaws at the mercy of
the Estates.   Soon it became apparent that there was
a plot to prevent the Captain-General from being able
to take advantage of his pact with Middleton.   For one
thing, and that the principal, the vessel the Estates
had promised to carry the Marquis and his exempted
followers furth Scotland did not come.   The days
passed, and those of us who looked on saw they were
squandered with delays which impeded the movements
of the Marquis and prevented him from getting into
touch with Middleton, who was clearly being kept
busied with other affairs by the Estates.   But move we
did, in spite of all these obstacles.   We reached the old

town of Montrose, which had been named as the port of
embarkation, as the month of August began to wane,
and chafed out our hearts there watching for the ship
from tide to tide. The inhabitants were not so much
openly hostile to us as indifferent. They shewed us no
hospitality. On the other hand, no one was overtly
offensive to us on the streets, or shewed resentment at
our presence if we chanced to enter a tavern.

One night the Red Sergeant and I watched as usual
for the coming of the Covenant ship. We had seen, as
we always did with wonder and delight, the great basin
of that landlocked harbour fill with the fresh tide, and
the scene change from one of deadness to one all sparkle
and life ; but over the bar the tide carried no vessel
to quicken our hopes. We were returning with dowie
spirits. As we passed a hostelry much frequented by
mariners, we heard the stave of a song sung by one
within who had a voice like a storm at sea. There was
something so infectious in the rumble of gaiety that
Evan and I paused and listened to it as it rolled out by
the open casement upon the autumn air. And, faith,
the fellow could pronounce his words, for they came to
us as clear as a clean-fingered pipe tune :

> " I love no roast but a nut-brown toast,
>   And a crab laid in the fire.
> A little bread shall do me stead ;
>   Much bread I not desire.
> No frost, nor snow, no wind, I trow,
>   Can hurt me if I wold :
> I am so wrapped and thoroughly happed
>   Of jolly good ale and old."

" Evan, man," I cried excitedly, " do you not ken it ? "

" What, the song ?   Not me."

" No, the voice.   There is only one man in the world it can be."

" And who is he, whatever ? "

" Why, lad, Gwyn.   The last time I heard him sing was in the Castle Wynd at Selkirk, the night before Philiphaugh, and here he is alive and hearty enough to sing.   I tell you it's a good omen.   Here wi' ye ; " and I dragged him to the open casement.

We looked in on a mighty man at his ease and all his lonesome.   He reclined in a great leathern armchair. His long legs were stretched before him on two other chairs, and by his elbow on a table, which bore the dishes of a supper but none of its food, stood a stonejack of liquor, for size like a jackboot.

" Gwyn, Captain John Gwyn," I cried, " we call you to account ! "

My certes, there was a change in him.   Evan himself could not have made a quicker cat's spring, or more deftly dropped the jug handle, to snatch up and level the pistol that was lying ready on the arm of the leathern chair.   For a moment or two his blue eyes flamed on us. Then he lowered his weapon and gave a bellow of a laugh.

" Lord save us," he guffawed, " it's the Covey, the Covey turned into a Cavalier, and, for his friend, a Highland chief more glorious than Solomon, with the Viceroy's colours to touch up his tartan.   'Zooks, lad, by that hail you gave, Jack Gwyn thought that he had overstayed his welcome and that his little bit of song might send him back to the vile dungeon at Newcastle, to be starved to death by the reprobate marischal there. But all's well, and the name you shouted, famouséd though it be, means nothing in this barbarous town ; so join me, hearties, and pass the hour in a barter of news."

Accordingly he had us within, when he had overcome our fear of drawing him into our troubles, by saying :

" Have no fear for me. This is a house for mariners, where, by good chance, mariners there are none, save the supercargo of Jens Gunnersen, whom you see before you. If mine host were to go back on a friend of the Norwegian, he would say good-bye to the free-trade wines and brandies which draw skippers and tarry britches to the house."

The Welshman himself was a passable counterfeit of a sea-officer. To my surprise he insisted on having our tale first.

The eyes of the honest fellow were kept fairly dancing as we unfolded our story ; and when he heard how the treasure had been salved and conveyed intact to the Marquis, he rocked with merriment at the fantastic way of doing it, but was generous in his praise of the spirit which had carried us through. " Cavaliers both, that's what you are, lads, and of the brand that succeeds. Now take me, born and bred to the trade. How do I succeed ? I tell you hard knocks and strange shifts

Jack Gwyn gets, and never a penny richer in his purse or bettered in rank is he."

" The day is not done yet," I said ; " but come, Captain, we are hungering to have your story."

" Story ! " he replied ; " there's little of glory in it, like yours, little but feints and shifts and subterfuges, such as a soldier thinks of with shame. But whither would you when the devil drives ?

" That day at Philiphaugh I thought I had said good-bye to you all and the treasure lost in that last onset of Leslie's horse. These fellows might have been schooled by Rupert, and I was lucky to be left, after their wall of steel passed, lying pinned under my shot horse. I looked and saw the fight was utterly over, and I separated from the few of you that remained. I was lucky enough to catch the riderless mount of one of Leslie's captains. God forgive me, I joined in the pursuit, bareheaded, lest my different headgear should betray me. Otherwise I was not specially distinguishable from some of the volunteers who rode with the Kirkcudbright dragoons. At the first chance I evaded the others and made for the south. By day I travelled the less frequented roads, by night fell on the plan of taking up my quarters in church porches. I was not at all so troubled to lie upon the bare stones in the near company of the dead as I was to dine with Duke Humphrey, the which I often did. Howbeit I made my way through Westmoreland, reached Lord Digby, was in his ill-starred expedition, fled with him to the Isle of Man, returned in time to the neighbourhood of Newcastle.

There I loitered, watching for a chance to help the King. The mayor, an exact fanatic, had his eye on me, and I might have found myself in the castle dungeon were it not for the kindness of some of the Scots officers. These had a soldier's feelings for myself and old Royalist soldadoes like me. Several offers they made to frank me into Scotland, and thence, if I wished, to Holland, for honourable service there. But Jack Gwyn, who trained the children of the King in their military exercises at Richmond and Windsor, waited on to help the King. At last His Majesty learned of me and how I could serve him. Robin Ker, it seems, had borne two letters to the Marquis from the King, and that openly, because their general purport was communicated by the King to the enemy. But a fortnight gone His Majesty desired to send a secret letter to the Captain-General, and whom did he turn to but Jack Gwyn? By the greatest luck, Halkett, our old friend Jens Gunnersen was lying with his sloop in Newcastle. I had but to ask a passage to get it. The sloop reached last night a little port named Stonehive. This day at noon I delivered the King's letter to the Marquis, and am here till it pleases the Marquis to use me as the bearer of his answer or otherwise. I am hoping that the letter I bore may tell of some good turn in fortune for the cause, and, if so, at last for Jack Gwyn.''

This was exciting news, of which it were well to learn the sequel. So, after we had passed another hour with our bluff, lovable companion, we made our way to Dairsie's quarters. Dairsie, one of the nephews solemnly committed to the Captain-General's care by Sir Robert, just before his death, was treated as a son by the Marquis, and so the likeliest person to know the purport of the letter, if the Marquis deemed his master meant it to be known to his intimates. As a matter of fact we learned from Dairsie that Montrose read aloud the letter, which was one of affectionate greeting and commendation, and ran on to the fateful postscript before he had realized its meaning. This postscript said, " Defer your going beyond seas as long as you may without breaking your word."

" Too late," he had groaned, " too fatally late ! " He appeared crushed in his very heart.

That night the Red Sergeant and I discussed the letter, and Evan put what I think was the thought of both of us.

" Gilbert, my dear, I think I can say I love the King, and it will not break my loyalty to say what I now say, and it is this. What a master to serve ! Here is the Marquis twice commanded to disband his forces. He obeys, though he has let the King know Seaforth has declared for him and can give him eight thousand claymores, and that the Irish can send seven thousand pikes. And now he tells him to delay his going. He invites him to make a fresh start when he has himself, by his previous command, ruined all. To delay now, to hang on waiting better fortune ! God above us, the only fortune would be his head grinning on the West Bow. And His Majesty cannot see it. He puts this man, whom he declares he loves like a son, at the mercy of his weakness and fear, and then, when there comes some fancy to raise his courage, he dares him, for that fancy, to yield himself, a man already proscribed, to the very nets his enemies are spreading for him. Oh, pity on the Marquis's tries at slumber this night ! It is a bitter business for a man of chivalrous heart to be commanded by a fool. Forgive me for the wild word ; but when I search my own heart, I find now clearer than ever that I serve the Marquis, and the King only as seen through that perspective glass, which magnifies his merits, the Marquis."

And so, very disconsolate, we got us to bed.

CHAPTER XXV

AN ANGEL TROUBLES THE WATER

I LOATHED that good town of Montrose during these last days of August. The Red Sergeant and I were on the tenterhooks of suspense over the Marquis, young Dairsie, and the others exempted from the pardon. Though all knew these to be the expiring days of grace, there appeared no sign of open menace. Indeed, the stillness on the part of the Captain-General's enemies was what affected us most. It was like that time of gasping which so often precedes a storm in high summer.

Evan remarked how, whereas we might have expected the Estates to fill the town with its troops, and so overawe us, we were left free to walk the streets and to wear more swords among us than did all the folk in the town taken together. But he pointed out that the hostelries were filled with men who seemed to have neither friends abiding nor business to transact in the burgh.

We could not doubt that these were the agents of the Estates, there to see to it that the letter of the pact was kept till the days expired. The Marquis and his little suite were to be allowed their run, but everywhere round them was their cage. The very stillness boded

that the lookers-on were confident they could not escape
from it.

" Gilbert," he would say, at the end of our strolls,
when we felt we were constantly spied on, though never
molested, " it looks as if the spells were on us.   I would
give my right arm to break this horrid net, soft as silk
and as cruelly strong, and be the mouse that sets the
lion free."

We dared not visit Gwyn again, lest we should draw
him too into the coil, and the big man showed a discretion I had not expected from him.   For, dearly
though he loved company, he shunned ours, and even
passed us, without giving us so much as a look, on two
occasions when taking his walk abroad.   And, pre-
sumably waiting for such answer to the King's letter as
the Marquis might send by him, he abode solitarily at
his inn.

Then there happened something which stirred the
pool of expectation for me, and, as of old, it was an
angel that troubled the water.

As I hung by the quay one day towards the end of
the month, a fishing-busch sailed into the estuary and
ranged herself alongside the jetty.   Listlessly I watched
the fishermen furl the brown sail and make the boat
fast.   Then, from the green-painted scuttle that broke
her broad deck, came forth two women.   My heart
missed a beat.   There was no mistaking the sturdy lass
who struggled to airt herself and her knapsack out of
the narrow doorway.   It was Eppie Tamson.   The lady
who followed her into the sunshine was Alison.

For a moment the two gazed, with a wandered look, toward the town. Then Ailie saw me and, with a little cry, started forward. I sprang on board and ran to take her hands.

"Oh, Gilbert," she cried, "do not touch me in kindness till you forgive me for this I've done. Hear me before you again call me friend."

The colour rushed into her face and deepened to her very throat. Timidity, such as I had never beheld in her, clothed her as with a garment.

There were none to note the manner of our meeting, or to overhear our words, save the busch's crew, and they were too concerned in making their boat snug to heed.

"What need for explanations!" I said. "Is it not good enough that you are here?"

"No, no," she cried out. "Even you must own I have done a bold thing. Others will say I have done a brazen and bad thing in running from the harbour you found me and in chasing you here, to increase your troubles. Ere I stir a foot in your company, you must hear my tale and give your judgment."

"The tale will make no differ," I answered. "But, if it must be told first, say on."

"Well," she began, like a penitent at the confessional, "all went well till Normand Hunter took a hand in my affairs."

"Ah!" I gurred, like a dog birsling at prospect of a fight.

"Stop," she pleaded. "That's not the way to keep

your promise and hear me out. Be just to the man.
He could not, if you will but think on the matter from
his side, accept without question my spiriting-away
from his house. He felt it lay on his honour to trace
me and get to the rights of the strange business. He
proved an eident seeker, but it was only a month since
that he succeeded in discovering my whereabouts. He
came by night to my asylum. In the most honourable
way he asked to be allowed to raise my case with the
Committee. He assured me he had good hopes of
getting me their quittance and permission for me to
return to Winterhope on his cognizances. I replied I
was sensible of his goodness, especially after the indignity
he had suffered on my behalf, but that I must abide in
hiding. He asked no explanations, took my decision
without arguing it, and assured me no person would be
wiser for anything he would do or say.

" But, it seems, the creature, Mungo Amos, had been
watching Polmood, and ferreted out enough to be suspicious we were somewhere near the Burghmuir. Eppie
here was our alarum, for she saw the skellum ranging
round in his search.

" What was I to do ? Well, I heard that your old
patron, Maister Henderson, had come home by ship
from Newcastle. I determined to seek him out and
throw myself on his mercy."

" But," I interrupted, " did you get no letter from
me, telling you the Marquis had secured a free pardon
for us ? "

" Oh," she burst out, in a pitiful voice, " I did not.

So I've acted over quick—and what I've done was needless after all."

" I will not allow you to say that," I answered. " Tell on.   How did you fare with Maister Henderson ? "

" I took my courage in my hands and went in the gloaming to his house, with Eppie as my convoy.   As we drew near, a gentleman came out and walked across the yard.   Eppie, who has got to have a by-ordinar' knowledge of the city grandees, says :

" ' It's Sir James Stewart, and, dod, the man's in tears.'   It was in truth so, and he went towards the gate in such a broken fashion that I felt a great fear, and, ere I was 'ware, cried out, when he would pass us :

" ' Oh, sir, has ony ill befa'en ? '

" He came out of his preoccupation and replied, after a moment's look at us :

" ' No ill, mistress, I trust in my heart no ill.   But were ye seeking the minister, may I ask ? '

" ' I am,' I said.   ' I would fain see him on a matter of importance that concerns my life.'

" ' Then, lady,' says he gravely, ' I grieve to tell you are ower late for that.   He's done with life and is standing before his Maker.'

" ' Ye cannot mean that he is dead ? ' I cried, in such distress that it must have touched him, for he went on :

" ' It is even so.   I have just closed his eyes, the eyes of my best friend, and a good friend to many.   We may mourn for ourselves, but it would be doing despite to his last testament if we mourned for him, who, just before the end, opened his tired eyes and bent upwards a glance brighter than the sparkle of any diamond, and then, like Stephen, fell on sleep.'

" ' Oh ! but this sudden stroke is heart-rending,' I murmured.

" ' Nay, 'twas not sudden,' he explained, as he made to take leave. ' Maister Henderson was marked for it when he landed from Robert Steward's ship an eight days since. When a waft of fever struck him here, the feeble flame went out. And his is the greatest loss Scotland has suffered since he that never feared the face of man went.'

" Gilbert, as we turned from that closed door, I was wae for you, losing your best friend without the reconciling word from him. And I was wae for myself, losing my hoped refuge in the time of storm. The city was a prison, but a prison with the door open. I thought I must go away from it, for any danger to me would beckon you back, only to put you in the toils as well. I persuaded myself the instruction to abide would be changed, did you but know my case. A landward journey I could not hope to make undetected. Then I thought of the sea, and the way in which the fisher folk keep clear of all State affairs and are intent only on making the pickle that serves them. I had the siller. Could we hire a wee ship and be carried to Aberdeen, or some port in the north where we should be unknown ? Eppie took up the idea briskly. That very night we bade farewell to Mistress Cowieson, and, like two gaberlunzies, with a change of dress and some victuals in our packs, walked through the darkness to a fishing-place just beyond Aberlady. There we found a skipper, who, for sixty pounds Scots, promised to land us in Aberdeen, and no questions asked. We beat about the sea for near a week, and never will I forget what Eppie endured. We had, indeed, little occasion to think of food, but the boat ran short of water and had to put into Stonehive. There the skipper learned that all the men left to the Marquis were here. Oh, Gilbert, when I heard that I could not reason. I took a short cut in place of the long way of my plan. Yet, as you value my friendship, I pray you be honest with me. Say I am a clog on your freedom, and, I declare, this same boat that carried us here will carry me out of your sight."

She was excited to a degree, and told her tale in rushes of speech that minded me of the hill burns. Then she stood passive, awaiting my judgment, as if she were a soul come for doom and I Rhadamanthus.

" Alison Laidlaw," I said, in as level a tone as I could master, " I thought you had more sense than to get into such a fret over one of the finest of ploys. This is the second convoy of a treasure, and it has ended better even than the first, for me, anyhow. So come your ways without a word further. You'll find, I think, you couldn't have timed your coming better for a return home in safety and with honour."

" Ah ! " She drew a long breath. Then a gleam of the old roguishness came into her eyes.

" Well," she went on, " since I have been forgiven, I must own I have not *entirely* opened my mind. Perhaps in the back of my head there was a thought that Aberdeen would not be so far from some friends of mine as other places I might have chosen. But I did not confess this to my self till, at Stonehive, you proved to be so wondrously near. It was there that I was tempted, and, like the daughter of Eve that I am, fell from my steadfastness."

" Adam had the logic, no doubt," said I sententiously, " but Eve had the charm."

So together, followed by Eppie, who, while studiously unconcerned, had yet missed not a word or look that passed, we made our way from the quayside to the town.

When I had secured a lodging for them, and seen them settled in quarters at a considerable distance from our own, I sought out Evan.

I gave him my news. He remained silent so long that I twitted him.

" Are you not glad she has come ? " I challenged.

" Oh, I am," he replied gravely. " Glad for our sakes, but sorry for her sake. It is not a place, or an hour, for a lady. As the way is open, you should set out with her for the south with to-morrow morning's sun."

" But ye ken how set I am on seeing the waygoing, Evan. I cudna leave wi' a licht hert unless I had first seen ye a' quit of what ye ca' the net. An' noo she's as keen as what I am tae bid ye fareweel an' furth fortune."

He hesitated. Then he began by calling me " Gil-

bert, my dear." I knew he never did this except when
his deepest affection spoke. It is an endearment which
never falls from a Lowlander when addressing a man
friend. Indeed I should distrust one of my own kind if
he used it. It would sound unnatural and extravagant.
But, coming from Evan, it always sounded like a word
of my mother. He had a touch of the woman in him,
and it never expressed itself except in his strongest and
most manly moods.

" Gilbert, my dear," he said now. " Listen to me.
There's something more precious at stake than your
pleasure or hers. There's her reputation. Now, do not
kindle, for she was obeying a right guidance when she
came, and you will guard her honour as we soldiers
would watch over the herald who comes into our camp.
The matter concerns not you two, who have the innocent mind. It concerns others. And, let me say,
Gilbert, the innocent mind is more than most of your
countrymen have. Here we are in a particular sour and
embittered town. Do not be deceived by the decencies
they have observed towards us. We are soldiers who
have had the worse of it. So there is a kind of respect
for us. They incline even to pity, because they are so
sure there is to be no escape for us in the end. But
introduce a woman as one of us, and at once suspicion
fastens on her. They have but one opinion of such of
these as appear in camps. It hurts me to say it, but all
the innocence in the world will not avail against that
imputation, even among the best of them. And the
worst ! Why, these, the understrappers of the Com-

mittee and the sweepings of the town itself, will jump
to one conclusion—that the lady is also a spy and here
of design to get us away out of their hands.   Should
the trap be sprung and we go free, I tell you, the lady
and you would be left to bear the brunt of their vengeance.   Well I know their idea of virtue.   It is to hold
sourly to what they call their own, and to blow on that
of any woman who dares throw in her lot with their
enemies.   Gibbie, be advised by one who knows the
meanness of those who are in a war, yet fight only with
their tongues till it is safe to draw on the defenceless.
Get you on the road for the places where you are both
known."

I own he shook me by the earnestness of his manner.
Yet his idea itself appeared to me to be little short of
ridiculous.   I told him I was firm to stay the day or
two that remained, and was confident nothing untoward
could happen to Ailie and me.

So he desisted from the attempt to persuade me, and
when I took him to Ailie, he did not show her a trace of
his concern.

Eppie and she had laid out their belongings, and the
knapsacks were pointed to with pride.   Ailie gave me a
jolt by her gay remark to the soldier :

" See, we carry them, as leaguer-ladies should."   I
question if she knew the meaning of the term.

" You will not be having to march far, then, for this
is like to be a standing camp," was Evan's way of
turning the awkward corner.

" Then I fear I shall be the more likely to prove what

I have been calling myself—an encumbrance," she rejoined.

Evan rounded that one with this :

" You will be a cheerful weight, then, like the burden which steadies a man when he has to cross a torrent."

But, in the days that followed, I found reason to believe that Evan's forebodings were only too well founded. At first sight of Ailie, the folk in the street looked at her with as much amazement as if she had been the fabulous unicorn. Then, apparently, surmise curdled into suspicion. There were leering glances cast at her. At times an odd word or two, caught in the passing, made my face burn. All the while Ailie was sunnily unconscious of anything save the pleasure of the reunion. After her wearisome time of confinement in Edinburgh, it was like a hairst-play for her to be free to walk abroad, and to share with our little company the excitement of waiting for that issue on which the fortunes of all hung.

CHAPTER XXVI

THE LOYAL SERVITEUR TAKES A HAND

THE last day of the month came, and on it sailed into the estuary the long-expected vessel promised by the Estates. Our party was now at such a desperate pass for time that the Marquis could not afford to send Sir John Hurry or young Dairsie to make preliminary arrangements. There was nothing for it but to embark without ceremony.

The Marquis himself headed the little procession. You could see by his very dress that he had studied to avoid being provocative. He was attired in a plain suit of black velvet with a collar of lace, a broad-brimmed hat having a single plume, and high boots of soft leather. He gave no suggestion of the campaigner, for the small sword he carried was little better than a toy. Hurry shewed no such consideration for the feelings of the folk who watched him or his probable convoyers. A steel cuirass covered his breast, and his sword stretched out behind his cloak and hit against the riding-boots, from which he had not even discarded the spurs. All the Captain-General's followers were sufficiently armed, indeed, and kept close behind him, as if suspicious. I, who accompanied them, as I expected to take farewell, unconsciously imitated their master in carrying only a light hanger.

Drummond of Balloch had gone on before and got ready a pinnace. In her the company was rowed over to the chartered vessel. She lay at anchor almost midway in the roads. Though high in the forecastle and the stern, she was so low at the waist that the Marquis, his half-brother Harry Graham, Hurry, and Dairsie were able to step from the pinnace right on to the deck. There, and not on his own poop, the ship-master stood waiting, while round him, lounging in little knots against casks and coils of ropes and the bulwarks of the vessel, was as discontented-looking a crew as ever man set eyes on.

The Marquis had removed his hat, and bowed as his feet touched the deck; but the skipper, without so much as lifting a hand in salute, burst out in what was evidently a rehearsed effort in rudeness.

" Maister, I suppose I needna say I ken wha ye are, or raither wha ye *were*, and what ye seek ? "

From the boat, where the rest of us sat, I saw the hand of Dairsie fly to his sword-hilt, and the hand of his master quickly but gently rest on it to check the lad, while he answered :

" I am James Graham, Marquis of Montrose, and I came to your ship, good sir, in the belief that she is the vessel appointed by the Estates to convey my friends and me from this kingdom. Am I not right in my thinking it to be even so, sir ? "

The fellow was a trifle abashed by so soft an answer,

but he was not to be put off playing the part for which he had been cast.

" Richt ye may be, maister, in jalousin' my ship was *appinted* tae that office ; but alloo me, John Mac-growther, tae inform you, James Graham, Markis o' Montrose, that tae *cairry oot* the appintment is anither maitter.   Man, the Estates may appint what the ship *Beulah* is tae dae ; but the waters an' the win's hae their say first.   I tell ye, she's hed the weather we micht hae expectit frae Heevin when sent on sic an errand.   Her riggin' is rottit an' her seams are as open as an auld basket.   I maun hae her re-riggit an' caulked afore I sail anither sea mile in her.   I winna risk my life for a' the markises in the warld, and, what's mair, my crew wadna pit hand on rope gin I did.   Isn' that sae, lads ? "

The sour-looking sailors gave a great rumble, in which oaths were the principal ingredient.   There could be no doubting that here was a most resolved company.

Lillie and Melvin and Guthrie, the old soldiers in the boat, were for rushing on board, clapping pistols to their heads, and having them heave up anchor or get their brains blown out.   Evan stopped them by a word.

" They would run the ship on the sands, and what better should we be ?   Trapped, that's what we are. Wait on the Marquis."

The Marquis stooped even to entreat, but Mac-growther stuck the stubborn chin of him out, and his men began looking impatiently shoreward, as if he was merely delaying their leaving a leaky tub by his gentle talking.

At last he courteously saluted the skipper, and saying to us, " Well, gentlemen, we have kept our part of the bargain," stepped, with a Hurry who was fuming and a Dairsie who was white in the chaps, into the pinnace.

So, a baffled company, we gained the shore and passed through streets, well lined with spectators, among whom the forms of those whom we had learned to set down as agents of the Estates were but too discernible, to our various lodgings.

On parting, command was given by the Marquis that we should gather at his quarters in a few hours' time, when he would advise as to what were best to be done. But if ever men looked like rats in a trap, that little company did. All but two of them. The Marquis held his head much higher than he had done when he walked down to the pinnace, and never did I see his face wear so settled a look of calm; and the Red Soldier, who had given counsels of passiveness that seemed to me strange as coming from him an hour since, trod the causeway as if it were the heather, and his eye was as full of fire as a gled's. Here were two spirits well matched, for their hearts rose in the hour of adversity.

It was, all the same, a dull companion I had in our lodging as, for once, the Red Soldier kept his thoughts to himself. I was glad when, as evening fell, I heard an unmistakable voice in the entry, and forthwith Gwyn came bursting in on us. He was vastly perturbed.

" See here," he cried, " I've broken out of my leaguer, and not for nothing ; word must be passed to the Marquis, yet I dare not go direct. So I've risked beating up my old acquaintance, Halkett, who is a free man, and you, Sergeant, who will carry my tidings. They are not good ; they are most damnably bad. I think I've served the cause by putting up at that rats' house down by the quay, for, though I've had it to myself till an hour since, then I had company in plenty. Jack Gwyn smelt trouble when he saw the tarry britches from the ship's boat met by some gentlemen at large on the quay, and all make for his tavern. It took his mind to go just then for his evening *passeggiata*, so he lounges out by the landlord who is watching the knot of oncomers from his door, slips round the corner, and then darts into the back court and gets down behind some empty puncheons that are by the rear window of the little living-room. A good disposition, for in comes the master of the ship, a great whiskered fellow, and two or three tallow-faced men in sombre clothes, like attorneys, for their private confab, while mine host is serving the ship's officers and their boat's crew in the inn kitchen. I cannot give you the Scots turn of their tongues ; but I understood the run of it.

" When the jugs had passed once and their throats were wetted, one of the soft-handed gentlemen hee-heed :

" ' It was a bonnie bit of work, Macgrowther. Eh ! I would have liked to stand on your deck and see how the peacocks looked when you plucked their feathers.'

" ' They looked like hens at the moulting, Maister Tait,' says he. ' I don't think you'll see them preening themselves much longer and offending the eyes with their braggery. Some of them were for attacking us and compelling us to put to sea.'

" ' And much good they would have done by that,' Tait rejoined. ' There are English ships of war ranging up and down the coast, looking like raging lions for their prey, the ship that is to carry this so-called Marquis. Furth Scotland or within it, I tell you, we have him and the whole cleckin' fast.'

" ' Well,' growled Macgrowther, ' but if your general appears he'll make me sail, for the ship is as seaworthy as on the day she left the stocks.'

" ' The General ? Oh yes, he would ; but the Committee is keeping him out of the way till the days of grace are past.'

" ' But isn't this the last day of them ? ' says the tarpaulin. ' Why not nab them ? '

" ' Oh,' chuckled he, ' don't you be uneasy, the twig's well limed. We must keep up appearances. As for the others, they may be allowed a day or two till General Middleton appears ; but with the arch-enemy, that traitor to Covenant and kingdom, we'll take no risks. If he is not lifted by us and jailed like the murderer he is afore the morn's nicht, he'll be so surrounded by the faithful and penned up by them, that a rescue of any sort will be impossible. Eh ! isn't it fine to think that he's scratching for the last time against the bars of our bonnie cage ? '

" I had heard enough," concluded Gwyn, " and here I am. I think you'll agree it is time for action, and that in a hurry. Now, here is my plan, Sergeant. You hie to the Marquis and put the straitness of the situation before him. Then tell him Jens Gunnersen is still with his sloop at Stonehive. Let him give John Gwyn the commission and he will get away to-night to bring the sloop here as fast as a journey by road and then winds and tides will allow. It may need days, but keep him safe from these wolves. I can surely trust a man of your wit to do that."

" You may trust me to do that," was all Evan said, and he was off with his news to the council. It seemed long to Gwyn and me ere he returned, but I believe he was back within the hour.

" The Marquis falls in with your plan, Captain," he reported. " For your safety it must all be done by your word of mouth, but he bids me say he knows you will do all a man can do. But haste you, for the sands are running fast."

Horse Gwyn could not have, lest his setting out should cause remark ; so the honest fellow took the road, and without further parley, on foot. I went with him a mile or two to set him on his way. Evan told me he was under orders to wait again on the Marquis.

On my return I stayed up late, yet there was no Evan forthcoming, and at last I went to sleep. In the morning I turned only to see that the Soldier's bed had been unslept in. I hurried to the Captain-General's quarters, and found them all in a hubbub. It was

Dairsie who told me that, after a late council had ended, the Red Soldier asked for a few words with the Viceroy. It seemed they talked so long that all the rest retired.

A few minutes before my arrival, the French valet of Lord Gordon, Lasound, who now served the Marquis, had come to say that, on entering the Marquis's chamber, he had found the bed unslept in and the Marquis gone.

When I told how the Red Soldier had not returned to our lodging, I put the cap on the company's consternation.

CHAPTER XXVII

MASQUERADE—AND MASKS OFF

THE consternation over the disappearance of the Captain-General was not to be wondered at. The Marquis was not the man to play at mysteries, and to go off at such a juncture without a word of explanation by tongue or pen! And yet, as I considered on the strange happening, in light of the news Gwyn gave as to the enemy's intentions, I seemed to see light. The Marquis knew his followers were for the time being safe, and that only his freedom was threatened. Now, if he could in some way lie hid till Gunnersen's sloop appeared without his absence being detected, it would do no harm to his followers, and yet afford him a chance to break through the fowler's snare set for him. Then, too, if his absence were discovered, it would serve his followers well, for they could in all honesty declare they knew not his whereabouts. Besides, I think it no shame to those gallant gentlemen who formed his little following to say that they did not excel in discretion. Hurry had a sharp temper, and Dairsie, dear lad, a most enthusiastic tongue. I saw, further, in the scheme, whatever it was, the Red Soldier's hand.

I will say Dairsie shone at this juncture. He de-

clared that, as the Marquis had bidden them rendezvous on Gunnersen's sloop, the Marquis would doubtless
join them there, and that he must have good reasons
for keeping dark his own particular plans. It was for
us to obey without question. Meanwhile we must give
out that the Marquis was indisposed, but we ourselves
keep up the illusion that the vessel of the fanatic
Macgrowther was the one string to our bow, and pester
the shipmaster with our importunities to set sail.

Harry Graham, who had a spice of mischief in him,
improved on Dairsie's plan by suggesting that Lasound,
the valet, should impersonate his brother. The French-
man was not unlike the Captain-General in build and
complexion, and we agreed that, while he would not
pass for his master in the street, he could give a
colourable imitation of him as he reclined, a semi-
invalid on a couch at the window, or passed to and fro
in his chamber. I believe the valet was the only man
of us who enjoyed the two days that followed. He
wore the best garments remaining in his lord's camp
wardrobe, and affected his walk and manner of holding
the head to admiration. Yet it was fortunate that the
town bailies, who accepted Dairsie's regretful report
to them of the Marquis's indisposition, and no doubt
passed the word at once to the spies of the Estates, did
not seek an interview, else poor Lasound's nobility
would have been shortened. But they did not. They
were so sure of him that they were content to play their
game of cat and mouse till the killing stroke fell.

After two days, Hurry, Drummond, Graham, and the

chaplain went to Stonehive by night and, as we afterwards found, joined the ship there.   The others of us
judged that, if they reached her in safety, we should
not have much longer to wait.

How my heart leapt as I saw the topsails of the
Bergen sloop shewing above the heads beyond the roads
on the afternoon of the third day.   In she came, and
then ran up into the wind as close to the shore as the
tide would let her.   I passed the word, for had I not
been aboard her at Morrison's Haven now near twelve
months before ?   The whole company was on the road
in a jiffey.   I think we fairly took our closest observers
by surprise.   There was some attempt to impede us by
jostling as we made our way to a boat that was all
ready at the quay ; but the little knot was well armed,
and the proscribed veterans, Lillie and Melvin and
Guthrie, in particular, shewed more than their teeth
and bared their blades.

" But whaur is he ?   Whaur is he ? " men muttered
to each other, as they missed the chief quarry of their
long hunt.   Where, indeed, was he ?   But we obeyed
orders and held on, a company of players with the actor
who does the title piece absent.   As we pushed off, if
hands were kept off us, eyes were devouring us, eyes
full of anger and amazement.   Few, if any, except we
who were then facing the shore, observed a young
servant fellow, with a portmantle on his shoulder, walk
down to the little stone jetty along from the quay.   He
was followed by a minister of religion, a well-set-up
youngish man, walking somewhat stately as if careful

of soiling his shoes, with their bonnie silver buckles, on the dulse and slime.

"This is your boat, Mr. Wood. This way, sir," the servant fellow called. They got into a cockboat, with the portmantle in the bow and the minister in the stern. The servant pushed off, and I noted that he rowed with great deliberation and very inexpertly. I could not but remark to myself on the contrast between that little peaceful boat and ours, so full of strange passion and unrestful hearts.

We had hardly cleared the shore when the angry mob that lined it seemed to find a leader. One of the lawyer-like fellows harangued but a moment or two, and in a trice another boat was manned and followed to cut us off. I vow we laid to our oars and fairly raced them for the sloop, which they now saw clearly to be our objective, and not the *Beulah*, as possibly most had imagined it was. We were on the deck of the Bergen vessel a good minute before they hailed her skipper.

"What do you want?" shouted Jens from his forecastle-head, where the anchor was at the hawse-holes, for he was lying with his topsail backed, ready for a start on the moment, should his party come off at once.

"We want these men. They are forfeited traitors," came back the leader's voice.

"Then you come to Norway for them," shouted Gunnersen. "I sail under the Norwegian flag, and if you come alongside my ship I drop a puncheon of

Schnapps through the bottom of your boat, and give you *gins* in plenty.   Sheer off."

" Stop, skipper," he persists.   " There are English vessels outside waiting to take these traitors."

" All right," rejoins the skipper, " I shew you my boot, but them my heels.   Away with you.   These gentlemen you call traitors are my guests, my honoured guests."

" Ay, but you've left your most honoured guest behind.   We'll see that he's served with the one meal that will be his last," cries the same voice vindictively.

" Are you sure I've left him behind ? " asks Gunnersen.

The cockboat had slipped round by the lee of the ship and was now alongside her waist on the weather side, plain to the view of both parties.   The servant lad lifted his valise on deck and handed up his master.   We gasped with amazement.   The cleric was the Red Soldier and his servant lad the Marquis.

The cockboat was swung along to tow at the stern of the ship.   The yard was braced, the sails filled, and, as she lay to her course down the roads, a sound between a yell and a groan came from the occupants of the shore boat.

" Get back to your plottings and your cold porridge," bellowed a great voice.

Gwyn had to fire that parting shot—Gwyn, happy as a schoolboy who is not alone playing truant, but playing it with the whole school, safe from the dominie's tawse.

The Marquis passed a word to the little group that had come with Gwyn and to us who had thus happily rejoined them. His face wore an amused expression, which it did our hearts good to see.

"My friends," said he, "you will forgive me the anxiety I caused you by making a mystery of my movements, since this little act of deception has succeeded so well. All the credit is due to Evan here. His mind conceived the plan and his art carried it out. He is the modern Proteus. I vow he looks as much to the manner born in the black coat and lace cravat of the real Mr. Wood as in the dress which will always frame his picture in our memories of him—that of the Red Sergeant."

Thereupon he took Evan in comrade fashion by the arm and, in what must have been the proudest moment life had yet brought to my friend, led him away.

It had been arranged that I should get ashore in the cockboat when the vessel had passed the mouth of the estuary. I went round, saying my farewells.

To Dairsie I gave good-bye with a strange sinking of the heart, as if an evil fate hung over the bright lad who had been my hero and was still my friend.

I found Gwyn a cordial for this depression when, without regret, we recalled all that had passed since, near a year before, he had deflected my path.

The vessel cleared the entrance to the great circular bay, and, just beyond the bar, Gunnersen threw her up into the wind and so took the way off her.

Under the break of the forecastle I saw Evan appear.

He had discarded the habiliments of the man of peace and was once more in his campaigning garb.

The moment for the sorest parting had come. Glad was I that it had to be so short, for there was a choke in my throat as I caught his hand and cried :

" Evan, will ye no think again on it, and let us face what is left of life together ? "

" Lad of my heart," he responded, " it's you must have the double sight. I'll pass the next bit of life with you, whatever, for it's ashore in that boat with you I am even now going."

If he had struck me in the face, I could not have been more dumbfounded. I knew how, up to the moment when last I had speech with him, he was set on following the Marquis, like a penny-dog, in exile.

" What ! " I cried.   " *You* leave the Marquis ! "

He gave his answer to this in a slow, deliberate fashion, like a boy repeating his conned lesson.

" Well, you see, the Marquis it is that has decided it. He has just told me I will best serve him here for the present. After I have done his will, I can cross direct to France, and so be there as soon as, or before, himself." And then, with a kind of jocularity, " Has he not just been telling you that I am the man he fancies for quick changes ? So, in with us."

In a maze I moved towards the stern. Not a soul on that deck had an inkling of the Red Sergeant's intention till they saw him seated with me in the boat. They gazed at him in wonderment. Then Sir John Hurry, with whom he had a close amity, called to him :

"What folly is this? If you go to that shore, lad, you go to your death."

Evan only smiled and waved his hand gaily.

As we cast off from the sloop, her lantern was hoisted on the bowsprit stay. The freshening breeze again filled her sails and sent the water slapping against her sides. So she moved into the deepening gloom of evening, till her sails became ghostly and only the lantern-light was seen clearly, like a solitary star.

A groan came from my companion. As I turned in alarm, he clapped his hand to his side.

"Ach! that was a nasty stitch," he said, laughing. "I must have racked a sinew in walking over the dulse with the Marquis."

CHAPTER XXVIII

"SCORE THE WITCH!"

WE landed on the north side of the estuary so as to avoid the harbour. As we made towards the town, I pressed Evan to give me more light on the sudden change in his plans. Then he opened his mind.

It appeared that, on the last stage of his journey from Stonehive with the Marquis, they had come on the encampment of our old friend, Jimmuck the Caird, a few miles west of the town of Montrose. Jimmuck had not dared shew face in the town, but members of his company had not the same fear of being recognized, and mingled freely with the crowd of strangers in the burgh. They reported that the alehouses hummed with clash about the Marquis and his party. No one was more in folk's mouths than the new-comer. Why was a woman there, and why had she appeared just in the hour of the enemy's dilemma? The secret agents of the Estates put her down as a spy. The town rabble, whose mind this idea inflamed, marked "the woman" as their special prey when the whole party came to the day of vengeance.

"Now, Gibbie," proceeded Evan, "this news of Jimmuck's was bad hearing for me, because I saw that, if my plan for the escape of the Marquis succeeded, the trouble would fall on her at once, and, what is worse, would fall on her when left without a single defender. We were even then on our way to the harbour, without time to pass the warning to you. I saw the lady blamed for having arranged the coming of Gunnersen's sloop, for had she not sailed into Montrose from Stonehive ? In the hands of an enemy, sore at being tricked out of its main prey, she would be in real peril. Gibbie, you are a good lad your lone, but it appeared to me you would be the better of having Evan with you in this. I bade Jimmuck keep a fire burning to guide us, and to look for us some time in the night, with horses ready for a dash to the south. I put my difficulty to the Marquis. He agreed there was but one thing to do—see you clear and then myself make for the country of the Keiths, where I may hope to get a cast over to France. So that's all the mystery that is to it. Jimmuck's men may be telling old wives' tales ; but I think they are not."

" Evan," I said, finding it hard to find words for my disgust at myself, " this danger, and the upsetting of the plan nearest your heart, are all my wite. Man, knowing the glaikit creature you had to deal with, you should have done more than advise me, yon day Ailie came. When you saw me so big in my own conceit, you ought to have *commanded* me to take your way of it. I am the gomeril who, when all was well, insisted on pulling away the props and bringing the house down on those I love."

" Ach ! 'tis nothing," he replied. " We are as we are made. This will come out right in the end. In any case, it had to be. Action is the best stopper on anxious thought. We must airt the lady out of that town within the hour."

As we walked, warm drops of rain began to fall, and, when we reached the burgh, it was to find it a place of semi-darkness. The few oil-lamps, which lighted the streets in winter time, were not used in the autumn evenings. The streets lay in deep shadow, save where open doors threw a flicker of light across them. And, indeed, many doors were open, and people stood in knots, like bees at swarming, clustered round them. Other groups were out on the causeway, as if it were a sunny summer's night. It took some unwonted excitement to draw folk from the ingleside to confer thus in the thickening rain.

We edged into the rim of one of the largest groups, where voices were specially vehement.

" It was her got the Norwegian doon an' made gowks o' us a'. That's clear, onywey," one said.

" Ay, an' it was her played the minister an' gat the man o' blood by, aneath oor verra een, as her flunkey," added another. " It's a tarrible peety she's gotten awa' wi' the lave."

" Na," interposed a third, " ye hinna the richt o' it there. The Jezebel's had the impidence tae come back. Fegs, I got a glisk o' her, as bold as brass, lookin' oot o' her windy, no an 'oor syne."

This was news indeed, but the fellow who had spoken

so confidently about the double of the minister could
not allow that as the limit of Ailie's power of disguise.

" Ay," he commented venomously, " mebbe she *wis*
there an 'oor syne, but hoo did ye ken she's no gaen
awa' on a besom ? It's ma opeenion the limmer's a
witch, an' a'm no alane in thinkin' sae. She ocht tae
hae her broo scored, at the least, even gin we dinna mak'
a job o' her wi' the tar-barrel."

A growl went through the crowd. " Rabble the
randy ! Ay, that's it. Rabble her, afore Middleton
comes wi' his sodgers. It's a graun' chance. The
bailies 'll be bedded, or blin', an' no ill-pleased gin we
hannle her the nicht."

A stranger to our land, who does not know how the
witch-madness works among the ignorant populace,
would not credit the absurdities and cruelties it fathers.
Under its spell, humanity and reason go by the board.
Most times its victim is some wretched carline, who will
be burnt at the tar-barrel, or tied to a stake below
high-water mark and left to drown. At other times the
victim is some object of popular aversion, who cannot
be reached except by raising the *fama* that she exercises
the power of sorcery. Even when they do not proceed
to the last extremities, there is a cruel practice termed
" scoring the witch." This consists in making a cut in
the form of a cross above her eyebrows. The blood
drawn is supposed to lift the spells cast by the dealer
in the dark arts, but the horrible brand remains to tell
all, for the rest of her days, that she has been counted
as one accursed by the community.

" Score the witch ! Score the witch ! " The cry
rang along the street. It pierced my heart like a sword.
I seemed to see Ailie's beautiful brow disfigured by the
cross of infamy. And, if you had observed, as I did,
how that crowd caught fire, as the heather does under a
wind, you would not mock at my fear for her.

Let it be said here that the mob which, in a shorter
time than you would believe, moved boisterously in the
direction of Ailie's lodging, was not composed of the
decent citizens of Montrose, but the kind you will find
in most any town, the kind that are ever ready for any
bangstrie and violence. The ringleaders were some of
the men who had pursued us in the boat, and a handful
of the tarry-britches from the *Beulah's* crew.

Evan and I did not linger after we got our warning.
We raced down a lane off the main street, reached the
lodging, and burst in.

Ailie we found sitting with Eppie, sewing at their bit
things.

The moment Ailie saw who my companion was, she
went white.

" Oh ! Do not say that you have failed," she cried.

" No, no," he answered ; " succeeded, succeeded
beyond all we could wish. And now the Marquis has
sent me to convoy you to safety."

" Me ! " she gasped.

In hurried sentences he explained the peril. Even as
he spoke, it was heralded by lights appearing at the
street-end and the cries of the approaching mob.

She did not bandy words. She took time only to pull

a gold piece or two from her little silken purse. These she laid on the table and joined Eppie, who was already following him whom she called the rattler.

There was a back entrance to the house that led into a yard behind. By this way we dashed out, passing an astonished landlady, all in a confusion over the fracas within and without her quiet dwelling.

" Mistress," cried Evan to her, " tell neither when we went nor how we went, and you will help this lady to win free from a horrid cruelty."

The dame must have done her best, and delayed our pursuers more than a little, for, running as fast as the intervening yards would allow us in the darkness, we cleared the outskirts of the town and reached the road westwards unmolested. Jimmuck's encampment was but four miles on, and, as Ailie and Eppie Tamson were moving at a pace which told they were hill-bred, it looked as if we were to have an easy flitting.

Suddenly the character of the night changed. The rain, which had hitherto been moderate, came down in torrents. Then a fork of lightning opened the sky. For a moment it lifted the veil off the whole country-side, and made it almost as clear to the eye as if it were noon. Before the thunder, which came on the back of it, followed, we heard a yell from the environs of the town. A fateful flash it was for us. Up till then our pursuers had merely been casting about for our direction. Now we had been seen, and the track for hunters and quarry was one and the same.

There is little romance in the spectacle of draggled

creatures running under a sky that teems whole water. Yet often I go back to our flight then, as an instance of how the will can take command and force the body to fight against the elements of Nature, when these appear to be in a malefic band with some cruel purpose of man. For the Soldier and myself it was just such an effort as men should count on. But these two girls! No nymphs, pictured on some ancient vase, fleeing from the satyrs, can ever, by their grace, convey to me such a sense of moral heroism as the remembrance of these forlorn figures, their soaked garments clinging to them as closely as masks, yet with faces set in a resoluteness which the staring eyes and gasping mouths served only to accentuate.

For all we could do, our pursuers gained on us. We could hear their cries and the beat of their feet coming closer at the end of every furlong. Ailie and Eppie were now lurching pitifully as they ran. It was hopeless to reach Jimmuck's camp.

" We'll have to stand and make a fight of it," Evan called out.

Even as he spoke we saw a ruined house standing a little to the right of the road. We gathered ourselves for a last effort and raced for it. The door was gone and part of the roof had fallen in, but it seemed to me a passably good place in which to put up a defence. Evan was not of that mind.

" We could hold this for an hour, possibly, to be all taken at the end of it," he said. Then he turned to Eppie.

" Will you stay by me, to let your mistress escape ? "
he asked.

" I will that," was the reply.

" Then, Gilbert," said he, " make haste with her to
the Caird's camp. You have time to clear, while we
make that trash think she is still in this hut."

" I will not go. I refuse to leave the spot," Ailie
cried.

" Then I *command* you." The Red Sergeant's tone
shrilled through us like a brazen trumpet. It shattered
in me the power to frame those words with which I was
preparing to second Ailie. As for her, I felt her cower
at my side, like one who has been cut by a whip.

" I obey," she said, in a broken voice.

" Now," Evan cried, " now," and pushed us out into
the night.

We were in time, and no more, for as we stumbled
by the back of the house, the mob reached the turning
from the road. At that moment the interior of the
cottage was lighted up. Evan had fired a heap of
straw which some homeless lodger had used as his bed.
The light shewed him standing in the doorless entrance.
Behind him, but clear in view, was Eppie. The straw
fire, after its one great burst of flame, quickly died down.
But it achieved Evan's purpose. The rabble began
running towards the house, and, as they ran, they
roared, " The woman ! The woman ! We have her."

One of Evan's pistols spoke. It stopped the rush.
Evan was to make a fight for time. My companion
groaned.

" He will be killed, *killed*," she gasped.

" No fear," I answered, as I pulled her on, though far from feeling the assurance I tried to convey, " these rottans value their skins. If they have a matchlock or two, they will require to blow the fuses, and so make easy marks for Evan's pistols. If they too carry dags, it will be strange should they have kept the priming dry, as Evan has. Any work will be sword-work. We can trust Evan at a bout of that."

We struggled through that night of storm. Light we saw in plenty in the flashes above our heads, but glimmer of camp-fire there was none. The downpour had been too much for Jimmuck's promised beacon. When we had wellnigh given up hope, there came the sound of horses' hoofs on the road ahead, and there was Jimmuck coming with his men to airt us to his camp.

Hurried explanations passed. Then Ailie burst in with an appeal to Jimmuck to ride straight to the ruined house and rescue the Red Sergeant.

" Ma sodger frien' ! " the Caird responded. " There's nae man leevin' I wad suner risk the widdie for ; but, dod, I daurna show face as the leader o' sic a fracas."

" It matters not. I will lead," came from the maiden.

" Ailie," I expostulated, " this is madness."

" Then," said she, " it is a madness becomes me, and, what is more, neither you nor any other man will hinder me. *This I will do.*"

I had seen the man in his commanding mood. Well, here was the maiden in hers.

She swept me aside and turned to Jimmuck's riders.
The Caird's men at that time were odds and ends of the
Lowland soldiers disbanded from Montrose's army.
They wore their old military cloaks, still retained their
side-weapons, and rode the best beasts in Jimmuck's
string.

" Wha are the folk that are rabblin' the Sodger an'
the lass ? " one asked.

Ailie gave a description of her pursuers that was
sufficiently kindling.   There was a murmur of consultation which ended in the spokesman saying :

" We're wi' ye, mistress."

" Then," cried Ailie, "_I want a cloak, a horse, and a
sword."

There was no checking her impetuosity.   In a minute
the draggled figure of the pursuit was transformed.
She sat a coal-black horse.   Her rain-drenched hair was
gathered under a Cavalier hat, well pressed on her head.
The long cloak, circled by a sword-belt, completed her
resemblance to a young officer of horse.

One of the lads, who stayed with Jimmuck, gave me
his mount.   I felt as if I were the actor in a dream
where the happenings are utterly beyond his control.
Yet there was an elation in my spirit, as Ailie shook her
bridle-reins and set the cavalcade off at a brisk canter
along the road which we had, but a few minutes since,
traversed like two woebegone pieces of driftwood on
the tide.

CHAPTER XXIX

"SPLENDIDE MENDAX"

IT was open country round the ruined house. We rode down on it at a slant from the point where we left the highway. As we approached, a confused shouting arose from near the door, and told me his antagonists had closed in on the Red Sergeant. Then we were on them. At that moment a flash of lightning made the night like day. It shewed us Evan leaning against a lintel, the while his sword made play and kept beyond its point a ring of men that encircled the doorway. To his antagonists that flash revealed a body of horse, apparently sprung out of nowhere, intent on riding them down. At its head was the officer, sword in hand, who at one and the same moment shouted to his men, " Halt ! " and obeyed his own order so promptly that the horse he rode was pulled almost on its haunches, with forefeet pawing the air and head jerked back so as wellnigh to hide the face of its rider.

Next moment came darkness again. But the tableau had bit the brains of all. Like a clap on the back of it, an imperious voice rang out :

" What means this ? Rioting in a time of peace ! Who are you that attack a lone man ? "

" He's a Malignant, maister," a ringleader of the mob

answered sulkily, " an' the woman he's keepin' frae oor
han's is a spy o' the Malignants. She connived the
escape o' the black Montrose. She's a witch, forbye.
An' noo they hae the bluid o' wounded men on their
han's."

" You can tell that nonsense to-morrow to General
Middleton, whose advance-party we are, and see what
will happen to you," came the response in a voice
which even I could not recognize, so low-set was its
note. Then it turned from the pose of cold contempt
to impatient scorn.

" You fools ! You poor fools ! " it went on. " There
are no Malignants since the pact. If you break the
peace, it's the mercies of the provost marischal you'll
get, and you'll find they are not tender. As for these
clavers about witches, General Middleton's the last man
in the land to be deaved with them. Come now, move,
move, and leave us to deal with these persons. I may
even put in a word for you with the General, when
this matter comes to be looked into, if you save us a
further ride on this most villainous night. This you can
do, if you rouse the provost and say that the General
and his cavalry will reach the town by eleven to-morrow,
and that he expects quarters to be in readiness then."

In the pause that ensued, I trembled at the thorough
way in which she played her part of the hectoring
officer, for she cried, " No more words from you !
Move ! " and began urging those nearest her with the
flat of her sword. Her utter confidence, coming on the
back of that tableau revealed by the lightning, of a

posse of riders like an officer's patrol, had its effect on the mob. Even the most ignorant had heard of Middleton's reputation as a martinet when irregularities were concerned, and none seemed keen to be noted by Middleton's lieutenant. There was a rumble of voices in excited consultation, the while Jimmuck's men were shouldering the mob aside with their horses, a task the ex-troopers appeared to find vastly to their taste. The crowd was melting away. In the end the knot round the door took themselves off slowly with many curses and grumblings, and slouched away townwards into the darkness. The Caird's men spread out in a screen and shepherded these, till they saw even the last stragglers footing it on the way homewards. The rescue, then, had succeeded in a manner beyond belief. The great moment for gratulation over it had come.

Ailie and I flung ourselves out of the saddle and were within the ruined house.

"Evan! Evan!" we both cried, as with one voice. From somewhere out of the darkness he answered faintly; yet he did not move to meet us. A chill of apprehension seized me. We must have light.

Ever since Gwyn schooled me, I was wont to carry that campaigner's friend, the candle. I struck flint on tinder and kindled one. Its feeble light revealed what turned our brimming cup into a bitter, bitter draught.

The Red Sergeant lay, where he had sunk on our arrival, in the corner just beyond the doorway. His face wore a ghastly greyness. Ailie read her own meaning into that pale ensign. She made not so much as a sound, but next moment her arms were under his shoulders and his head resting on her breast.

Eppie broke the silence with a disconsolate wail from a corner, where she had had the charge of loading the pistols.

" I didna ken. I niver kent that he was e'en hurtit. Eh, mistress, he maun hae been hittit a half-'oor gane, whan they fired they mouskets. I mind, noo, he stachered than in the entrance, and, ever syne, he's been leanin' on the jamb. I thocht it wis his wey o' fechtin', an' wha cud hae tellt by the poust he pit intill't, that the life-bluid wis drainin' oot o' him ? I cudna lod they pistols fest eneuch tae lat him keep the trasherie back ; but, whan they cam', siccan a rainbow he made o' his swerd. Oh, wae, wae, that there sud be sic a dulefu' endin' tae his stan' ! "

I had crossed to Evan's side. The flicker of a smile came on his face at Eppie's recital.

" It was a good stand," he murmured, in a horrid, gasping voice, " and I could not have better comrade in it."

His doublet was wet with blood. He groaned as the three of us now removed it, and opened up the saffron shirt. I saw then the place where a musket-ball had entered the upper part of his chest.

" Do not trouble with me," he said. " There is nothing to stanch. Evan's sped, my dears."

" No. No. No. Do not say it. For pity's sake do not say it," Ailie pleaded ; and, though she did not sob even then, her tears fell like rain upon his face.

" What have we here ? " he whispered, with a touch
of his old raillery. " Not the lady on the horse framed
in lightning ! That sight of you, risking all to rescue a
friend, as you did first at Talla Linns, were a better
one for him who is making a happy end."

" A happy end ! " she answered brokenly. " Oh,
never, never will I forgive myself that you came to this
in a brawl over miserable me. A brawl ! You that
loved to be in high enterprises only, to sacrifice yourself
in so pitiable a fashion. You have wasted the precious
thing to save what was not worth the saving. Your
heart went with the ship. Your tale to Gilbert was a
blindfolding of our eyes."

" Listen to me, lady." He moved uneasily, as he
prepared to get but the right start so that the web he
would weave might follow to its pattern. " You have
it wrong, for you do not know my real mind. I was,
indeed, set on following the Marquis till we had our
journey together. It was then he pictured to me the
time we were like to have when we reached France from
Norway—himself and the rest of us deaved by the
delays of kings' courts and the plottings for place of
the little men among us. I saw, for the first time, that
it might be years before another expedition could be
attempted, and that it was like to be a forlorn hope. I
thought of the great Montrose like the king of beasts in
a cage at a show. I could not place Evan at all in that
scene. Then there came over me a great longing to
see the home-straths, and to feel the winds blowing
round the shoulders of Ben Wyvis. All I needed was a

good excuse. Your difficulty came as the very white day itself. It delivered me out of my darkness. Never was a man more happy than when I got the express command of the Marquis to help my friends. But there was no word of rejoining him in France. Freely I own I said that to save my pride and keep my place in the regard of Gilbert here. But for this ending I would have been going north to-morrow, back to the old, shiftless life of the wanderer. This expedition finished Evan's hopes as a soldier, and, surely, you would not have had him gutter out some day, soon or late, as a skulker in the hills. No, better for him to go out in a flash, even as you came to-night. That thought is wonderful contentful to him, as it has ever been to the race from which he springs."

His lie was a great effort and an exhausting. Yet such was the lightness of his manner in the telling of it, that even I could hardly have detected how it tried his spirit to cast, like Saul at Gilboa, the shield of the mighty thus vilely away.

Ailie had watched him, while he spoke, with an expression in which anguish and wonderment fought with each other. When he concluded, she said never a word, and Evan checked any from me by adding :

" Why do you waste time ? You risk everything anew by lingering here. You ought to be twenty miles on the road south before these ravens come again, as come they will the moment your stratagem is discovered. Speed to the Caird and start your journey."

" And you ? " asked Ailie.

"Put me where I can see the sky," was all he said.

"You'll see the sun itself, and that for many a day," Ailie returned, in a quiet, firm tone. A minute later she galloped off, with two of our bodyguard, to bring Jimmuck and a wagon.

When we heard the thud of the horses' hoofs, Evan had a word for my own ear. "It is good she has gone, for, Gibbie, I want a promise. You'll never turn for her that *sgeul*, which I spun for the lightening of her mind, into a fairy tale?"

"She will do that herself, Evan."

"Not if you hold steady to my way of it. If you do not hold to it, she will dwell on this little act of mine as if it were a sacrifice. That would be gall to her heart, so never give it voice for ever. It is happy I am to be doing it for the two I love."

What could I do but pass my promise? The man so manifestly thought himself in the article of death that his words had the sanctity of a last testament.

And, indeed, when Jimmuck appeared, with the selfsame wagon which had carried the treasure from the Greymare's Tail to Loch Lomondside, it looked as if hope were vain. Even Jimmuck was clearly dashed by the first sight of that ash-grey face, drenched with a moisture that made the chestnut hair hang dank over the brow. Not a word did he utter till he had examined the wound. Then he cried to us:

"We'll cooper him up yet, hinnies;" and to Evan, "Sodger, what dae ye gentles ken o' wounds? Tak' a houp o' this." He held a phial, filled with some dark-coloured tincture, to the Red Sergeant's lips.

With an amused smile, as if to pleasure his whim, Evan took a draught.

" Keep you quaet as a moose noo, frien', for twa-three meenuts," said Jimmuck, " an' the lave o' ye, hearken tae me. It's no magic ye're seein', but plain sense, helped a wee by ma grandda's balm. You folks wad hae lutten this lad dee, an' the lad himsel' wis no a hair the wiser, for a' he's a sodger. Sodgers ken aboot wounds in men ; but me, I ken o' wounds in horse forbye. Whan I wis a callant, I aince saw a wheen lairds in their cups daur ane of their company tae ride his blood-horse up the ootside stair o' a mill for a wauger. He was a young birkie, an' mettle. He pit his munt at the stair fower times, and fower times it refused. The young laird, lauched at by the ithers, drew his hanger in a rage, stabbit the beast, that wis wiser nor himsel', i' the shoother, an' left it lyin' i' a puil o' bluid. Half an oor aefter, Jimmuck hed that horse on his legs, led it cannily awa', hoosed it i' a stable, an', inside a week, wis ridin' it as his ain, for the laird wis ower muckle ashamed tae claim it. Noo, that mousket-ba', that wis makin' ye think o' a quick journey tae the mools for oor frien', riped bluid in plenty, but touched a mortial pairt nae mair than did the whinger o' that young laird. The bleedin's stoppit, an' the wee kick o' strength, tae help what's left, he'll get frae that houp o' ma grandda's balm. In a wee we'se get him tae the camp, an' syne anither sook 'll aiblins mak' him fit tae be convoyed

cannily i' the cairt. Dod, Sodger, there's no anither
man in Scotlan' I wad hae drawn ma grandda's balsam
for. Twa things, his Eskdaile souple an' that wee tate
o' balm, wis a' the fortun' the auld caird left me. The
secret o' the balsam he took wi' him tae the cairn on
Lilliard's Edge, whaur his banes rest. A wis hainin'
the wee drap against ma ain ill 'oor ; but, Sodger, ye'll
maybe no need tae toom the boddle. Onywey, ye're
welcome, even gin ye dae."

To this day I cannot say whether it was because we
had been deceived as to the gravity of the wound, or
because the Caird's potion possessed the virtue he
claimed for it, that the Evan we knew began to come
back to us, as if borne on a tide that slowly made.
What I do know is that, on the night when we were
already full fed on wonders, Jimmuck, half an hour
after he had read us his lecture, carried the Red Sergeant
in his great arms to the wagon. There he held him, as
if he were a babe, suffering none else to help, while the
wagon was driven at a snail's pace to his camp.

When we reached the place the storm had cleared off.
The early September night became bright with stars, as
if to cheer our hopes. All night long, in the covered
cart, lighted only by a stable-lantern, Ailie and I fought
for Evan's life, with the Caird watching like a faithful
mastiff. Just before dawn, as the landscape began to
show itself under that lightening, which is not yet light,
Ailie motioned to me to take her place and steady the
head which was now recognizably that of a man on
the mend.

"Ay, ye're richt, mistress," the Caird murmured appreciatively. "He can traivel, and, lod, it's high time mair nor him wis on the rod for a safer bit."

We thought we were to bear the Soldier south with us. But here came a surprise. He declared he was for the country of the Keiths, if Jimmuck would carry him to the coast, where he could hope for a vessel to France.

"But——" cried Ailie in astonishment, recalling his tale in the ruined house.

"Ach," he replied, "am not I the weather-cock that turns to every wind? You see, I've changed my mind once more. I'm out of taste for idling, after all, and think it would be a better life for me among the brisk blades across seas."

The born play-actor that he was! A shade of disappointment crossed my lady's face, but I, did I not read him? His service to us ended, he was now free to follow his beaten lord. The purpose lay naked to me, behind his rôle of the flibberty-gibbet.

We would not hear of parting company till we had seen him safe. Yet there was no miraculous recovery, and three weeks passed ere we stood on the shore of one of those sandy coves which bite into the rocky coast of Buchan, where we found a skipper willing to give the Soldier a cast over to France.

A lean, gaunt Evan it was that walked painfully to the boat, but still the steady player of his new part as the conscienceless soldier of fortune. His gaiety fitted him like a glove. Well he saw it was no hour for emotion. He bade us farewell as if he were going to a

merry-making, of which he would give us the news the
next morning.

The boat stood out to sea.   As she rounded the rocks
on the edge of the little cove, the last sight we had was
the sun glinting on Evan's bared blade, which he first
raised in a grave salute and then waved in a gay
flourish, ending in a thrust which pointed south.

" Weel, that's the braw lad coopered up an' awa'
aince mair on his traivels," Jimmuck remarked.   " Lod,
I wush I hed his company in his ain country, for it's
that airt Jimmuck maun haud till the folk i' the sooth
turn a wee less camsteerie ; but there's naething tae
hinner ye gangin' sooth, gin ye keep clear o' the toon o'
Montrose an', maybe, General Middleton."

This, indeed, we did on the morrow.   All that journey
the bridles of our horses seemed to carry bells.   We
knew at what cost to another they tinkled, yet felt it
were ungracious to muffle their music in sad thoughts
of one who had given us our happiness with the lightness
of a flower sowing its perfume on the wind.

So the music lasted till we reached the valley which
the Red Sergeant's coming had made wonderful for us,
and to which he, by his last motion, had certainly
pointed us home.

CHAPTER XXX

SIM CLEGHORN SPEAKS AN EPILOGUE

I TAKE up my story on a day wellnigh four years farther on. I had gone down from Cramalt to try the Megget pools below the Winterhope burn with the May-fly, which was a full week late in hatching out that year. In the season and on that stream a fishing-wand, a length of horse-hair, and a hook, dressed with the golden lure sporting its wings of gauze, should open Paradise for the angler. But wow, sirs, if ever mortal had reason to endorse the dictum of Horatius, that a man who changes his sky does not change his thinking, it was I.

Those last days of May in the year 1650 were to me packed to the full with dolour. They had witnessed the closing scenes in that last essay of the great Marquis in Scotland, when he put his all to venture for the new King as he had done for the old.

Men told how Seaforth, through his indecision, failed him, and how a creature of Seaforth's betrayed him; but if you want the spring of Seaforth's failure, you have to look to the royal master, bowing like a reed to self, like the ancient Herod, and careless, as that princeling was of John Baptist, who should go to

prison and death for his whim.   Did he not sign away
Montrose's life with a flourish of the pen in the draft
treaty with his loyal servitor's enemies at Breda ?   I
may yet live under that monarch's rule, but, if such is
my lot, may I never eat his bread, any more than share
the bannocks baked of the meal of Assynt's Neil, that
he got as the Judas who actually betrayed the friend
who trusted to his faith.

Oh ! but events moved fast.   April the 27th saw that
fateful fight at Carbisdale on the Kyle of Sutherland,
and May the 21st saw the great Marquis launched from
this little life into the eternal world at the Mercat Cross
of Edinburgh.   What a stound the news sent to my
heart ! With the eclipse of that life, like a young sun
with only thirty-seven years of shining, it seemed to me
that a world of honour and simple faith had ended.   It
pierced me with pathos to think even of the man's
nobility of soul as he went.   All men, even his enemies,
were talking of it, as the news sped from district to
district, how in the Tolbooth, where the men of the
town guard filled the air with the tobacco smoke he
loathed and wrangled over their drink, on the last night
of life, the Marquis wrote a poem breathing high courage
and religious fervour ; and how, on the day itself, he
dressed like a bridegroom and trod the street of doom
with a majesty which awed the spectators and a courage
which moved their hearts ; and how, forbidden to
address the crowd, he yet spoke to the magistrates and
those round them words, clean of all malice to his
enemies, of loyalty to the King who was so unworthy

of him, and of humble faith toward the God in whom he trusted ; and how his last words were a prayer to that same God for his country. Well might the crowd sob, as it did ; yet, in truth, the people's tears were more a prophecy of their own woes than a chrism over his, for these were ended, and a new way of looking at him, in which honour of his memory grew and grew, was begun.

Yet it was not of him, whose influence I apprized whenever my thoughts turned from common things, that my mind was full, as, without more interest than a stock, I cast the flies on the pools of Megget. It was of another very dear to me, like the Marquis in fate, but unlike him in that he made, if print spake truth, an end dishonouring to his manhood. Of the friends, known to me in the campaign five years gone, who had borne part in this emprise, their fortune varied. Gwyn had gone to Orkney with Harry Graham, after the latter had failed to join his half-brother in time to help at Carbisdale with his five hundred recruits, and afterwards, with his usual good fortune in small things, escaped in an open boat to Shetland, and thence in a herring-busch to Holland. Sir John Hurry, the major-general of the Marquis's army, was captured, and, though report declared he professed himself " penitent," he paid the price of failure like a true soldado on the day after his leader suffered.

Of the Red Sergeant I could hear nothing since the day of the fight on the Kyle of Sutherland ; but of my intimate, Dairsie, alas, I had but too much news. First came the cruel intimation, given on the very day of dule on which the Marquis suffered, that the Committee of Process found him guilty of treason, that the House approved the report and sentenced him to have his head chopped off at Edinburgh Cross the next day at two in the afternoon. Hot on the back of the story of the Marquis's sacrifice came tidings that, as a " Malignant " and " delinquent " unpardoned, the young Spottiswoode had gone to the block.

Horrible as was the thought that such should be the end of all Dairsie's enthusiasm and fair dreams, it was not that event, known to me now for three days, that filled me with the anguish from which I tried to escape by passing from pool to pool in Megget. There was the bitter drop of dishonour to my friend's memory added to the cup of misery.

The night before the laird of Polmood had ridden over with a broadsheet, which he got the day previous, as it was being hawked in the streets of Biggar. It professed to be " Captain John Spottiswoode's Petition to the Estates of Parliament before the Pronouncing of his Sentence." This thing, printed on greyish paper with blunt type, he had left with me, I trow in great sadness. I bore the broadsheet in my bosom that morning, and needed not to take it out and re-read it, for its phrases had burned themselves into my brain as if my friend had branded me with the ensign of his shame. It was a cringing, whining voice, utterly unlike that of the Dairsie whom I knew. In it he blamed the upbringing, on which he had ever prided himself, for

having involved him in other men's guiltiness and
fortune, and for leading him into the labyrinth of error.
He pictured himself and some other gentlemen as made
but the bridges for men with ambitious designs to pass
over, and lamented that they could not free themselves
for the time from that slavery. He told how, not only
were they weary of that service, but were to leave it so
soon as opportunity could serve for their safe retreat.
" There were never such a company of bedlames driven
into a poynfauld as we. There may be a little honesty,
but beat us in mortar, you shall not find a dram of
right understanding, of poor, nay, of common sense
amongst us all . . . God (in whose place ye now sit) of
all His attributes delights most in mercy towards the
sons of men ; do you so and I am assured it shall never
repent you."

True, one saying reminded me of Dairsie. The
broadsheet declared that, if the block on which he
might chance to lay down his head would make one
step to advance the King to his father's throne, the
King might, with the victim's blessing, tread upon it.
Yet what will men, and especially those in the flower of
life, not utter, I mused, when faced by the cold abyss of
death ? Dairsie could use wild and whirling words even
in what was summer weather for him. And here was
the ugly grey broadsheet, declaring that, as he felt the
rigor of the killing frost steal on him, he worked himself
into a frenzy and inveighed against it in untempered
words. I wished, oh ! how I wished I had never
handled the hateful thing, so that, if I must have grief,

it should yet be but a pure passion of regret as I thought of Dairsie ending, without even the scurviest crying shame on him, as the great Marquis had ended.

My doubts were resolved in unexpected fashion.

"Hey, maister, it's you I'm seekin'," a voice said, and, looking up, I saw, beyond the little screen fringe of rocks that fringed the pool, the visage of Sim Cleghorn.

I knew him on the instant, though I had not set eyes on him since the day when he broke for ever my youth by bringing me Dairsie's message in my lodging at Linlithgow. Sim it was, his beard more grizzled, but with the same impudent, saturnine expression, yet a Sim draggled and unkempt as I had never seen him in the days when he rode head-high as the Spottiswoode steward. A skulker, but a bold skulker at that, Sim looked now.

"Man, Sim," I cried, tossing my fishing-wand on the bank and fairly leaping towards him, " ye bring news. Dinna say no."

"Ye've got the richt o' it, Maister Halkett," he responded dryly. "I fund yer braw hoose an' saw yer braw leddy. Doon by the waterside, she said ye were ; an' tae the waterside I've come, as I've gane the roads like a gangrel body in hairst, wi' looks frae een asklent, an' feint a kindness or a lift, me that disna owerly lo'e usin' my feet oot o' the stirrups. An' a' for the bit news ; an' here it is."

He pulled from below a sort of baldric that he wore across his chest a letter.

" The young maister gaed it tae me that last morn in the Tolbooth, alang wi' ane for his ain folk, saying,

' Sim, give both by hand for a last service.' I've been
to Fife, an' noo I'm here ; an' wi' yer lairdship's leave,
I wad be gane."

He spoke with a sullenness which was bitter ; but I
knew this gnarled fellow and his lealness to his master's
house, and that his churlishness toward me was a
reflection of his grief for the young master, who might
have been alive before him, as I was then.

"Bide," I said, and took the letter. There was no
seal to break, and I could conceive that it had been
written to the light of a guttering candle where the wind
blew in through the bars of the prison window.

"Gibbie, lad," it ran, "this is to take farewell, for
the morn I go as his Highness went to-day. I have
been casting back much on the old days, and, though I
repent nothing, either of the course I took or this its
end, I thank my Maker that, though you were led for a
little into peril, yet by good hap you and your lady have
suffered no scaith through your kindness toward me.
Man, that thought is balm to my heart now. I can
think of you in peace and with a blessing. Do not
imagine, however, I have turned preacher. A great
deal of my good state of mind comes because, by a
gracious act of their mightinesses, my jailers let me
have a short audience of his Highness the day before
he was summoned for his journey towards the scaffold.
A great rock in a weary land I found his Highness. He
was so composed that he listened with a fatherly
patience while, not finding words of my own, I said my

adieux to him in Sir Henry Spottiswoode's verse. Whereupon, though his hands were tied with cords as a malefactor, he leaned forward and kissed me, while the tears stood in his eyes for me. Do you marvel that, with such an example, I stood up to the Committee of Process, though, I fear, it was not with the meek spirit of his Highness that I dared to defy them and all their house. How I shall end on the morrow I know not, for I am but flesh and blood ; but this will come to you by the hand of honest Sim Cleghorn, who, you mind, learned us to ride on the same garron, and I doubt not he will tell you the truth of that matter. There are some bits of verse of mine which I have sent to Dairsie. Will you see, for old sake's sake, that they do not lie for always in the charter chest ? Farewell, dear Gibbie. A happy day be yours. DAIRSIE."

Ah ! there was the real Dairsie, true even to the little touch about the poems.

"Sim," I cried, pulling the broadsheet from my breast, "there speaks your master ; but who speaks here ?"

"Oh, that liein' screed ! The hand is the hand o' young Dairsie, but the voice is the voice o' some clerk-buddy in the Council. It was a good stroke tae mak' the young maister an awfu' example of the sinner that repenteth, ay, an' fouls his ain nest in the repenting. But the young maister maun hae got some sough o' it, for at the Mercat Cross he was in a maist furious rage, ca'ed them a' what, and, whan they wad hae him confess at the last tae his fault, turned as dumb as he had afore been wud, and dee'd like an icicle for coldness, an' calm as Sir Robert himself. I tell 'e, he dee'd a true son o' the hoose.

" Hech, sirs," the retainer went on, changing his mood, as if high emotion were to be indulged in only by spasms that surprised himself, " tae think o' this deevelitch warld ! There's Maister John, heir o' an auld name and mony an honour, gane like a cannle flame blown oot, an' here's you, that were but a fairmer's son, noo a laird, rich in lands an' a leddy, forbye a safegaird whilk keeps the monsters that devoured him frae as muckle as bark at ye. An' yet, ye were in the same broil fower years syne, an' it was me set you on the errand that brocht ye fortune an' this fine doonsettin'."

He rolled his eyes round the glorious cup in the hills which is the very heart of Megget. I took no offence at his impudent, grinning way. A sore, sore heart was beating under that travel-stained coat of his.

" Sim," I said, " it is a devilish world, but there are good angels in it. A good angel met me early, but you know from your Bible that it was not always the best men who were met by an angel, but often the worse, for they needed the angel. The best men have ever followed, not an angel but a star. Dairsie's great master did. I believe Dairsie himself did, and we'll need to wait till the end of a longer day till we find whether, indeed, they have not fared best."

" Oh, mebbe," he said, with a humph, as I led him towards the old house of Cramalt.

CHAPTER XXXI

A BREEZE BLOWS IN FROM THE NORTH

WHEN the hairst is in, and the rivers, running brown in spate, warn of the wilder weather that is coming, the Egyptians make for their winter quarters at Kirk Yetholm, and the tinker clans seek the shelter of a roof up and down the Border country.

It was in making his way to Midholm, the hamlet that lies on the south side of the great ridge beyond the Selkirk hills, and commands such a vista of the Cheviots as you get nowhere else, that Jimmuck the Caird came up, by Talla Linns, to Cramalt. He camped in the haugh, where the Winterhope burn runs into the Megget, as though the place belonged to him. In the October sun he rode down on Barefit to Cramalt, and the sight of him brought back the day, in the same time of the year, when first he came to the bothie below the Linns of Talla.

Ailie and I had just been to Loch Skeen to see Yiddon Amos, for the old man was failing. Ailie went to persuade him to give up his work on the wild hills, and take his ease in a cottage hard by the house, where she and Eppie would see to his comfort. But, for once, her words failed to move him. The old man had replied :

" Mistress, I've listened tae the roar o' the Greymeere for forty year, an' I winna lea' this bit till I hear the Voice that is like the sound o' mony waters."

She came home a hantle dashed in her material plans for Yiddon, yet elevated in spirit by the thought the old man gave us as his reason.

The days since she came back to her home a bride had sped for us under a happiness so great, that we did not mark the click of time's shuttle. She was the Ailie of our days of adventure, with alternate moods of merriment and seriousness, that chased each other like the fashions of an April day. " Magerful " she declared she was no longer, as there could be now no excuse for a woman, with a lord and master, to break bounds like an untamed girl. Indeed, this boast was no mere daffing. It both humbled and thrilled me to know that, of a truth, this creature, with brain and temper finer far than mine, actually looked to me as to a master-spirit. Yet, while I knew she kept her resoluteness on leash, to spring into service at a mere word of mine, and did this with happy grace, there were depths in her that I could not fathom. Ever since that night and morning on the wind-swept moors outside Montrose her spirit seemed at times to walk alone. She went beyond my consubstantial world. Yet she was not conscious of my dullness to these moods. She always seemed to think that I could follow the flight of her fancy.

Though I am soberly religious, I have ever some sense of bondage in my beliefs. Ailie had a sense of spiritual reality which I lacked. Instead of bondage, she breathed

the air of liberty, and was like a child wandering along
banks of primroses and gathering the blossoms care-
free. She had, in these moods, a power of sensing
things, on which I would twit her as proof that the
enthusiasts in the town of Montrose had not been so far
wrong in taking her for a witch. But, unlike the
pronouncements of the carlines, Ailie's premonitions
were always associated with the tender and beautiful
aspects of life, so that I never feared their coming, or
the issue of them.

You could not tell what would make Ailie waken my
dull mind with the flash of her fancy. Yet was it to be
wondered at that the sudden sight of Jimmuck, following on our visit to Loch Skeen, should bring from her
such a flash on that day ?

As we stood together at the road-end, we saw him
riding down the glen. Suddenly Ailie clutched my
hand and, in a voice full of excitement, said :

" Gibbie, he brings a message from the Red Sergeant."

She gave a sob, the first I ever heard break from
her.

" Hoots, lassie," I replied, " if ye're richt, it's guid
news, or Jimmuck wadna luik sae weel pleased."

I had reason for my comforting assurance. Any one
less like a messenger of woe than Jimmuck it would be
hard to imagine. The ingratiating leer, which passed
as the Caird's smile, overspread his scarred face and
puckered it till his eyes almost faded from sight. The
famous kerchief, of which he was as proud as is a
chieftain of his eagle's feather, or one the own brother

of it, was knotted round his neck.   Below it Jimmuck
now wore a tartan waistcoat of the most glaring colours,
fully exhibited, for a new jerkin of moleskin, with silver
buttons, was worn open so that it should not dim any
of the glory.   A contrast he presented to our visitor of
the spring, poor Sim Cleghorn, with his draggled garments and hunted look.   Here was the old jauntie
Jimmuck, without a care in the world, or fear for king
or cadger.

Yet, when within the house, his outdoor air of ex-
pansiveness appeared to ooze away after he had com-
plimented the lady as looking brawer than ever as a
" merrit wife," and me as turning into a real Border
laird.

The entrance of Eppie with a refreshment rallied him.
He inquired what speed the dour farmer of Gameshope
was making in his wooing of her, to be told tartly that
the farmer was at least a decent man, and not notour
for riotous living, like some folk.   Whereupon the Caird
unexpectedly declined this invitation to a flyting-match,
and betook himself solemnly to his glass.   I believed
the rogue found delight in fending us off, as long as he
could, from any story he had to tell.

Ailie broke Jimmuck's unwonted constraint.

" Ye hae some news for us, Jimmuck, but ye're unco
sweer tae tell't."

"What, me!"   He hesitated.   "News, say ye?   Oh
ay," he added, after a pause, " I wis near forgettin'.
Ye hed but ae unfrien' left, that pushionous crittur,
Mungo.   Weel, noo ye needna fear even him."

" Why that ? " I asked.

" The Shauchlin Herd's hed a lang rin, for sic a draff-pock as he wis, but he got his stopper frae Muckle Joseph a week gane, near Earlston. There wis wirds, and mair, atween the twae. At a' events Mungo's body wis ta'en oot o' Tweed anaith Dryburgh. Some held it wis juist a drooned corp, ither hed it that the neck hed been broken. Ony gait, it wis a puir feenish for a lad wha hed been sae chief wi' the big folk in Embro'. But, lod, I wad hae likit weel tae hae heard the click o' his neckbane. He wis a naisty whittret, an' auld Yiddon hisna muckle tae murn."

" Yiddon need never be told," said Ailie. " Why add vinegar to the waters of his full cup ? I have only sorrow for the poor creature himself. Oh, Jimmuck, the treasure was that wretched man's undoing. The treasure ! It brought happiness to my man and me. To whom else did it bring anything but sorrow and death ? "

" Dinna sey that, mistress," the Caird cried. " The treesur fair made yer auldest frien', Jimmuck. I aye look on that fracas wi' the baron-bailie buddy as the stert o' ma fortun'. Gin it hadna been mair healthy for me tae jouk an' lat that jaw gang by, I wad niver hae seen the raal Hielan's—Ross an' Sitherland—wi' their braw fairms an' their folk sae keen on guid horse, an', maist ferlie o' a', them makin' their ain strang waters, wi' ne'er a gauger tae speir what for. I tell 'e, Jimmuck wis a wee chief than, though I'll no sey but it wis a sairious drawback tae find the lasses wi' their nebs

in the air at ma free mainners. Still an' on, wi' the
luckpenny I gat ower the treesur, I gaithered mair an'
lived crouse. But, noo that this last stramash is past, I
fand masel' youkin' for the auld wey an' they bits o'
roads an' hills. An', eh, it dis ma hert guid tae sey ye
sae cantie an' safe oot o' a' yer tribbles. It's no a' oor
frien's that hae sic a doonsettin'. Ane we ken o' is like
tae be a broken man for mony a day."

"Jimmuck," cried Ailie, with a heartiness which
made the Caird's pock-pitted visage creash with gratifi-
cation, " never, never will Winterhope here and I forget
what you did for us—and for one dear to us. Ah ! "
she went on, with a catch of the breath, " I knew you
were keeping something close. It's news of him, the
Red Sergeant."

" Ay," replied Jimmuck, " like the laddie that nibbles
roon' his oatcake an' keeps the crowdie in the middle
for a last guid bite. There's naething waesome, ma
bonnie dawtie, in what I hae tae tell. Ye maun ken
the clamjamfrey in the Hielan's is ower an' by. The
lads there are aye in het water, an' whan it's a wee aff
the bile, sit by an' watch the pot heatin' aince mair.
Them that focht against the Marquis hed seemingly only
hauf their hert in't ; an', whan Strachan's sodgers gaed
sooth, they were for leevin' an' lettin' leeve. On the
back o' Beltane I wis comin' frae the Muir o' Ord, the
braw market for nowt an' horse, and wis sellin' my
string tae the tacksmen in the fine fairms roond a muckle
mountain ca'ed Ben Wyvis, whan wha sud come into
my camp at the Black Rock o' Balconie but oor frien'

the Red Sodger. I'd gien mony a thocht tae the lad, for, certes, I aye likit him weel, an' wis feared he maun hae been kilt in the fecht at the Kyle o' Sitherland. Gled wis I whan I saw him as crouse as a muirfowl on a May mornin', though he wis in the hert o' the Munro country, whaur they're Covenanters frae the chief tae the gillie wha hauds his stirrup. No but that he wasna wae. He had cut his wey, wi' a handfu' o' ither lads, oot o' Carbisdale by the hechts o' Craigcoinichean, which the lave oucht never to have left. It was days afore he cud find the roondaboot wey the Marquis had taken. He hurried tae save him frae the claws o' Neil o' Assynt; but, though his men surroonded the castle of Ardvreck, tae lift the Marquis, Holbourn hed been afore him, and the Marquis was brocht tae Leslie at Tain. The Sodger followed hot-foot tae the east country, but was just in time tae see the Marquis, on his wey sooth, pass through Beauly, and gairded sae strongly that it wad hae needed a regiment for a rescue. The Sodger near grat as he tellt hoo the Marquis, in an auld ragged plaid, sat on a shelty, wi' rags an' strae for a seddle, a tow for a bridle, and his feet fastened aneath the garron's belly. Thereaefter, for himsel', he took tae the hills roond Ben Wyvis, an' says he's as safe amo' the cottars as he wad be by Loch Maree."

" Had he no word for us, Jimmuck ? " I asked.

" Ay, there's a bit letter," said he. " He bided the nicht an' gaed awa' like a laverock at the dawin'. Here it's, an', fegs, it took him a time to write wi' a goosequill; an' the brown colour o' the ink tells ye what *it* is." He drew out what had been an old army order. On the back of it was scrawled :

MY DEARS,—

Jimmuck will give you fuller word of me ; but this is to bear my love to you both. We may well be past shyness, and say it boldly. Let no thought of my distress mar your happiness. It is no ill lot is mine. Though the great star has set, there are still stars in my sky. Yours I think of as still lit with the glamour of the days which we spent together. I may yet see you near, when the road to Talla becomes as safe for me as are the corries of Wyvis. If that is not to be, I will write my memoirs, as the Welshman declared to me he would write his, and it may serve to amuse your children to hear the later doings of one who is sure of a place in your hearts,

                    The Red Sergeant.

" It's to us both," said Ailie, her eyes shining with moisture. " And, Gibbie, you'll let me keep that."

" I will indeed," I answered.

She took the crushed billet, with its curious ink soaked into the soft paper, and put it in her bosom.

" He wis daffin' aboot writing the meemors, I'm thinkin'," remarked Jimmuck.

" Ay," I replied. " It was an auld joke o' his that he wad hae tae tak' my pairt o' scholard, sin I had forhooed it. But I wish wi' a' my hert his ither threat, tae tak' the road tae Talla, may be nae jest. If he did, he wad be safe frae ilka soul in Megget."

Next day we watched Jimmuck and his company pass
Cramalt on his way down Megget. There was a flourish
of his great hand to us and a parting word to Eppie
Tamson, bidding her drop the dour man at Gameshope
and give a call on a far blyther lad at Midholm. We
heard his chuckle as the douce lass made a face of disgust for reply.

The Caird's coming had sharply awakened the memories of our days of adventure, and how the Red
Sergeant had been their guiding spirit from the first,
till they ended in the crowning of our love. There was
one thought in our hearts. Why had *our* cup been
filled so full, while his was left so empty ?

As Jimmuck and his train disappeared over the dip,
Ailie and I looked round the encircling hills, golden
with the yellowing bracken. Then we looked in each
other's eyes. Silently we clasped hands, and stood,
thus handfast, as if plighting our troth anew. It
was as if something sacramental, like the draught
from the well of Bethlehem, had come to us in Evan's
letter.

This was the thought we shared. For myself, I went
on to ponder how I, the prosaic man, who blundered
into a life of adventure, had yet been met, at the end of
it, by outward prosperity and with inward blessedness
in her who is to me the one woman in all the world.
I could not understand why those who plod on, more or
less blindly, should reap a harvest, while those who
follow a star so often find the fields bare. Then I
remembered that Evan himself declared he found the

fields sown with light. He had passed on his message to us in that faith.

Since that day some years have gone by.

The constraint put on us, when we returned from our course against the law, cut us off from public affairs, so that we were like dwellers in a castle where the drawbridge has been lifted. We had seen too much of politics to be sorry that we were thus sequestered among the people of the vales, who have never thought the less of us because of our adventures. Now, however, I seem to see the signs of changes in the State, that are like to bring me more liberty to serve it with any little wisdom in affairs I may have acquired.

But there are times when we ourselves lift the drawbridge and, without twinge of conscience over duties undone, rejoice in a little world that is all our own.

When in winter the wind bores its way up Talla, hurls the snow against the slopes of Winterhope, and haps with it the windows of Cramalt, we listen to its voice by the light of the blazing fir roots. Then Ailie takes out the crushed army-order paper, which, as if it were a jewel of price, is guarded from every eye but ours.

It stirs us to tell the story our children never tire of hearing, the story of how their parents came out of another storm into this peace.

They love to hear of Captain Gwyn and Dairsie, of their rough friend, Jimmuck, and that knight without reproach, the great Marquis. But it is of Evan they long most to hear. We do not stint them. If there is one desire above another in our hearts, it is that a waft of his courage, his chivalry, his charm, should breathe again in them, and they, in turn, pass his spirit on to the generations following. For there are some forms of failure that are fairer than what men commonly count success.

Yet their mother and I long for something more than that bodyless influence of him who is, in such singular fashion, the friend of each. Our hearts, for all their happiness, would lift themselves with an added thrill did there come a rap on the door, and, when the latch was lifted, there were to step over the threshold, and into our lives once more, the Red Sergeant.

THE END

PRINTED IN GREAT BRITAIN AT
THE PRESS OF THE PUBLISHERS

www.ingramcontent.com/pod-product-compliance
Lightning Source LLC
Chambersburg PA
CBHW030244030726
47493CB00023B/581